GREENGAGE SHELF

Part three in the Greengage Series

EMMA STERNER-RADLEY

SIGN UP

Firstly, thank you for purchasing Greengage Shelf.

I frequently hold flash sales, competitions, giveaways and lots more.

To find out more about these great deals you will need to sign up to my mailing list by clicking on the link below:

http://tiny.cc/greengage

REVIEWS

I sincerely hope you will enjoy reading Greengage Shelf.

If you did, I would greatly appreciate a short review on your favourite book website.

Reviews are crucial for any author, and even just a line or two can make a huge difference

DEDICATION

For Amanda, the person who makes surprisingly brilliant vegetable tray bakes for someone who hates vegetables.

ACKNOWLEDGMENTS

During the writing of this book I had eye strain, wrist pain, chronic acid reflux, crippling pain throughout the right side of my torso, AND cancer. (Ridiculous, I know! I just don't know when to quit!) I still had to work and writing in the sweet, funny, warm universe of Greengage helped a lot.

The people who made that possible helped even more. They were: Amanda, who was patient and positive at all times. And in general was my rock, my comfort and at times even my nurse.

My editor Jessica Hatch and my proofreader Cheri Fuller, who both had to help me unravel the mess I created during months of recovery. You two gave me much needed encouragement and your invaluable writing advice.

My wonderful family for giving me both space and support. And of course, the friends who popped out from the most unexpected corners to check up on me.

This includes my faithful readers who kept interacting with me and remembering me even though I didn't have any books out for a long time. I can't name you all here but know that you held me up and kept me writing. My books are my legacy and you helped me by telling me that I (and my books) weren't forgotten. That meant everything to me.

One last sad thing before we move on from this maudlin note from the author and into a silly and (hopefully) funny book.

In memory of
Malin Sterner
1973-2011
Jag saknar dig.

There! Now, let's travel back to Greengage.

NOTE FOR READERS

This book includes footnotes, if you're reading on an ebook then you can click the small number next to the text where displayed. If you're reading a paperback, flip to the end of the book for a list of endnotes.

Chapter One

RHINOS AND RELUCTANT DETECTIVES

K it frowned at a speck of mud on her jeans. It was in the exact shape of a rhino. She wiped at it, obviously just smearing the rhino into a huge blob. This was all her fault. Well, mostly her fault.

If she hadn't agreed to sort out the matter of Widow Caine's books, they wouldn't be in a muddy ditch right now. Or rather, they wouldn't be if she hadn't made them leave the cottage in that ridiculous way. Kit was aware of that. She was also aware of Laura sighing, quietly but demonstratively.

Kit's girlfriend, Laura, was a sweet soul who would never blame or harangue her for taking this little mystery on. Be that as it may, Laura clearly wasn't happy about her expensive dress being muddy while her favourite heeled boots had switched from their original, stylish grey to mud brown.

Kit got up, adjusted her glasses, and held out a hand to her girlfriend. Laura took it and stood. Other than the look of annoyance, there also flecks of mud on Laura's face, almost blending in with her freckles. The difference being that the freckles were half-hidden by make-up while the mud stood tall and proud on those soft cheeks.

"You know, this isn't *only* my fault," Kit tried. "If you hadn't asked for the recipe for the shortbread, we probably wouldn't be here. We'd have gone home long before this all kicked off and left in a normal way no less."

"That's true, dearest."

That was all her girlfriend said. The silence spoke the rest.

What had brought them to this damn ditch in the first place was a visit to Widow Caine's cottage on Nettle Road to start off the investigation. Because Kit had solved a few tricky situations on the island of Greengage since she arrived a year ago, she'd been asked to look into a mystery regarding some books that had been moved around in the widow's home—and one that had been stolen.

They'd gone to Nettle Road right after Laura finished up at the office of her family fruit farm[1] and picked Kit up from her job at the library. When they arrived, they were told the whole tale of how the books had been neatly arranged one day, then moved about, and then moved about again. Finally, one had gone missing. A copy of *Journey to the Centre of the Earth* by Jules Verne, to be exact.

Kit remembered reading it as a teenager but had no clue if she had liked it. That was back in the day when she tried to wow the other girls with her speed reading. The result was that none of them were impressed and that Kit had read loads of books she didn't remember anything about. Had there been a moose in this one? Or was that some other book?

Telling them the whole mysterious tale over shortbread

and weak tea was the owner of the books and the cottage, Widow Caine herself.

Kit clicked her tongue as she inwardly scolded herself. *I have to remember to call her Alice. Not "Widow Caine" like people do on this island, which is still stuck in the forties. No wait. The twenties. Or maybe it's in completely its own time period. Possibly a parallel universe.*

After Alice told them the story, she divulged that the only suspects, meaning those who had visited the cottage around the time that the Verne book was stolen, were:

Phillip Caine. Alice Caine's oldest son at fifty-four years of age. A former Wing Commander in the Royal Air Force. He was retired now due to a back injury, which left him in chronic pain.

Jacqueline "Jackie" Caine. Alice Caine's daughter-in-law. Aged forty-five. She'd been a theatre costume designer back in her native Edinburgh. She quit her job and moved to Greengage when she married Phillip in the late nineties.

Anthony Caine. Alice Caine's youngest son at forty-nine years old. Formerly living in Devon but returned to Greengage two months ago, after losing his job as an architect.

Caitlin Caine. Alice Caine's youngest grandchild. Aged thirteen. The only of a sibling group of three to not only still live with her parents, Phillip and Jackie, but to remain in Britain. Her older brothers both live abroad. According to her grandmother, Caitlin "needs a spot of attention."

Liam Soames. Alice Caine's neighbour. Twenty years old. Known to the police but has lately been "improving his ways." Liam, while not a family member, did odd jobs like mowing the lawn and, recently, mending the fence. He had a spare key, just like Alice's two sons. Jackie and Caitlin would have been able to access those keys as well, of course. Liam's key, however, was to the backdoor.

All that information had been great. So had the shortbread. Their exit, on the other hand, was decidedly not. They had needed to leave in a rush, out through the window. This was due to a knock and a booming voice saying, "Mother? Let me in. Jackie has my key," which indicated that suspect number one—Phillip, who Alice regretfully admitted was her main suspect due to his refusal to let her investigate the bookshelf mystery—was at the door.

It had been Kit's idea to jump out the window. That way, Wing Commander Caine wouldn't know his mother had asked someone to look into the missing book affair. At the time, diving through the window had seemed like a fun way to add a little action to the venture. Except, outside of that particular window was a steep slope, which led to a muddy, roadside ditch. The one which she and Laura were now wearing as a crusting shell over their clothes. Kit knew that Laura would've suggested they tell Phillip that they'd only popped in for tea or something, if Kit hadn't jumped out that window with the *Mission Impossible* theme playing in her head first.

At least Widow Caine had been happy that they left with such stealth, whispering out the window that it made her happy to see them taking it so seriously.

Alice. Her name is Alice, you numpty.

Kit looked back at the cottage. "Isn't it weird that even Rajesh calls Alice 'Widow Caine?' I mean, they're the same age, and he even dates her on and off, doesn't he?"

"I'm not sure 'date' is the correct term, dearest."

Kit snorted. That was how a posh, well-brought-up person like Laura would say that Rajesh, Kit's boss at the library and her former landlord, slept with every eligible woman over sixty on Greengage.

Laura picked up again. "But yes, it is odd that no one uses her first name. Another one of those old-fashioned habits Greengage clings to that you always laugh about, I suppose."

Kit winced. *There's the offended voice. How do I smooth this over?*

"Babe, if I ever laugh at Greengage and Greengagers, it's the way you can giggle at your family members. You still love and respect them even if they're acting silly."

Laura was dragging her fingers through her bouncy curls, trying to get some mud flecks out. "Family members? Does that mean you finally feel at home here?"

"Yeah. I mean, I'll always be a Londoner. That's the way I was raised." Kit scanned the quiet, leafy street. "Still, this sort of feels like home. Like… a new home."

"New? You've lived here for more than a year."

"I don't mean 'new home' as in that I've recently moved here." Kit adjusted her glasses while thinking of how to explain what she meant. "It's more like if you've grown up in a house and moved to a flat. It takes a long time to get your subconscious used to it. Everything is different, but with time, it starts to become your natural base."

Images of her little cottage popped into her head, and sure enough, that feeling in her chest was the safety and comfort of home. And the knowledge that she'd filled the place with books and posh teas. No more sticking to one bookshelf due to cramped London apartments; no more sticking to regular tea due to high London prices.

Meanwhile, Laura had retrieved a pack of tissues from her pocket and was using one to wipe at her dress. She scowled at the mud and put the filthy tissue back in her pocket. "Never mind. I'll get it dry-cleaned next time I'm on the mainland," she said with a brave smile.

"I promised Dad I'd go to London to see him soon," Kit said. "We can have it dry-cleaned then."

Laura gave her a quick kiss. "I'm sure that will be fine. Let's head back to the car."

Her little Volkswagen Beetle had been parked at the bottom of Nettle Road. That was one thing which was the same in London as here on this island. Never enough parking.

"Anyway, what do you make of your little case, Miss Marple?" Laura teased as they walked.

"I'm hardly a Miss Marple, or any other kind of detective, for that matter." Kit paused to groan. "This is really not my thing. I'm a librarian. Sure, I help friends figure out if their boyfriends are cheating on them and solve people's money issues, but I don't unearth missing things. Not even books."

"Missing *book*," Laura corrected gently. "Only *Journey to the Centre of the Earth* has been taken, remember?"

"Mm. If we're taking Alice Caine's word for that it's actually gone."

Laura furrowed her brow. "Why shouldn't we?"

"Well, I mean, she's not young. She might be getting confused or forgetful. Or maybe her loneliness has her making up stories to get company and attention?"

"Widow Caine is sharp as a whip and certainly not lonely. Yes, she misses her late husband, but she still has friends. Not to mention her children and grandchildren."

Kit shoved her hands into the pockets of her leather-jacket. "Mm. True."

Laura shot her a glance. "Are you sure you want to wear that?"

"What? I always wear this jacket. Unless its freeze-your-bum-off winter."

"Yes, but darling, it's summer."

Kit noticed she was picking up the walking pace. "It's a cold day. And only June."

"Cold? Dearest, it's 22 degrees."

She stopped to make eye contact with her girlfriend. "Hey! This jacket with my vintage blue Converse is… my signature outfit."

Laura watched her from under those long, mascara-clad eyelashes. "Do you need a signature outfit, my love? Is it part of your detective lark, now? Like Sherlock Holmes' deerstalker or Hercule Poirot's moustache?"

Kit wanted to play along with the banter, but she didn't have a proper comeback. She didn't want to be the island's famous detective. She did, however, want to wear her jacket. Even if she was beginning to sweat a little.

Laura almost managed to hide a smile. "Still, it does make you stunningly sexy. Now, get in the car so we can have a shower and something cool to drink before dinner."

"Great idea! Remind me to wash my Converse first."

"Sure. You're lucky that your shoes can go in the washing machine. My boots look ruined."

While Laura mumbled something about having the car's interior cleaned later, they got in and drove up the hill up to Gage Farm and the adjacent Howard Hall, Laura's family home. On its grounds was the old work-man's cottage Kit was renting from her. *Home.*

The smell of mud made Kit open the car window. Somewhere in the trees a bird sang as if it were really trying to tell them something. Or trying to woo a partner, perhaps? Animals were still a bit of a mystery for a Londoner like Kit. Unless the animal in question was a pigeon or a rat. They mostly just wanted to not get run over. Or a chance to steal your chips.

Kit spotted Mrs Morney, who lives about five houses down the road. She was walking her sausage dog at a pace not much faster than a hungover snail. She and the dachshund turned and began walking home again. Kit heard the old lady say, "That's enough, Bronwyn. You've had your long walk today already. We won't go all the way to the square this time."

Kit made a mental note of that as she considered whether or not to inform Rajesh. After all, she had to protect her investments in their new hobby of dog walking bets.

She leaned back and thought about borrowing some clean clothes after the shower with her girlfriend. And about what might drive someone to steal a book.

Chapter Two

UPDATING RAJESH

The next day, Kit peered out at the crowded library. It was nice to see the place so packed, even if most of the people weren't there for the books but to hear a famous naval hero called Admiral Warshaw speak about his brave adventures at sea. That talk was scheduled for 3:30 p.m. It was 11:00 a.m. now and the library was full of elderly Greengagers, all with a glint in their eye. The men, who were in the minority, were buzzing about hearing Warshaw's thrilling tales of combat and survival at sea. The ladies were all buzzing about handsome sailors and the fact that they had never seen an actual admiral before.

Kit wished they'd stop asking her when he would arrive and if their newly blue-rinsed hair looked nice.

Rajesh appeared at her side, patting his big belly to the tune of "Rule, Britannia." "So. Next Sunday, my money will be on Honoria Shaw. I took her out to dinner last night, and she said her Pekingese, Mewly, is in heat and needs loads of walking."

"Why is Mrs Shaw's dog called Mewly?"

Kit instantly regretted asking the man who'd named his bulldog mix *Phyllis* a question like that.

"Dunno. Perhaps it mewls? It's always locked in the kitchen when I call on Honoria."

Oh, so it's Honoria now, huh? It used to be Mrs Shaw. Looks like Romeo here has a new favourite.

She squeezed her lips together to not smirk at him. "Either way, your bet is on Mewly and Mrs Shaw, then? I'll jot down how much you're betting when I have my break."

"Good stuff. I'll get back to tidying the shelves."

He wandered off, and Kit wondered what old-lady-dog combo she was going to be betting on come next Friday. Perhaps Mrs Morney and her sausage dog, since they clearly had two walks yesterday and might spring for three walks on a Friday. Especially if the weather was nice.

He and Kit had started a betting pool on which of the old dears walked their dogs the most. The ladies all ended up in the town's square at some point, which happened to be Greengage's gossip central and where a drinking fountain for dogs was placed. So, Kit, Rajesh, and Phyllis would saunter down there every Friday when the library was closed. They'd find a bench, place their bets, and then mark down the ladies strutting past with their adorable dogs. Phyllis might give them all a friendly bark, if she was awake and not snoring her wonky-toothed head off.

The trio would take walks around the square and buy teas and coffees during lulls, always keeping an eye on the dog walkers and the score sheet. The person with the losing bet had to bring a posh lunch for two to the library the next day. It wasn't scientifically laid out or a very sensible pastime, but then that was in the Greengage spirit. Besides, it gave the inactive Rajesh some more exercise and Kit something to do while Laura was working.

Suddenly, Rajesh waddled back toward her.

"Ah, forgot to ask how things went with the pretty Widow Caine? Had someone moved her books about, or was it all a load of old tosh?"

Kit slapped his arm lightly. "Don't say that. Of course it wasn't tosh!" She didn't mention that she herself had voiced doubts to Laura. After all, Laura had been right. Alice Caine was to be trusted until proven otherwise. Being friends with Rajesh had taught Kit not to count someone out due to them being over sixty.

"All right, Katherine. Keep your hair on!" Rajesh replied, as usual ignoring that no one else used Kit's full name.[1]

Kit stared into space. "Someone moved the books. Took one by Jules Verne, too. No clue why. I have my list of suspects, though."

"All right, let's hear it." Rajesh crossed his arms over his chest. "I can tell you the things about the suspects that Laura and Widow Caine will have been too polite to say."

"Okay. Widow—I mean, Alice said that she worried it might be her oldest, Phillip."

"Ah, yes. The man who gives the brave Royal Air Force a bad name. Stuck-up, strict, rude git. Why does she reckon it was him?"

"Firstly, he's often at her house borrowing books, especially lately. Laura hinted that he might be wanting to spend time away from his wife."

"I should think so. He and Jacqueline fight like cats and dogs."

"Secondly, Phillip is also the one who keeps protesting against investigating this bookshelf mystery, which is why

Alice worries he has something to hide. She says all her family think she's making it up and that she shouldn't tell anyone, but Phillip is apparently the most adamant."

"I bet he's the loudest about his opinions," Rajesh said with a grimace. "Greengage's proud RAF officer with a chip on his shoulder always thinks he's right and that everyone should listen to him, even if he has no clue what he's talking about. That might be why he keeps pushing this, because for once his mother won't obey him."

Kit pursed her lips and hummed. "Maybe. Laura hinted, in her polite way, that Phillip wasn't a pleasant bloke. Is that because of the constant back pain?"

"No, he's been boorish since he was a little nipper. Phyllis hates him."

Kit nodded gravely. Rajesh's lazy bulldog might not be good for much, but she did have a good sense for which people to avoid. "I see. Anyway, his wife is a suspect, too. Maybe he's covering for her? She had access to the key and knew about those few times Alice wouldn't be in."

"Jacqueline Caine? Ha! Good-looking woman, of course, and a flirt to boot. It caused quite a stir when Phillip married a woman nine years his younger." He gazed up at the paint flaking off the library ceiling. "They met when he was stationed in Scotland, I think. He brought her here and left her alone while he went back to the mainland and his Air Force duties. He came back once in a while to scold her for flirting with all the blokes. Oh, and to knock her up."

"Rajesh!"

He tore his gaze away from the ceiling and his reminis-cences. "Fine, fine. 'To have children.' There, suit your sensitive ears better?"

"Yes. You should show some respect."

"Why? They don't respect anyone unless they're bloody aristocracy. Both Phillip and Jacqueline are middle class but like to pretend they're posh. Jacqueline once lectured me for half an hour for pronouncing Shostakovich wrong."

"Jackie," Kit said, using the nickname even though Rajesh wouldn't, "has seemed a bit guilt-ridden lately, Alice claims. But who knows if that has to do with the books."

"More likely to be about her array of lovers," Rajesh replied with an eye roll. "One of them being her brother-in-law, if rumours are to be believed."

"To be fair, Greengage has crazy rumours for everything. I mean, someone even spread a rumour that I was a witch because of my 'weirdly' blue eyes."

Rajesh grinned. "Ha! I fanned that rumour as much as I could. Said you won Laura over by putting a spell on her. Ruddy funny! The rumour about Anthony sleeping with Jacqueline probably has merit, though."

"How so?"

His gaze went back to the ceiling, as if that was where he stored memories these days. "Anthony Caine. Twitchy and tetchy bloke. Gossip says he lost his job as an architect because his ideas lacked imagination."

"Do you believe that?"

"Sure, Anthony is more ambitious than clever. He always wants more, he's never content. He was the same as a nipper. He got in trouble for stealing his brother's things and solved it by crying until everyone pitied him instead. That little weasel."

Kit clicked her tongue. "He's forty-nine and quite tall now, so he might be a weasel, but he isn't a little one. Well, no matter whom he sleeps with, he's got a key to Alice's house and knows her schedule."

"Right. So, who else could've gotten in to mess with the books?"

"Well, Alice thinks there's two other people with the opportunity."

"Let's be having 'em."

"The first is Liam Soames, the young bloke who lives next door and helps mow her lawn and do other odd jobs. He's apparently got a key to the back door so he can put tools and such away in the utility room when he's done," Kit said as she leaned against the library counter. "Alice says her family seems convinced he's only helping her so he can rob her one day."

"Yes, they would think that of a working-class lad who was thrown out of school," Rajesh grunted. "I remember the likes of them disapproved of my lower-class background almost as much as that I was an immigrant back in the day. Snobby bastards!"

"Mm. The prejudice towards Liam seems to have escalated now, since he's been out of work for quite a while and is openly struggling for cash." Kit tapped her lip, trying to remember who the remaining suspect was. "Oh, and of course there's Caitlin Caine, the granddaughter."

Rajesh shrugged. "Don't know much about her other than that she's Phillip and Jacqueline's smallest brat and rumoured to be as spoiled as her older brothers. I assume the others aren't suspects, since neither of them could stand to live in the same country as their parents?"

"No. They haven't been back to Britain for years. This business with the books has been in the works for about eleven months. It was at the kitten races last summer that Alice asked me if there was something strange about someone's books being moved about, remember?"

"Ah, yes. Why did she wait this long to ask you to look in to it?"

"Her sons kept telling her not to involve people. That it was probably Liam rooting around while looking for money, some friend borrowing books when she wasn't watching, or that she imagined it all."

"I see. What changed?"

"Last week I ran into Alice—"

Rajesh's bushy eyebrows shot up his forehead. "Surely you've seen her around during the past year?"

"Yes, but it was only last week, when I stood behind her in a really slow queue at the post office, that we got to talking and I got a chance to ask about whatever happened with the shuffled books."

"And?"

"She told me that nothing had changed since *Journey to the Centre of the Earth* disappeared, no more mysterious events but also no explanations. Despite this, her kids wouldn't let her ask around about it."

"So, she'd buried her head in the sand?"

"Well, as the books stopped being moved, she simply let the subject go and waited for the Jules Verne to pop up somewhere. Still, it seemed to really weigh on her when we spoke, so I convinced her to let me check into it."

Rajesh scratched his badly shaved chin. "Do you have any clue to why the book was taken? It's not even Verne's best work."

"Says you," Kit said while gently elbowing him. "And no, I don't know why."

"Hm. Was it a first edition or valuable in some other way?"

"Apparently not, no. I even asked Alice if there could've been anything important scribbled in the margins of the book or if it might have contained a note for someone. Anything out of the ordinary, really."

"And?"

"No, she says it was a common, unmarked, empty book as far as she knows."

Rajesh hummed. "And there were no signs of a break-in?"

"Nope. No one had been seen sneaking around either. There'd been no contractors with access to the house and no unusual guests. Laura was with me and asked about that twice. Still a negative."

"Does Widow Caine tend to leave her doors or windows open? Does she ever forget to lock the back door?"

Kit lifted an eyebrow. "I should ask you. You've dated her."

"Yes, but I was let in through the front door, Katherine," he admonished. "I don't tend to enter through ladies' back doors."

Kit suppressed the dirty double entendre which she couldn't allow her gutter mind to entertain. Smutty jokes didn't always go down so well on Greengage. She saved them for her best friend, Aimee. Sadly, that would have to be shared via phone as Aimee lived a ferry ride away, in Southampton on mainland Britain.

Rajesh sucked his teeth. "You know, there is another person who would've had a key to that cottage last summer."

"Really? Who?"

"Rachel."

This got Kit's attention. "What? Our Rachel?"

"If by 'our Rachel' you mean the lively, ginger pub owner who is best friends with your girlfriend, then yes."

Friends. Laura and Rachel had been a little more than friends back in the day. It was only due to their teenage flirtation that Laura even suspected she might not be straight. It had taken falling in love with Kit last spring to cement that the well-known, well-loved heir to Gage Farm was a women-preferring bisexual—a series of events that had also been helped along by Rachel. The pub owner was a chatty, funny, extroverted sweetheart who was loved by everyone on Greengage. Surely she couldn't be a suspect?

"What does Rach have to do with this?" Kit asked.

"She's related to the Caines in some roundabout way. It's a small island, everyone is someone's second cousin or seventh aunt. Unless you're one of the rare people who were born somewhere else, like you or me."

"Okay, how does that make Rach a suspect?"

"I was getting to that, Katherine! She's not only related to Widow Caine, she also helps her out a bit. For example, Rachel cobbled together those big bookshelves that hold all of Widow Caine's books, with some advice over the phone from that hutch ladylove of hers."

"Butch, not hutch," Kit amended mechanically. She took her glasses off and rubbed the bridge of her nose.

So, Rachel built the bookshelves. This meant she had probably handled the books more than any of the suspects. That was a coincidence which was hard to ignore.

"The shelf building must've been a little before you moved here," Rajesh continued. "Rachel whinged for weeks about how hard it was to put the shelves up and how she knackered her back putting all the books in place."

"Hm. Well, I mean she wouldn't have a key to the

cottage for that," Kit argued. "She would do it when Alice was home. Besides, she could smuggle out the book then and there, no need to mess with the books later on, right?"

"No, I suppose not. She did have a key, though. Back then, Alice was helping Anthony the Weasel fetch some things from where he used to live. Stuff that had been with some ex, I think? She was with him as moral support for a day or two, so Rachel borrowed Liam's key."

"Why his key? Does she know Liam?"

"Oh, dear me, yes. Poor lad, everyone knows he has a bit of a crush on Rachel." He clicked his tongue. "Anyway, Rachel still pops by the cottage to help out once in a while, I believe. Changing light bulbs and such. The small stuff that Widow Caine wouldn't want to bother young Liam with."

Kit was itching to go talk to Rach about all of this. Never mind the other suspects, Kit's first stop would have to be Pub 42, the modern gourmet pub that Rachel and her long-term partner, Shannon, owned with the other gay couple of the island, Josh and Matt.

The third couple, Kit reminded herself. She and Laura were the first and foremost rainbow couple on the island as far as she was concerned, even if they were the newest.

Kit's thoughts were interrupted by a screechy, older voice saying, "Excuse me, miss. I am so sorry to bother you."

Detective work and workplace chitchat would have to wait. Kit slipped back into full librarian mode while Rajesh slunk away, probably to flirt with some of the ladies present.

Kit adjusted her glasses and smiled at the woman, whom she recognised as the grandmother of Laura's assistant. It was a small island, indeed.

"You're certainly not bothering me, madam. I'm here to help."

There was real relief on the woman's face. "Thank you. I have been searching for a book, using those clever computers of yours like Rajesh taught me, but they keep saying the title is on the shelf." She gave a grave shake of the head. "I'm afraid it's not, however. I've checked three times!"

"I'm sorry to hear that. Sometimes books do get misplaced. Or someone in the library might currently be reading it. I'll try to help you find it. What's the title?"

The lady leaned close to Kit, bringing a waft of herbal throat pastilles. "*A Guide to Better Orgasms for the Elderly.*"

Kit fought with every ounce of her librarian strength to not let any surprise be displayed on her face.

Control yourself. Better orgasms are a good thing to be searching for at any age. Besides, you have to be unfazed and professional!

Kit amped up her smile. "I see. That will be in the non-fiction part of the library then. Come—hrm, I mean, *follow* me, and we'll have a look together."

Chapter Three

SHELVING ROMANCE AND THE TEDDY BEAR TECHNICIAN

I t would be a lie to say that Kit enjoyed her evening run. She missed the high-tech gyms back in London where she could be on a cross-trainer with her e-reader in front of her. Everyone around her would be wearing the same ridiculous breathable outfits and be equally sweaty. Instead, she was now out in public, pounding the uneven pavements while listening to an audiobook, which wasn't the same thing at all. Especially not as the narrator had just gotten to a tear-jerking scene where the main character's dog died. How was anyone meant to get in some good cardio while listening to that?

Kit stopped the audiobook and instead searched her phone for some music with a good beat. She nearly fell backwards, though, when she looked up and saw a big mass of auburn curls come hurtling toward her. Or, well, a person with said locks. Laura brushed the curls away from her face and tamed them into a ponytail. Her breath was shallow, and she had the wild-eyed look of someone who had forgotten their anniversary, left the oven on, *and* promised to give a presentation at work on a subject they knew nothing about.

"Dearest! Thank goodness I found you. I've been trying to ring you, but I know you miss calls when you're jogging."

Kit drew in a long breath so she wouldn't pant at her girlfriend. "Running, not jogging."

Laura waved her hand dismissively. "Yes, yes, whatever. I need to talk to you about my uncle."

"The recluse who lives with his equally reclusive adult kids in some sort of hut on the other side of the island?"

"The very same," she said, catching her breath. "Although, his recluse ways have faltered a bit. He has to go to London a couple of times a year, to check up on a business in which he is a silent partner. It seems last time he was there, he became involved with a teddy bear repair technician."

"He became involved with a what?"

"Do keep up, dearest. A teddy bear repair technician. Which isn't important right now," Laura announced, to Kit's disappointment. "What *is* important is that he dated this woman for about a week, at which time he found out that she was not only married, but that her husband was a former heavyweight boxer. A jealous one."

Kit whistled low. "Ah, all that'll put an instant stopper on any romance."

"Exactly. Uncle Maximillian hasn't had a partner since his late wife. Mainly due to his hatred of crowds and people in general, which means he rarely meets anyone. He is also rather… eccentric."

"Eccentric? By normal standards or by Greengage standards?"

Laura looked pained. "Both."

"Whoa."

"Exactly," Laura said. "He dropped in at the office a few minutes ago. I thought he wanted to check on Gage Farm, even though he isn't involved in the family business anymore, but what he actually wanted was to lament his failed relationship and say he needs a change."

"A change?" Try as she might, Kit couldn't figure out where this was going. All she had to go on was the nagging unease in her stomach, which felt like she'd eaten a kilo of vibrating marshmallow.

Laura avoided her gaze. "I'm afraid so. The change he has in mind is going back to the comfort of where he grew up, occupying one of the dusty guestrooms in Howard Hall. Oh, and remind me to thank my *helpful* cousins for this. They suggested that it might distract him to do a good deed for someone else, naming me as the prime victim—I mean, recipient."

"A good deed?"

"Yes. He decided that the act of charity will be advising me on how to run Gage Farm and shadowing me on a daily basis to see where improvements can be made. In short, he'll be glued to my side until his heartbreak heals."

"Okay. Wow. Yikes."

"Precisely."

"Sorry to hear that, babe. Not only because you'll be stuck with him but also because it sounds like he disapproves of how you're running Gage Farm. I mean, unless you really like him, his advice, and his company?"

Laura's full lips pressed into a thin line. "I've tried to like Uncle Maximillian my entire life. I'm ashamed to say I can't."

Kit almost reeled. "Have you got a fever or something? You always find the good in everyone."

"Yes, and there is good in him as well." She waved her hand in the air as if searching for examples. "He's interesting, well-meaning, and, um, well, he's harmless at least. He's also, as I said, eccentric. He can be selfish and highly strung, too," she admitted, looking pained to do so. "For example, if his heart is broken and he sees a happy relationship, he's likely to become disagreeable and impossible to be around."

"What do you mean?"

"After his wife died, whenever a family member or friend would display joy over being in love, he would give speeches about the injustice of the world and not stop until his throat got too sore to carry on." Laura looked heavenward. "He'd also sit and sigh loudly whenever there was a love song on the radio or someone mentioned romance or relationships."

"Well, I mean the guy was grieving, right?"

Laura gave her a weary glance. "This behaviour carried on for sixteen years after my aunt passed away. It's continued on, but on a smaller scale, ever since."

"Whoa. Okay." Kit ran a hand through her sweat-soaked hair and was grateful the night air wasn't cold. "Now, he's heartbroken again."

"Yes."

"And he's coming to stay with you?"

"Yes," Laura whispered this time.

Kit groaned. "Let me guess, you're going to do the sweet and dutiful thing and take him in even though you don't want to." She groaned even louder. "What's more, you're going to ask me if we can keep our relationship on the down-low for a while to stop him from making your life a misery every time we kiss each other."

Laura seemed to deflate with relief. "Exactly! I'm so glad I didn't have to explain all that. Kit, I know that'll be making you pay for the fact that I feel like I have a duty to the people around me, and I'm terribly sorry for that. I swear I will make it up to you. I just… I can't refuse him."

Kit sighed. "Fine. I won't have the argument about your sacrifices for others again. I'll play along until the old git feels better. I will, however, put my foot down if you tell me that I can't see you at all during the time he stays with you!"

"Oh, gosh no, I'll still see you," Laura quickly reassured her. "We'll only shelve the kissing and romancing for a while. I can't imagine not seeing you."

Kit tugged at a fistful of her sopping hair, as if this whole situation was to be blamed on it. Honestly, though, what could a mop of sweaty, short, black hair do against an irrational uncle and a girlfriend who always stepped up and helped?

Kit's mind went back to Christmas. It had been their first holiday season together, but several work emergencies at Gage Farm—as well as Greengage's events committee, which Laura chaired—had kept them apart for most of December.[1] That incident had taught Kit how to deal both with being away from Laura and with coping with her overly generous nature. Well. Sort of.

Kit accepted her fate and smiled at her girlfriend. "Well, we've been together for more than a year. I suppose we can do with some time apart—and some sneaking around—without joining your uncle in the lonely hearts club."

"I think so, too. Besides…" Laura's gaze flicked down

and then up again so that she was watching Kit from under the veil of her long, blackened eyelashes. "It might be fun to sneak around, stealing kisses and touches. We'll be like teenagers. Or forbidden lovers."

Just like that, Kit's heart began to pulse its appreciation for the doe-eyed seductress in front of her, a pulsing which soon echoed faintly between her thighs. "You're right, babe. As usual. Just don't let this go on for too long or let him take advantage of you, okay?"

Laura smiled. "I promise. I also promise that I'll make it up to you. How does a romantic holiday sound? And maybe some new lingerie?"

"For you to wear or me?"

"Whichever you prefer, dearest," Laura said, low and tempting.

"Then I'd like for you to wear it. Can it be mainly made of lace and quick to take off, please?"

Laura's sculpted brows shot up her forehead. "Well, I'm not going to say no to that." She paused. "Obviously, I'm never really comfortable with my body. However, I am *very* comfortable with how you react to it. Especially when it's in nice underwear. Besides, I quite like the idea of clothes being easy to get off."

There were so many naughty jokes about "getting off" and "being easy." However, Kit decided to keep away from more sex talk for the moment. She didn't want Laura to think that her only worry about them shelving their relationship for a while would be the lack of sex.

Instead, she smiled and said, "That's that sorted then. Was there anything else you wanted to chat about?"

"No, I don't think so."

"Alrighty then." Kit put her hands on her hips. "Are you going to join me for the rest of my run?"

"Yuck. Dearest, you know very well I only run if I'm being chased. Or someone's selling waffles with Häagen-Dazs on. With greengage jam. From Gage Farm, of course."

Kit rolled her eyes but knew from experience that Laura wasn't joking about happily sprinting for her favourite dessert. "Yeah, yeah, fine. So, I'll carry on running, and you…" She trailed off. "Hang on. Can we get back to what the hell a teddy bear repair technician is now?"

Laura rubbed one of those perfectly plucked eyebrows. "I believe it's someone who repairs damaged teddy bears. I don't know if she's employed by a toyshop chain or if she works only for serious teddy bear collectors and connoisseurs? You'll have to ask Uncle Maximillian."

"Ah, so I can meet him, then?"

"You'll have to if you're going to hang out at Howard Hall and have lunches with me and such. I think I'll introduce you as my best friend."

"Only for now, though, right? I've been out of the closet since I was a teenager and I don't fancy going back into it," she said, unable to keep from sounding as stern as she felt.

"Oh, dearest! No one is expecting you to go back into the closet. That's not why we're pretending to be just friends."

"I know."

"Do you? Because I need you to know without a doubt that I'd never hide the fact that I'm bisexual. Or that you're a lesbian." She took Kit's hand. "And I despise having to hide that I have the best girlfriend in the world. It's only to protect my uncle's broken heart."

Kit gave a reluctant smirk. "And your sanity while he lives with you."

"Yes, that, too," Laura said, shame making her slump. She stood right back up to add, "I'll tell Uncle Maximillian everything about us soon. I'll even explain why I felt the need to disguise our relationship and how badly that reflects on him."

"Yeah?"

"Absolutely! I'll tell him the moment he is either recovered from his heartbreak or at least ready to move out."

Kit stretched her left calf. Her legs were tightening up, and she needed to get moving again soon. "I just don't get how he can have missed what happened with Dylan, Sybil, and us. It was the talk of island for months!"[2]

"He's a hermit, remember? He knows little of what's happening on Greengage. Or in the rest of the world for that matter. What's more, he doesn't care. Unlike Aunt Sybil, he has no concern for gossip about the Howards or for maintaining the family name."

Kit shrugged. "I guess that's why, then. Well, I should keep running before my legs seize up and my pulse drops too much."

Laura grabbed her waist with a possessive fervour and pulled her into a kiss, a long, intense one that made her toes curl.

When they broke apart, Laura whispered, "Or you can come home with me for a hot, steamy shower, so we can make the most of the time we have before my uncle moves in."

Kit hummed with pleasure. "Sounds like one hell of a great way to make sure my pulse doesn't drop. Lead the way to your car, love."

Chapter Four

A HOTPOT AND RACHEL IN HOT WATER

K it finished locking up the library by fiddling with the alarm system that must have been installed before fire was discovered. Or possibly a few years earlier.

When she was finally done, she called Laura.

"Laura Howard speaking," answered that sweet, warm voice which still made Kit tingle all over.

"Hey, babe."

"Dearest! Oh, wait a moment, my assistant is waving something under my nose." There were muffled words like, "I'm afraid I can't sign that. Why? Because they've put in exclamation marks instead of full stops in every sentence. It, well, with the risk of sounding horrible, it looks like an excited Labrador drew the contract up." The assistant mumbled something which sounded like agreement and then Laura's voice was clear on the line again. "Sorry, Kit. We've got a new client, and they're… rather unprofessional. I secretly suspect they're all twelve."

Kit laughed. "Whoa there, grandma. You're only thirty-one. You can't be judging people for being too young."

"I can if they write professional documents filled with exclamation marks in which they have used 'there,' 'they're,' and 'their' incorrectly at every chance."

Kit bit her lip around a smile. "Fair enough. Anyway, I wanted to check if you'd mind having dinner at Pub 42 tonight? I've got to talk to Rachel."

Laura hummed pensively. "I think Imelda would boil me for tomorrow's dinner if I don't eat the Lancashire hotpot she prepared for tonight."

Howard Hall no longer had servants. Laura had done away with all that when she took it over from her aunt Sybil. The cook, the capable Mrs Imelda Smith, had however refused to leave. Instead, she'd gone from being "Howard Hall's cook" to being "private chef to Laura Howard." Even though she now only came in to cook up dinner, she still refused to scale down, creating feasts better suited for when the manor was filled with people as opposed to now when it was just Laura and occasionally her obnoxious brother, Tom. Well, and Kit, whenever she finished up early enough to make it to the banquet. The leftovers always ended up being the next day's lunch at Gage Farm's office or at the library. Usually both.

"All right. I'll pop over for some Lancashire hotpot, too, then, if that's all right? After that we can walk down to Pub 42 for a drink."

"Walk?" Laura whinged. Kit could imagine how the idea of exercise was making Laura's normally upturned nose scrunch up even further.

"Well, yeah, I don't drive, and I expect you'll want your usual gin and tonic?"

Laura gave an almost obscene moan. "Ahh, I could kill for some Sipsmith gin right now. Preferably straight into the veins."

Kit flung her rucksack over her shoulder and began her saunter through town. "You can afford a more expensive brand of booze, you know."

"Why? I love this one."

She slowly shook her head. "Never mind. Just thinking you should treat yourself, since you can afford it."

"Don't start this 'you're rich' business again. My ancestors were rich. I'm up to my ears in the costs of running a fruit farm and distillery in this modern age and economy." Laura's voice sounded strained with stress. "Not to mention the upkeep of the Hall."

Kit bit her tongue to keep herself from saying, "Sell the place." She knew Howard Hall was all Laura had left of the parents who died when she was little.

"I know, I know. Okay, honey, I won't get involved in what booze you drink. I'm just planning to ply you with some while I discuss the bookshelf mystery with Rach."

"With Rachel? Oh yes, you said you needed to talk to her. What about? Why her?"

"Is that jealousy I hear?" Kit teased.

"No, you plum! It's confusion. What does Rachel have to do with all of this?"

Kit filled her in on what Rajesh had said.

"Gosh," Laura replied. "Right, I see why you need to talk to her. She might have seen something."

Kit crossed the street, heading for the hill which would lead her out of the busy part of the island and up towards Howard Hall. "That's what I'm thinking, too. Rajesh thinks she should go on the suspect list, though."

"Rajesh is cynical and suspects everyone of everything. Rachel would never steal or meddle with Mrs Caine's books."

Kit pushed her glasses up her nose. "Alice. She told us to call her Alice."

"I know," Laura said, "but when you grow up curtsying to a lady and calling her Mrs Caine, it's hard to knock that habit on the head when you're an adult."

Kit was about to reply when she heard someone in the background scream something about the printer leaking ink over tax forms.

"Ah, blast it! I have to go," Laura said, her voice back in boss mode. "Bit of an emergency here, I'm afraid."

"No problem. Go take care of that. I'll meet you at Howard Hall when you've finished up."

"Smashing. Fancy a movie after we've been to the pub? I'd like to cuddle up with you and watch something diverting tonight," Laura said quickly. There was still wailing and cursing in the background. Kit wasn't sure, but she thought someone said that the ink was leaking through their trousers and into their knickers? That sounded worse than the ruined tax forms.

"Sure," Kit said. "As long as I get to hold you, I'm happy to watch anything."

"Great. Got to go! Love you."

With that Laura hung up. Kit put the phone in her pocket and rolled some work stress out of her shoulders.

The beauty of the scented, thick-aired summer evening kept Kit smiling during the remaining walk up to Howard Hall. Or perhaps it was the promise of the Lancashire hotpot and a certain set of freckles almost covered by expensive make-up on full cheeks. She shivered with pleasure as she thought of those freckles. Her Laura. She was going to hold her so damn close tonight.

Kit picked up the pace, nearly tripping over a rhododendron branch extending away from its mother plant. It was pretty and all that, but Kit wasn't having any of it tonight. It could never be as pretty as Laura.

"Petals off the Converse, purple pest. I've got places to be," Kit admonished it and continued her daydream-fuelled march up the hill.

After dinner, Kit and Laura took that walk back to town and into Pub 42. Kit stepped inside and took her first lungful of the pub's particular scent of food, alcohol, and their usual air freshener, which lay above the other smells like a sandalwood-scented blanket.

It was so packed tonight that Shannon barely had time to nod to them as they entered, being too busy serving up plates of burgers, fish and chips, and the pub's claim to fame, quesadillas, a dish which to Kit's shock was exotic for Greengage.

"Kit! Curly! Popped in for a cheeky drink, huh? Brill," Rachel shouted from behind the bar. Laura rolled her eyes at the nickname that Rachel only used when she wanted to mess with her old friend but didn't comment. While they made their way through the small pub's few tables, Rachel added, "So glad you guys are here! I was literally about text you, Laura."

"Really? What about?" Laura asked.

Rachel pulled her into a hug, strands of her long, ginger hair falling forward and mixing with Laura's auburn curls like they were trying to make a colour chart of reds.

"I need your help," she whispered in Laura's ear, just loud enough that Kit could hear it, too. Next it was Kit's turn for an emphatic hello hug and a kiss on the cheek. "Actually, Kit, maybe I should've texted *you,* considering you're the one who sorts out people's problems and tricky situations around here."

"Okay," Kit said, stepping out of the hug. "Do you have a problem or tricky situation, then?"

"Shh. Keep your voice down," Rachel hissed. "It's Shannon. She's livid with me, and I've got no idea why."

Kit pushed her glasses up the bridge of her nose in her usual tic. "That sounds more like something the two of you should talk about and sort out on your own, doesn't it?"

Rachel frowned. "Normally, yes. Right now, though, she won't talk to me. None of my usual tricks to cheer her up are working."

Laura made a sympathetic noise while Kit asked, "When did this start?"

"Well…" Rachel trailed off, adjusting her skimpy halter top with fidgeting hands. "I suppose it was the day before yesterday."

"Okay," Kit said. "What happened?"

Finding a little of her usual cheerful mood, Rachel snorted out a laugh. It wouldn't have been a flattering noise from anyone else, but somehow, she made it sound charming and vibrant. "I sort of got a bit plastered. More than usual, that is. I blame the Jell-O shots. They taste like sweets but get you drunk in two secs. They're dangerous!"

Shannon slammed down an empty bottle of Worcester sauce on the bar while clearing her throat in an embarrassed sort of way. Her dark skin nearly hid what Kit thought might be a blush. "You were more than drunk, Rach. You were pickled to the goddamned gills." Her eyes only quickly flitted up to Rachel's face and then back to the floor.

Kit flinched. *No eye contact. Whoa. That's a bad sign.*

"When you get a chance, refill this." Shannon pointed to the sauce bottle and then went back to the table she had been tending.

Rachel watched her go with a furrowed brow. "Guys," she whispered to Laura and Kit, "I think I might've really fouled up that night. Two days later and Shannon won't tell me what I did or said when I came home. She only gives me the silent treatment."

"That's not like her," Laura said. "She's usually good at communication and telling you exactly what hare-brained thing you did, because I'm sure it was exactly that—hare-brained."

Laura was right on both accounts, Kit mused. It probably was hare-brained, and Shannon *was* usually good at communicating. She was about fifteen years older than Rach and much calmer and more patient. She tended to handle Rachel's revelries and occasional faux pas with ease. What could Rach have done to deserve this?

Rach grabbed Kit's arm. "Mate! Help me! This is the sort of thing you do best. After all, you helped us with Pinky last Christmas.[1] Please figure out why she's mad at me and how I can fix it. She's the light of my life, I can't have her angry with me. I'll do anything!"

"All right," Kit said. "Chill. I'll try to ask her at some point."

"Thank you! But don't tell her I asked you to."

"Of course not. I'm not daft."

"I know, I'm just so worried," Rachel said, pushing a ginger strand back into the messy up-do it had escaped from.

Josh, one of the other owners, sashayed out of the kitchen. "Laura! Kit! Have you come here so I can poison you with my cooking?"

"No, I'm afraid we've eaten," Kit said with a theatrical pout.

He looked her up and down. "You look like you could do with another meal. Have you lost weight?"

Kit tried not to preen. "Maybe, but I've gained it in muscle. I've been working on my abs."

He put his hands on his hips. "Ugh. Do you have to walk around like some sports magazine model and make the rest of us look bad?"

"Blimey, I'm not *that* fit," Kit shot back.

Josh made a sceptical noise. "You know, I used to be quite fit and look after myself so I thought I could teach my future child how to lead a healthy, active life. Except, ever since we adopted precious but very high-energy Clark…"[2] He paused to yawn, giving Kit a moment to think about how sweet Josh and Matt were with their new son. She couldn't help wishing her parents had been like that.

Josh picked up where the yawn had interrupted him. "…since then, I can't get the motivation to do anything physical except play with Clark and go on our walks to the park."

"That counts as exercise," Laura interjected.

"Yeah, but not as much as my body is used to. I'm thrilled that we have such a speedy system for adoptions in this country, but I wish I would've been given more time to prep for this busy, exhausting life." He patted the slight rounding of his stomach. "Or at least some warning so I could find new ways to stay healthy."

Kit knew nothing about being a parent but could spot an opportunity for a workout buddy when she saw one. "Why don't you leave Matt and Clark on their own one

Sunday and come over to my place?" she asked. "We could lift some weights together? Or go for a run?"

He pursed his lips. "Not really my bag. Weights are more Matt's thing. Can I bring my Pilates DVD and we can do that instead?"

"Why not?" Kit said fast, worried he'd change his mind. "I'll try anything once."

"Which is why Laura dates her," Rachel said, looking far too pleased with the innuendo, right up until Laura sighed at her like a patient older sister.

There was a sudden clanging noise and a curse in a deep male voice coming from the kitchen. Josh muttered his farewells and hurried towards the sound.

"I wonder what Matt dropped this time," Rachel said, eyeing the recently closed door. "I swear, ever since they got that kid, neither of them sleeps. It's made them clumsy. Still, they seem content. Those two were born to be dads."

Thinking about parents and children brought Kit's thoughts back to Alice and her sons, reminding her why she was here. "Oh, Rach. I actually came by to ask you about something."

"Ooh, interesting. What was it?"

"It's about Alice Caine's books," Kit said.

Rachel adjusted the strap on her skimpy top again. "Huh?"

"About you being related to Alice and apparently helping set up her bookcases," Laura clarified.

"Yeah, both those things are true. Why on earth have you come here to ask me about that?" Rachel said with a laugh.

The *Jessica Jones* theme song sounded, signifying that Laura's mobile was ringing. She excused herself from the others and went over to the pub's farthest corner to take the call.

Kit concentrated on Rachel. "I wanted to check if you know anything about what's been going on with Alice's bookshelves. I guess you knew they'd been tampered with?"

Rachel hummed pensively for a couple of seconds. "Do you mean last year when she was saying that someone had moved her books around?"

"Yep, exactly."

"Sure, I remember that. Didn't one of the books get nicked as well? Who would do that? Especially to someone as nice as Alice?"

Kit leaned in. "So, you know nothing about—" Her sentence was interrupted by Laura coming back with the air of someone who had been told that all desserts have been banned by the police.

"Bloody hell, are you all right?" Rachel exclaimed.

Laura stared into space. "No. He is... He has... I mean, I knew he would. It's what he does. But so soon? Without warning? And with all the changes?"

Kit put a hand on her shoulder and caressed it. "Sweetheart, you're making no sense. What are you on about?"

"Uncle Maximillian. He has moved into Howard Hall right this minute and is now wondering if he can rearrange the layout of the ground floor. Or rather, he's not so much wondering as currently doing it."

Kit made a split-second decision. The book mystery could wait. Right now, she had to make sure that the love of her life didn't find her home, and the keepsake of her deceased parents, turned into an eccentric uncle's play area.

She squeezed Laura's shoulder and then let go. "That's it, we're going to Howard Hall and stopping him right now! Rach, I'll have to talk to you about this later."

They headed for the door as Rachel called after them, "Good luck! Oh, and please don't forget about my… problem."

Kit shouted back that she wouldn't, and they left.

Chapter Five

THE DUKE OF WELLINGTON SAID WHAT?!

They hurried up the hill until the Georgian manor house that was Howard Hall loomed in front of them. It was one of those June evenings when the balmy air smells of honeysuckle and sun-warmed strawberries. However, if she was being less poetic, Kit would have to admit that it might be Gage Farms' nearby orchards that she smelled. She breathed in and for a second almost forgot that they were on a mission. The look on Laura's face brought her back to the present with a jolt.

Kit took her hand and held it tight. "How could your uncle just move in like that? And start shifting your stuff around?"

"I'm afraid that's Uncle Maximillian for you. He has the same forcefulness and propensity for action as Aunt Sybil and my father had. Sadly, he also has the eccentricity of Father and Sybil, but ramped up to the top level."

Kit fell quiet as she tried to imagine someone being more eccentric than the barmy aunt that used to run Gage Farm and Howard Hall.

"So, you're not surprised by all this, babe?"

Laura brushed a thumb over Kit's hand. "Surprised, no. Upset? Yes."

They shared a quick kiss before Laura opened the big, creaking door to Howard Hall. From inside came noises of furniture scraping across wooden floors and a man huffing, badly out of breath.

"Uncle Maximillian?" Laura called out while she took off her shoes.

"This armchair is without a doubt better suited for the east side of the room," a man's voice shouted back.

"Hello to you, too," Kit said under her breath.

They ventured farther into the house, following the noises of furniture being moved. They found the culprit pushing a wing-backed armchair around in the library, Kit's favourite room in the house. Sure, it wasn't as big as the fancy mansion libraries one saw in movies, but still, the fact that there was a room dedicated to books here made her librarian's heart soar. She couldn't quite see why there was a need to shift the cosy, old armchair, though. More importantly, she *certainly* couldn't see why it was a good idea to stack a bunch of old dictionaries in a corner and place a half-eaten sandwich on top of them.

Kit obviously couldn't see it herself, but she was sure her face was as scrunched up and disapproving as a raisin arguing with a political opponent.

The pest who was pushing the poor armchair around halted to stare at them. "Ah, Little Laura. There you are. Jolly good. Oh! And you brought Susan."

Kit and Laura looked at each other and in unison said, "Susan?"

Maximillian Howard —a short man with cottony, combed-over tufts of white hair and the shape of someone who stayed in his house and ate as many pies as his house-keeper could serve him —kept staring at them.

"Yes, silly girl! Susan." He pointed to Kit.

"Uncle Maximillian, I'm not sure who Susan is. This, however, is Kit. She's my—"

"Best friend," Kit filled in.

It wasn't a lie. Laura had been her friend before they became a couple, and she was still her best friend. If they spent a couple of weeks focusing on the platonic part of their relationship to not hurt this old man, who mattered to the family-orientated Laura, Kit was fine with that. In fact, she now saw the need for it. The man in front of them was clearly as loopy as an inbred kitten on catnip. He'd picked up the half-eaten sandwich, taken a bite, and then replaced it. However, instead of putting it on top of the dictionaries like before, he'd now wedged it between two of the volumes. This had made the sandwich's gloopy filling spill all over the poor dictionaries. Kit swallowed down a few curses.

Huffing and puffing, Maximillian ignored the intro-duction and fixed Laura with a perturbed look. "Poppet, I think moving this armchair is all I have energy for tonight. Tomorrow, however, we must discuss the glass cabinet and how much of it I can use. I have this new fox, you see. It requires a home."

"Of course," Laura said patiently. "If I'd been aware that you would move in tonight, I could've made more room for you before you arrived."

"Ah, yes. Well, as Wellington always told his troops, with family you should never warn of your approach. Unlike when you attack the French. It's bad for the blood."

He turned away and began moving the armchair again.

Kit nudged Laura in the ribs and whispered, "What? The Duke of Wellington? The one who beat Napoleon at Waterloo? 'Bad for the blood?' He can't have said that! What's your uncle on about?"

Laura stepped back so they could have a whispered conversation out of his earshot. "Yes, I believe that's who he's referring to, and no, I can't imagine Wellington ever said anything like that. My uncle makes things up. We play along. I should have warned you, sorry."

"Have you… Had him checked out? I mean, by a therapist or a GP?"

"Yes, both. All the doctors were very thorough. All his tests showed normal results when it came to his intelligence and brain patterns."

Kit watched him wrestle with the armchair, moving it in circles now. "Good. As you said before, unique behaviour does run in your family. Still, it seems rampant with this guy."

"Mm, afraid so. The psychologist said Uncle Maximillian's behaviour stems from a daydreaming personality type with disregard for the outside world, combined with a somewhat strange childhood and, well, a need for attention."

In front of them, Maximillian was realising that his sandwich was beyond rescue. It was squished between an English dictionary and a French one, neither of which would ever be the same again. He grunted at the books, but then chuckled and began wiping them down with what looked like a monogrammed silk handkerchief.

"So, he's not really as much of a plant pot as he seems?" Kit asked. "But puts it on to get attention?"

"Something like that. I believe he doesn't care what people think about him but knows that acting eccentric helps keep people away and lets him get what he wants. Is that an unkind thing to say?"

"Seems pretty accurate to me."

Laura sighed. "His behaviour has worsened in the last couple of years. Now I can't tell how much of it is for show and how much he has truly lost connection with the real world. Either way, he's perfectly lucid and sharp when he needs to make decisions about finances or the businesses in which he is a silent partner. In other words, he's fine. Merely eccentric."

Maximillian abandoned the dictionaries and said, "These will need cleaning. And I fear I shall require a new sandwich."

Laura stepped closer to him and gave him that beaming smile of hers. "I'm sure Kit wouldn't mind cleaning the dictionaries, considering she's a librarian and a book lover. You and I can go rustle up another sandwich."

He smoothed down his comb-over, which had come unstuck while moving the armchair. "Yes, yes, jolly good! We will do that later. First, back to my fox. Have you seen it, Susan?"

"Um, it's Kit, not Susan. And no, I haven't seen your... fox," Kit said, nearly able to hide her confusion and scepticism.

A curl tickled her ear as Laura leaned close to whisper, "It's not a live fox. He's an amateur taxidermist."

Kit sucked in a breath and whispered back, "You mean he stuffs dead things? And now wants to keep them in glass cabinets in your house?"

Maximillian was tutting at the sandwich-splashed dictionaries and didn't seem to notice their whisperings.

Laura winced. "I'm afraid so. Well, he gets an expert to do the actual stuffing, but still." She rubbed her forehead. "We used to have a lot of taxidermy here, including deer heads on the walls. I got rid of the last ones when Aunt Sybil moved out. It appears they're going to be restocked."

"Ugh. Bloody marvellous," Kit muttered.

Laura faced her uncle and said, "Neither I nor Kit I have seen your fox, but I'm sure we can find a nice spot for it."

Sure, a nice, dark place where no one will see it, Kit thought.

Maximillian shook his head, upsetting his comb-over again. "No, no. You misunderstand me, dear girl. I wanted to find the fox so I could give it to Susan. As a gift. Like a present. For Susan, don't you know?"

Laura took an audible, long breath. "You mean Kit?"

"Yes, Kit. Or Susan. The beautiful young lady next to you," he said with a dismissing wave of the hand.

"Uncle, while that's very kind of you, I don't think Kit wants that fox." Laura's voice had lost some of its patience. She rubbed her furrowed brow again.

Kit couldn't stand the look of unease on her face.

"Choose your battles, babe," she whispered. Then she smiled at Maximillian. "Sure, I'll happily accept the gift."

He clapped his chubby hands. "Jolly good! I shall fetch it."

As he hurried out of the room, Kit took Laura's hand. "Babe, you have enough on your plate with him shifting stuff around in your house and his sudden moving in. I'll accept the dead fox and figure out what to do with it. I'll head home after I get the thing and leave you to focus on this mess. Perhaps you can swing by the cottage when he's asleep?"

Laura shot her a glance.

Kit stepped back. "Whoa. What does that look mean?"

"It means that my uncle doesn't sleep much and always insists on having the bedroom next to mine. Sneaking out will be very hard. He's already promised he'll be with me all the time I'm at work and most of the time when I'm not," Laura said, gritting her teeth between sentences.

"Bloody hell. Um, okay, so when will I see you?"

"Every chance I get. That's not the problem, though. The problem is meeting up without Uncle Maximillian."

Kit shoved her hands in her pockets, trying to not appear as dejected as she felt. "You mean we can't even meet up alone in my cottage?"

"Dearest darling," Laura said, her voice softening. "We can try. However, it's on the same grounds as Howard Hall and Gage Farm. Maximillian will follow me wherever I go. It's not like I can shake him on that two-minute walk."

"He'll go with you everywhere?"

"Well, not into the most crowded places, as he is a bit of an agoraphobic. But anywhere not too busy, he'll follow me, I'm afraid. He doesn't understand personal space."

Kit's heart ached. So called "not too busy" places were exactly where she preferred to be with her girlfriend. When they were out in public, everyone on this island wanted to talk to Laura Howard. They needed her to help influence the local council, fundraise for charities, and just come to their parties to lend some aristocratic glamour to the event. Not that Laura was an aristocrat, but she was the closest that Greengage had.

Kit had known all this when she decided to be with

Laura. She knew that Laura felt responsible for the entire bloody island and was too kind to say no to anyone. It was one of the things Kit had fallen for.

And I'm certainly not the type who tells my girlfriend what she can and cannot do. Or tries to change her, she contemplated.

Still. There was a part of her that wished Laura would stop trying to do everything for everyone else and think about herself for a moment. Because if there was one thing Kit was sure of, it was that if Laura got to choose, she would always pick being alone with Kit. They weren't one of those independent couples who only met up once in a while. No, they'd both concluded that being together was better than being apart. It was just such a shame that the unselfish Laura so rarely felt she had the right to choose.

Kit shook off the brooding. This was temporary. Soon they could go back to being one of the island's most close-knit, affectionate couples. Besides, Laura had promised to make it up to her with a holiday and some lacy lingerie. That was worth waiting for.

She stole a quick but passionate kiss. "Well, we'll simply have to make the best of it then. Like you said, sneaking around could be fun."

Approaching heavy steps told Kit that Maximillian was coming back.

"You're an angel, and I can't wait to reward you for that," Laura whispered seductively right as her uncle returned.

He held out a strangely lifelike fox with bright red fur and a vicious look on its face. It was mounted on a slab of wood, which would make anyone have a vicious look on their face, Kit presumed.

"Here we are," he said with pride. "A handsome chap to brighten up your home."

Kit took it with hesitant hands. "Ah. Yeah. Thanks, Max, I—"

"Maximillian," Laura hissed.

He puffed out his chest. "Never Max, dear girl. That is a name for dogs and children. You have time enough to say the remaining letters of my name."

And you have time enough to figure out that my name isn't Susan, you bonkers twit, Kit thought.

Out loud she thanked him again and said her good-byes to him and Laura. As she walked out with the fox held at arm's length, there was only one thought in her head: *I've got to hurry home and email Aimee. If I call her to tell her about all of this, she'll laugh so much she won't hear the whole thing.*

She stared at the fox and decided to leave him out of the email. She was hoping to stick this thing in the closet and pretend it didn't exist.

Chapter Six

MUSTARD HEATHEN AND THE BROOM CLOSET PRISONER

The overly loud birdsong and the fact that it wasn't scorching hot suggested that it was early morning. Not that Kit had needed that proved. Her sleepiness was evidence enough.

I should've had a second mug of tea. Possibly a third one, too, Kit thought as she stepped out of Laura's red Volkswagen Beetle by the entrance to the library.

Kit held the door open to get a last kiss from Laura before saying, "Thanks for the lift."

"Dearest, you don't have to thank me every time. I like having this extra time with you in the morning. Especially now that we have to see less of each other."

"Mm."

Laura's face fell. "Please don't be sad. Remember that I promised to make it up to you. Lacy lingerie and a romantic getaway. That was what you wanted, right?"

Kit couldn't help but grin. Suddenly even the loud birdsong was less irritating. Nothing could be truly annoying when the mental image of a holiday alone with Laura in sexy underwear beckoned.

She waggled her eyebrows a little. "Sure. Don't you want that, too?"

"Absolutely," Laura purred. "I've already picked out the lingerie in question. How does a black negligée with white lace trim sound?"

"Bloody delicious," Kit panted. She cleared her throat. It was too early in the day for her blood to be running this hot. "Anyway, I need to start opening up and you should get to the office before Maximillian wrecks it."

"All right. Have a lovely day, and I'll speak to you tonight."

"Sure. Love you."

"I love you, too," Laura had time to say before Kit closed the car door.

The red Beetle drove off, following the speed limit as perfectly as always.

Kit turned and nearly bumped her nose on a man's chest. She peered up and saw a tall bloke wearing retro horn-rimmed glasses and a posh suit jacket over a roll neck. He had angular features and fingers that tapped against his leg as if he were late to his own funeral. Kit had only seen this man in the crowd at a local theatre production, but instantly recognised him as Anthony Caine. This was the bachelor former architect, Alice Caine's younger son and a likely suspect in the weird case of who moved an old lady's books around. And then nicked one.

"Mr Caine, isn't it? Um, good morning. Fancy seeing you here."

"Yes. Quite. Call me Anthony. And you're Katherine Sorel?"

"Well, yes, but almost everyone calls me Kit."

"Right," he said in an uninterested tone. "I wanted to have a quick word with you."

"Okay. I'm about to open the library, but I've got a couple of minutes."

"Good. It's about this ridiculous business regarding my mother's books." He ran a hand over his neat hair and seemed to be pondering his next words.

Kit took the chance to observe him closer. His pale blue eyes were so intense and his face so animated. He carried his striking height and slender build well. No doubt a lot of straight women would find Anthony Caine attractive. Kit found him unnerving. He was constantly fidgeting or moving in some way, as if he was phasing in and out of their world and had to leave soon. Also, he smelled of the strong mustard which had stained his lapel.

Wholegrain mustard with breakfast? Yuck. Heathen.

Anthony adjusted his expensive-looking jacket. "It's all a load of nonsense, of course. Mummy probably moved them herself while searching for a certain volume, got distracted, and forgot all about it. It's certainly nothing she should be asking the local librarian to look into."

He calls her 'Mummy?' Phillip always calls her Mother. There's probably something telling in that.

If Kit had imbibed enough tea, she might've figured out what it was. Now she only knew she was struggling not to yawn in this snob's face. "It's not a problem," she said. "I like helping people. It's sort of my trademark thing." Kit chuckled, but Anthony refused to let her break the ice.

"I see. Well, if you must persevere with this silliness, I should make something clear. Mummy said that you were focusing on every person who had a key to her cottage?"

"Yes, I suppose I am."

"Well, I haven't told Mummy this, but my key is gone. She gets stupidly worried about where her keys are and who has one, so I didn't mention that I lost mine about two years ago."

Kit fought the urge to shove him. "Well, I personally can see why an older lady living alone might worry about that. Do you know where the lost key might be?"

He straightened. "It's not with some undesirable person if that's what you're implying. If it was, I would have Mummy change her lock, of course. No, I lost it and all my other keys down a drain in Marseille when I was there on a business trip. Not only is the key in France, it's also buried under gallons of filth. Quite safe."

"I see. How do you get into your mum's cottage now?"

"I ring the doorbell, and she opens," he said in a tone which questioned Kit's intelligence. "I would have no reason to go there unless it was to see Mummy."

"Right. Gotcha. Well, thanks for sharing the info. Mind if I ask if you know anything about the missing book, *Journey to the Centre of the Earth*?"

He gave an elegant shrug. "It's a ridiculous, old fantasy book that we were forced to read in school."

"Sci-fi, actually," Kit said out of professional habit. "Do you know anything about the particular copy of the book your mother owned, though?"

"No. Nothing at all. I can't even remember seeing it." He started to turn. "Now, I really must be going."

"Huh? Oh, yes, of course. I need to open the libr—"

He cut her off with, "I'm sure we'll meet again," and left.

Kit watched him stride away, equal amounts of stress and haughtiness in every step.

"Yeah, so, bye then," she muttered.

She shook her head and turned to fiddle with the alarm system. All the while, her mind was set on how easy it would be for Anthony to borrow his brother's key. Or to mess with the bookshelf while his mother was busy in the kitchen. Alice might not leave a guest alone long enough for them to rearrange bookshelves and then steal a book, but a son in the house? He would have more time alone to do whatever he pleased. Still, that didn't answer what motive Anthony would have to mess with those books. Nor what motive anyone else would have. What was so special about the book that went missing?

The alarm system finally beeped its surrender, and Kit pushed her sleuthing aside to focus on work.

It was seven o'clock on a beautiful June evening and Kit was locked in a broom closet.

She had spent an evening in worse places, sure,[1] but she still wasn't happy about being a prisoner in this cramped, dark space which smelled like lavender wood polish and dust.

She was only in here because of that bloody pest, Maximillian. He'd needed to go to his home on the other side of the island to retrieve a favourite hat, so Laura had taken the opportunity to invite Kit over for some quality time.

There had been a good three minutes of serious, sensible conversation until they found themselves frantically kissing against the wall. Then they were doing more than kissing. Next, Maximillian stormed in exclaiming that his hat wasn't there and accusing Laura, or possibly some schoolchildren, of stealing it.

At the sound of him opening the front door, Kit's plan had been to step away from the wall she was currently pushed against, brush herself off, and pretend they'd been arguing or something like that. The problem was that Laura, for all her good sides, panicked when she felt guilty. Hence, when that door flew open and those heavy steps stomped in, Laura opened the nearest door and pushed Kit in. Sadly, it had been the broom closet.

Now, Kit rolled her eyes as Maximillian and Laura talked on the other side of the bloody door. There was no natural way to step out without awkward explanations or a damn good excuse. She literally had to *stay in the closet* until Maximillian left or was distracted by something.

There was no silver lining here.

There was no easy way out of this.

There was a large amount of frustration settling in the pit of her belly.

There was… a huge, fat fly in here with her.

At least she hoped it was a fly. It was hard to tell in the darkness. Maybe it was something that would bite or sting her?

Great.

The beast fluttered by her ear, and she flapped her hands to chase it away. This only seemed to antagonise the flying little shithead. She suddenly recalled a picnic where Laura had indicated a really annoying bee and said, "If you scare it or annoy it, it will only bother you more and finally attack. Try to ignore it."

That was all fine at a picnic with a knowledgeable country bumpkin to advise her, but how could she ignore a miniscule monster that was locked in the same teeny-tiny space and appeared equally peeved about it? Kit swatted at it again. She wasn't trying to kill it, just trying to convince it to keep to its own corner.

Stay by the mop, you little wanker!

Kit could hear Laura and Maximillian discussing the evening's dinner. As if they had all the time in the world to discuss gravy and broccoli. As if there wasn't someone stuck in a flippin' broom closet nearby! For a second, Kit's undying love for Laura flickered the tiniest bit.

The insect buzzed by her chin, heading up to her nostrils, and just like that, Kit was done with all of this. Without thinking, she struck at the bug. She didn't hit it. Instead, she walloped her own face. Her nose, to be exact. And she hadn't pulled any punches. Her nose throbbed as if she'd been smacked by a boxer. She tried to be quiet. She was usually good at that, be it in sexual circumstances or stealthy ones. Now, however, the skill failed her, and she bellowed a heartfelt "OUCH!"

She clamped her hand over her mouth and stared at the closed door.

All was silent.

Except for the buzzing insect of course, as it was now more annoyed than ever.

Then Kit heard the unmistakable voice of Maximillian Howard saying, "Do my ears deceive me, or did the broom closet just yelp in pain?"

"What? I… Um, I… what?" Laura said most helpfully.

Kit squeezed her eyes closed and pursed her lips together. She was praying to whatever ridiculous rom-com deity might be listening that Laura's uncle wasn't going to open the broom closet door and ask why she was in there shouting.

It became clear that there was no such god. Or if there was, it didn't answer prayers. The door opened and Maximillian's wide face came close to Kit's. He peered at her for a moment and then said, "Susan, are you quite all right?"

"I'm fine, thank you, Maximillian."

"Oh, good. Are you aware that this isn't the bathroom but in fact a broom closet? Did you stub your toe? You should've brought a light in there with you, you know."

For a moment Kit considered doing what she would've done back in London. What she would've done in her normal and sensible life, the one which had ended when she moved to Greengage. In any other place, with any other people, not only would she have avoided this weird situation completely, she also would have been able to simply tell the truth and put an end to this nonsense. Be that as it may, this was Greengage, where strangeness was more normal than normalcy itself. This was Laura, who never wanted to disappoint or hurt anyone.

And, if she were honest, this was the new Katherine "Kit" Sorel. A woman who no longer assumed things, people, or situations would be rational, easy, or have any modicum of common sense.

Therefore, she took a deep breath and said, "You're right. That wasn't the bathroom, which was why I was shouting. I was angry at myself for getting lost."

"Ah, excellent," Maximillian said with a reassured smile. "I was worried since it sounded like a yelp of pain."

"It certainly sounded like a shout of aggravation to me," Laura said in a relieved voice.

Maximillian looked at Laura, then at Kit, who was still slightly behind the small, dark-wood door of the broom closet. Then he looked down the hallway to the bathroom, which had a door which was not only much larger than the one for the broom closet, but also greyish-blue. He gave a brief shake of the head.

"Well, I am glad we got that sorted out. I shall let you proceed to the bathroom which you will find behind that powder-blue door." With a slow, clear gesture he pointed to the larger door. "When you return, I have a gorgeous specimen of a squirrel that I had stuffed just last week. I think you will enjoy it, Susan."

"Kit," she corrected.

"Yes, that, too," he said with a glazed look.

An awkward silence descended on them. Or rather, it descended on Kit and Laura. Maximillian appeared the same as he always had.

"It fell off, you know," he said out of the blue.

"What did?" Laura spluttered.

He gave her look as if he doubted her intelligence. "The squirrel, dear girl."

"Oh?" she squeaked.

"Yes. Fell off its branch. Right outside my house. Dead as a doornail, it was. I suspect a heart attack, perhaps from a broken heart, like the one from which I suffer. There have been times when I have thought of my lost love and felt as if I were falling off a high branch myself."

He was staring into space and so missed the glance that passed between Kit and Laura as they both tried to figure out what to say. They were saved the effort by him adding, "Anyway, I did the only thing you can do. I respectfully picked the poor creature up, said a silent prayer, then had it stuffed."

"Uh-huh. That's terrible, poor thing," Kit said. "Do you mind if I go to the actual bathroom, now?" She didn't need to go, but she certainly needed to not listen to this conversation anymore. It was giving her a headache.

"Of course. Never let it be said that I stood between a woman and her need to powder her nose. Here, allow me to escort you to the bathroom to ensure you find the right door this time."

Kit couldn't be sure, but there was a hint of a giggle coming from Laura as Maximillian took her arm in his and guided her towards the bathroom with the air of someone showing a child where her potty was.

Kit gave up. This evening was going to be bonkers. All she could do was roll with it. Oh, and try to get out of being given that damn squirrel.

Chapter Seven

TRIMMING THE VEG PATCH

The library was quiet that morning and Rajesh was busy discussing politics with some man in the reference section, so Kit managed to get some shelving done. As she worked, she switched her thoughts between the case of the missing book and the wonderful fact that she'd convinced Maximillian to leave the squirrel with Laura last night. She'd claimed that its fur was almost the same colour as Laura's hair, so they belonged together. There was a risk that Laura wasn't happy about that little move. Still, since it was due to Laura's priorities that they were in this weird situation, she'd have to put up with it.

When Kit got back to the counter, there was a pink Post-It note stuck to a pen. It hadn't been there when she went off to shelve the books. It read: *Caitlin Caine been arrest for shoplifting. Wasn't charged cos of dad's money. Not first time she's stolen shit. Bet she took that book.*

She had to read it twice because the handwriting was sloppy. A little too sloppy, enough for it to look as much of an act as the bad grammar. Was this left by a rubbish writer or by someone covering their identity? Furthermore, who was invested enough in a missing book to sneak into the library and leave her a weird note? *Further-furthermore*, why did the library's Post-It notes always smell of cabbage?

"Excuse me," a voice piped up on the other side of the counter. "I'm looking for a book. I saw it here last week and rifled through it. All I remember is that it was bluish and had dead people in it."

Kit arranged her features into an expression that didn't show how often this sort of question led to a wild goose chase. In all fairness, though, she did like a mystery. "All right, sir. Let's see if we can find it."

She tucked the note into her pocket and led the man to the crime section, hoping he was talking about a fiction book. If not, she knew what she'd be doing for the rest of the day. The only books with more death were in the history section.[1]

It was after lunch, and Kit was helping a twentysomething woman with her job search. When she stepped away to let the jobseeker type in her personal information, Rajesh swung by with the book trolley.

"Katherine, everything all right? Hang on," He gave her a pitying look, "You're thinking about the fox, aren't you?"

"Huh?"

"You better say 'pardon' or 'excuse me.' If not, you know Mabel will tell you off."

She grabbed his sleeve. "Don't go ratting me out to Mabel Baxter. Anyway, what were you on about?"

"I heard through the gossip mill that Maximillian Howard gave you one of his stuffed corpses."

Kit didn't even roll her eyes at how fast word travelled here on Greengage anymore. "Oh, the taxidermy fox, right. I nearly got stuck with a squirrel last night, too. Poor little creatures. Anyway, the fox is horrible. I don't know what to do with the damn thing."

Rajesh peered down at the book trolley as he considered it for a few seconds. "You know, if I were you, I'd send it to your friend on the mainland. Aimee, isn't it? She likes peculiar things."

Someone was struggling to use the self-service machine behind them, making it beep like a fire alarm when you burn even the slightest crumb of toast. Rajesh abandoned Kit to go help out.

Kit considered the idea of sending the stuffed fox to her sarcastic, fun-loving, childhood friend. She realised with a grin that, if the roles had been reversed, Aimee would've already posted the barmy thing to her.

Right. She'd ring Aimee tonight and, because she was the considerate one in their friendship, actually *ask* if she wanted the fox. Then, she'd either send the fox off to Aimee or bury the animal, which is what should've happened in the first place. Kit shivered as she considered that the animal was probably killed simply to be stuffed. As horrible as it was, if the poor thing amused Aimee or her toddler, George, then at least its death had served some small purpose. If she threw it away, the fox would've died for nothing. Besides, after Aimee had an incredulous chuckle at Greengagers' habits, she'd no doubt bury it. It would give her a chance to teach young George about death, the circle of life, and the cruelty of humans.

That was that sorted. Now, Kit's mind could return to that note.

The jobseeker coughed. "Excuse me? I've filled out my personal information now but need some help with this one where it says: 'Name your best traits as an employee.' It only gives the options *Yes* or *No*."

Kit blew out a breath. They never covered stuff like this when she got her qualifications.

ॐ

That evening, Kit was about five minutes into a phone conversation with Aimee. Thus far, they'd greeted each other with loving insults, checked how the other was doing, and discussed George's sinus infection, including where Kit's godson liked to place his boogers.

She put a hand over her eyes. "Yuck. Can we stop talking about this now?"

"I suppose," Aimee said. "So, what else is new out there in the rural parts of the land? Is it mowing the fields season?"

"Mowing? Aimes, even you know that's the wrong terminology."

"Fine. Are you picking buttercups? Harvesting granola bars? Trimming the veg patch? Sitting with your binoculars and checking out a great pair of tits?"

"Aimes, what the hell?!"

"What! Tits are birds, aren't they? They just happen to be funnier ones than wrens, sparrows, and, I don't know, pheasants."

"Can we find an actual topic of conversation before I lose the plot here?"

"But I'm having fun," Aimee whinged.

"Change the topic or I'll start talking about your disastrous love life," Kit said.

"*My* disastrous love life?" Aimee spluttered. "What about yours? Don't think I've forgotten that email you sent me after you met Laura's uncle. He sounded like a real… what's a nice word… original!"

Kit groaned. "Can we please not talk about that whole weird situation?"

"Fine." There was a slurp on the line, and Kit grimaced. Aimee was a monster with her tea-slurping. "What about your amateur sleuthing? Found any juicy clues about the missing book?"

Kit took the crumpled, cabbage-smelling note out of her pocket. "Yes," she said, lost in thought for a moment.

"Great. Wanna share? Or should I start guessing? My bet's always been on a cypher."

Kit dragged her focus off the note. "Huh?"

"A cypher. Like a code."

"I know what a cypher is, Aimes. I just don't get what you're on about."

"I think the reason the book was nicked was that it was used as a guide to decipher secret messages. Either between criminal partners or between secret lovers."

"What?"

Another slurp of tea. "Yeah. Why not? Didn't you say one of the suspects might be sleeping with his brother's wife? Tony, was it? Maybe they use the Jules Verne book as a code-breaker for secret love notes."

Kit furrowed her brow. "Firstly, it's always Anthony and Phillip, not Tony and Phil. Apparently the only one allowed a nickname is Jackie, Phillip's wife. Secondly, a cypher is a bit advanced for your run-of-the-mill middle-aged, middle-class cheaters, isn't it?"

"Maybe, but it's a more fun theory than that someone borrowed the book and forgot to tell the old dear about it."

"Yes, and more fun than the idea that the grand-daughter might have a kleptomaniac streak," Kit said, smoothing the crumpled note. "Besides, it's not all about the missing book. It's the fact that someone repeatedly rifled through the books before anything was stolen. Like they were looking for something."

"Hang on, babes. What's that about the grandkid?"

"Caitlin Caine. I got an anonymous note about her at the library today."

"Saying what?"

"That she was caught shoplifting but was bailed out by her father's money."

"He's that rich?"

Kit puffed out a breath. "First of all, let's not assume that the note wasn't a complete and utter lie from start to finish. Secondly, yes, he is. He's got not only the money he made in the army but also an inheritance from a long-dead uncle. Both he and his brother are rolling in dosh."

"That scarpers the money motive then."

"Not necessarily. Even rich people want more money."

"True," Aimee said after another slurp. "I still think it makes cheating or the 'possibly thieving child' motive more likely."

"Teenager," Kit corrected. "I don't think we should call Caitlin a child at thirteen going on fourteen."

Aimee scoffed. "That depends on the fourteen-year-old in question, mate."

"True. I really need to meet her and the rest of her family."

"Yes, you do. Also, scope out that neighbour people

say is up to no good. I've read enough old detective novels to know that it's often the rough neighbour."

"Uh-huh, and how many of those were told by middle- or upper-class writers who criticised the working class?".

She could hear the smile in Aimee's voice. "Ah, there's my social justice warrior."

"Aimes, I'm only trying to be sensible here."

"Fair enough. You still have to meet and question the bloke, though, right?"

"Of course. Although, 'question' sounds a bit serious for a missing book. No one's been murdered or anything."

"No, if they had, the police would be dealing with it. In this case, you get to play detective, Kit. So, go full hog and question people left, right, and centre, including the bad-boy neighbour!"

"Sure, but I'll start with the family. Rajesh, Laura, and even poor Alice seem to think that it's more likely it was one of them." Kit chewed her lower lip as she remembered her boss's theory. "Speaking of Rajesh, he mentioned that Rachel also had access to the books. And, it seems Liam has a crush on her."

"Okay. How is any of that relevant?"

Kit scratched her ear. "Don't know yet. It's probably not. Rach wouldn't mess with anyone's belongings and certainly never steal."

"Of course not. Even I know that anyone saying she would is talking bollocks."

"True." Kit snapped her fingers as her memory kicked in. "Hey, speaking of bollocks, would you like a weird present?"

"Like Greengage weird?" Aimee squealed.

"Yep."

"Always! Half of my social life at work is telling stories about Greengage craziness and showing Ethel Rosenthal's[2] weird knitted animals and itineraries for kitten races, all to prove I didn't make the stories up."

"Brilliant. Then I'm posting you a stuffed fox. You can keep it for laughs. Or bury it, which is what I was planning to do."

There was a long, heartfelt wail on the line, and Aimee swore under her breath. "Sounds like my offspring has woken up and remembered how ill he is. I have to check on him. I'll call you back later, babes."

"Sure. Tell him Auntie Kit loves him and hopes he feels better soon."

There was no telling if Aimee heard the last bit or if she'd already hung up. Kit looked down at the pink Post-It note. Who had dropped that off? Was the bad grammar and rubbish spelling intended to get her thinking it was Liam, assuming he was as uneducated as Rajesh said? She shook her head. That was far too obvious. She needed to meet the other suspects. Not because she thought she could convince them to leave handwriting samples for her to compare. Or that they'd even used their actual handwriting while writing this. But maybe she could tell if see if any of them would be the type likely to leave anonymous notes. Was there a way of telling that with people?

That would have to wait. Right now, she needed a cup of tea and some sneaky, flirtatious texting with Laura. Unless Maximillian was reading over her shoulder, like he had been the last couple of times.

He's such a rude, old git.

As if her phone knew she was thinking about texts, one came in with its usual ping. Kit quickly checked it, hoping it would be from Laura. Instead, it turned out to be Rachel asking if she'd spoken with Sharon yet.

Kit winced. She had forgotten about that. She texted back a sincere apology and promised to get to it soon. Trying to figure out how to broach a sensitive subject like two lovers fighting, she headed for the kitchen and that much-needed cup of tea.

Chapter Eight

CODSWALLOP

K it was running again. Her feet were pounding the pavement with a steady beat while she mentally went through the books on her "to be read" list. She was considering bumping a fantasy book up the list, as lately she'd been going through a lot of contemporary romance novels. Still, if she had to be separated from Laura more than usual, she might need all those extra doses of romance.

She walked past Steve Hallard's corner shop and remembered that she was out of yoghurt.

You're scratching around to find a reason to stop running because you hate it. Just go home and do some squats or something. Screw this bloody cardio and getting fresh air.

She turned and ran toward the hill leading up to her cottage and the weights that awaited her there. Her phone buzzed. She slowed her pace and checked the screen. It was a call from an unknown number, one of the few things Kit liked less than running. She allowed herself half a second to grumble and then answered it.

"Good evening, this is Wing Commander Phillip

Caine. I believe we should have a quick chat about my mother. Is now a convenient time?"

Kit stopped dead, her brain recalibrating to this unexpected call. "Hello, Wing Commander. Nice to meet you, uh, I mean talk to you."

"Yes, yes, likewise I'm sure. I asked if this is a convenient time for you?"

"Oh, right. No, not really. I'm out for a run at the moment. Can I call you when I'm back home?"

"Yes. I have a previous engagement in about an hour. If you can ring before then, we should have plenty of time for a fast conversation about this ridiculous book affair."

"Okay, Wing Commander."

"Good. I suppose you may call me Phillip," he said and rang off.

"What an honour. Oh, and bye," Kit grumbled at her blank phone screen.

She thought about the quick exchange. Why would he encourage her to call him Phillip when he loved his fancy title? Was this his bad attempt at being polite and charming so that he could win her over? Or convince her of something? There was only one way to find out; she'd have to talk to him some more. She picked up the pace towards her cottage. At least now she had a valid excuse to stop running.

Back home, with a glass of water at hand and her breath back, Kit pressed the latest number in her phone's call list.

"Wing Commander Caine," a stern voice barked after one beep.

"Hi. This is Kit Sorel calling you back. You wanted to talk about your mum?"

"Oh, yes," he said, voice less like rocks against concrete now. "Thank you for returning my call. I trust you enjoyed your exercise?"

Kit scratched her hair, wishing she had showered before calling. "I'm glad to have it done, let's put it that way."

"Of course. Physical exercise is important. A strong, healthy body leads to a strong, healthy mind. I'm glad to see you are aware of that."

"Sure," Kit said. Her brain was working overtime trying to figure out what this was all leading to.

"As I have my prior engagement coming up soon, I shall get straight to the point: Mother and this codswallop about a missing book."

"Do you think it's codswallop?" Kit asked, sipping at her water.

"Of course. There's nothing mysterious here. Only an elderly lady with too much time on her hands. I keep telling her she should do useful things with her remaining days. Perhaps bake or sew. Something appropriate for a woman. Of her age, I mean."

Kit clamped her lips shut to keep from saying something she couldn't take back. *Don't judge until you know him better*, she reminded herself, although that ship had pretty much sailed. He seemed like what Aimee would call a TWHUA.[1]

She took a swig of water, making him wait. "Well, if there's nothing mysterious to it, I suppose it can't hurt for me to have look into it? After all, I'm a librarian. Finding books is what I do."

"What?" he snapped, sounding as if he had already

finished with this conversation. "Oh, yes. Very droll. Nevertheless, you should save your… talents for your work."

With that tone of voice, his words sounded more like an order than a suggestion.

Kit shoved her glasses up her nose. "Your mum wants me to try find the book and figure out why someone moved all her books around. Twice." She took another drink of water, slurping almost as much as Aimee to wind this bloke up. "It leaves one with questions, Phillip. Were they looking for this particular Jules Verne book? If so, why? Or were the two actions not even connected? So yeah, I think I'll help her, as I promised her I would."

"What?" he blustered. "Why would you carry on with such a pointless farce? You're young, or rather young at least. Don't you have something better to do?"

Kit nearly choked on her water. "I—"

He carried on speaking over her. "You have a job, albeit an insignificant one. You also have the fortune to be romantically involved with a woman who, for all her faults, comes from one of the oldest and most prominent families on the island. A Howard, meaning she is far above your station. Surely all this is enough for you?"

"Phillip," Kit said through gritted teeth to keep from biting his head off. "I'm not doing this because I'm bored. I'm looking into this because your mother is worried and wanted my help."

"You *were* looking into this. You'll stop now. Your digging around and following us, like some amateur sleuth from an old movie, will be a bother. None of us have time for it. We are an important family, heavily involved in the administration of this island. I am even considering running for MP next year."

Kit thought of a hundred responses. At least fifty of them included how Laura, who this twit had been rude about before, did more for this island in a week than he had done in his entire life. She pushed them all away. She couldn't afford to alienate him this early if she was going to keep digging into this case. Which she was, no matter what this pillock said.

"Okay. How does that relate to me seeing if anyone has broken into your mother's house and nicked one of her books?"

"I told you, we don't want you asking us questions and cluttering up our social life. Now, I have important things to tend to. Don't make an enemy of me over the follies of an old woman and an even older book. Goodbye, Ms Sorel."

Not trusting herself to answer without using the f-word or one of the many c-words, Kit stabbed the phone screen to hang up. Steaming hot anger was pumping through her veins, but it soon dissipated as she saw she had a text from Laura. She clicked it and read:

Guess what the fopdoodle has done.

Despite herself, Kit chuckled. "Fopdoodle" was the Victorian insult her girlfriend used for her younger brother, Tom. Kit tried to imagine what Thomas Howard might do when unsupervised and wrote back:

Spent all the money he borrowed from you? Swindled someone? Tried to seduce some oil tycoon's teenage daughter?

It took quite a while before the reply came in:

Your swindling suggestion was closer to the mark. He's being detained in a police station in Monaco over some shady business deal. I've sent the family solicitor over there. We'll see what comes of it.

Kit gaped at the screen. As if Laura didn't have enough on her plate without his foolishness. He'd been detained? In Monaco? This was over the top even for Tom. Kit texted back, saying that she needed more info and asking if she could come over.

Laura's reply pinged in a few seconds later:

I think that could work. I've checked and Uncle Maximillian is on the phone to one of his business partners. He'll be busy for hours.

Kit flung the door open and headed up to Howard Hall, which brooded against the purple velvet of the late summer evening. Laura was waiting for her by the door.

When Kit arrived, she pulled her in by the collar of her shirt and kissed her.

That took a while. Such important things can't be rushed.

After that, Kit was invited in, handed a glass of red wine and sat down on the high-end leather sofa. She tried the wine and then locked eyes with Laura. "So, your brother is in a prison in Monaco."

"Police station, not prison, but yes."

"Sybil Howard, your dictatorial aunt, is terrorising the French countryside with your ex-fiancé, a man half her age and half her intellect."

Laura put her wine on the table and walked over to sit on Kit's lap. "Yes."

"Your doughnut of an uncle is haunting your days while his kids, your adult cousins, are in hiding and living off their daddy's money in his needlessly derelict house."

Laura grimaced. "Mm-hm."

Kit wrapped her arms around the curvaceous beauty in her lap. "Can you promise me that you won't go bonkers like everyone else in your family?"

"Well, my parents were mostly normal. Whatever normal is. However, I know better than to make promises like that." She ran her fingers through Kit's hair. "If you want me, you'll have to take me as I am, with the risk of me going all March Hare on you at any moment."

"Ooh, Alice in Wonderland reference. You do know how to woo a bookworm."

Laura laughed and leaned in to nuzzle noses.

"Oh, before I forget," Kit said, fishing the Post-It note out of her jeans pocket. "Here's the latest development in the case of the missing book. Well, except for Phillip

Caine calling to tell me to drop the case. The Post-It was left on the counter at the library."

Laura read the note while Kit reached for her wine glass and drank a couple of mouthfuls. Whatever this stuff was, it tasted really nice.

"Interesting," Laura said, handing the note back.

"Yep. Do you happen to know which of our suspects might have written it?"

Laura played with Kit's hair as she mused on that. "I think Phillip and Anthony went to Cambridge, so they *should* have better writing skills than this. Still, who knows? Jackie helps edit the reviews page for the *Greengage Gazette*, so I doubt it's her."

Kit was trying to think straight despite the pleasure of those gentle fingers brushing through her hair. "So, unless it's one of them trying to disguise their writing, that leaves Caitlin, who might not be bothered by writing properly but is unlikely to write this about herself. That leaves… Liam?"

Laura tensed in her lap. "Liam Soames didn't write this."

"How do you know that?"

Laura straightened and avoided her gaze in the way Kit knew to mean she was offended or irate and trying not to show it.

"Because, well, Liam used to send anonymous messages to the events committee."

That explained it. Laura was the head of the Greengage events committee and was well loved by all for it. Well, except for those who didn't like charity fundraisers, kitten races, village fetes, or Christmas markets.

Laura squirmed. "The letters, or notes rather, were vile things full of bad language and complaints about everything we did. Someone saw him drop one off, and I confronted him about it. He seemed truly apologetic about the anonymous nature of the notes and the curses and slurs, but not about the complaints themselves."

Kit pulled her closer, suddenly feeling protective even though she knew Laura could take care of herself.

Laura adjusted her position in Kit's lap and kissed the crown of her head. "Now Liam emails me to inform me how the village fete, kitten race, or what have you is bothering him. Anyway, his handwriting is nothing like that, and he is well versed in the use of proper grammar when he wants to be. He didn't write this."

"Unless he's trying to make it look like it wasn't him?" Kit suggested.

"Oh," Laura nodded, "whoever wrote it, I'm willing to bet it was someone trying to pretend it wasn't them."

"Yep. I bet you're right."

Kit took advantage of how close they were now to bury her nose in Laura's sweater, breathing in her scent and hugging her tighter. Laura made a content little purring noise in the back of her throat before running her fingers through Kit's hair again. The house was quiet. The delicious wine warmed Kit's belly and made everything seem rosy. Laura felt supple in her lap, and her fingers were so tender. Their cuddling couldn't have cemented their love more clearly if they tried. It was a perfect moment.

A door, sounding like it was upstairs, slammed open.

And there's good old uncle Max to ruin the evening.

"Laura! Where is the paperwork for Gage Farm's sales to the mainland?"

"Down in the office," Laura called back.

He made a sound somewhat akin to a cat getting its tail stomped on. "That's inconvenient!"

Laura closed her eyes and mumbled, "Perhaps Aunt Sybil should've locked him in the wine cellar when they were young. She always said that was her one regret from childhood."

"Dear girl," Maximillian bellowed, still upstairs. "If the paperwork must be in the office, then so must we. We shall have to go inspect them so I can pass the final figures on to Declan Bainbridge while I have him on the telephone."

"Is it too late to lock him down there now?" Kit asked.

"We had to sell the wines and use the cellar to store jars for Gage Farm years ago. There's no room for uncles down there," Laura whispered back. She raised her voice to tell Maximillian that she'd be there in a minute.

"I'm sorry," she said after planting a kiss on Kit's forehead. "I'd offer to let you come with us, but it's sure to be boring and complicated, not to mention longwinded, and you have work early tomorrow."

"Yep, and I bet he'll give me a stuffed animal if I stay."

Laura levelled a sardonic eyebrow at her. "There's always that risk."

"Right, I'm off then."

Laura stepped off her lap. "Okay, dearest. Let yourself out. I'll call you to say goodnight later. I love you."

"I love you, too."

After a quick kiss, Laura walked out, leaving Kit standing there scrubbing a hand over her face.

Damn all Howards, save for Laura.

Still, she had said she was fine with their current situation, and fine she would be. She had promised to take Laura the way she was, and this was it. Laura was the sort of person who didn't tell barmy old uncles to hang out with the jars in the wine cellar for the rest of their lives.

Kit tottered home to lose herself in a book. Or maybe some TV. Either way, it'd be accompanied by a big glass of Diet Pepsi and vodka. In her pocket lay that Post-It note, acutely reminding her that she was no closer to a solution for Alice.

Chapter Nine

ANTS IN YOUR BRA

I t was a Friday. That meant that Kit, Rajesh, and Phyllis had taken their usual walk and then settled down on a bench by the square. They were now ready to see how their placed bets would fare in regards to the older ladies and their beloved dogs.[1]

So far, Kit had picked only losers, and Rajesh was winning big. The fact that he was romancing half the contestants did seem to give him an unfair advantage.

The mid-June sun was beaming down on them, making Kit's head burn. She wished her hair wasn't so dark. Did blondes have cooler heads?

She ran her fingers through her tresses, trying to get a breeze onto her suffering scalp. It reminded her of another annoyance. "Oh, by the way, I spoke to Phillip Caine on the phone yesterday."

Rajesh grunted. "That must've been pleasant."

"About as pleasant as ants in your bra."

"I have no idea what that's like, but I can imagine it's better than talking to Phillip. That man. Ugh. I bet the R.A.F. were happy to see the back of him."

"Probably. He told me to drop the case, as there is no case."

"Big surprise," Rajesh muttered. "It's a shame the Caine boys turned out so bad. Both their parents were always lovely."

"Speaking of the two brothers, did I mention that I met Anthony Caine prowling around the library at early o'clock?"

"No. What did he want?"

"About the same as his brother: to tell me that this whole business was nonsense, but he was nicer about it. He also wanted me to know he didn't have a key."

Rajesh harrumphed, making Phyllis wake up and bark. Kit leaned down to scratch behind the dog's soft ear. Phyllis grunted contentedly, relaxing again.

"The Caine brothers are adamant about me dropping this," Kit said.

"A good reason to dig deeper," Rajesh said with conviction.

"I will." She patted Phyllis' head, smoothing the warm, tufty fur before adding, "You know, what fascinates me is that if Anthony is so sure there's nothing shady going on, then why race up to the library so early in the morning to tell me that he no longer had a key and therefore couldn't be a suspect?"

Rajesh sniggered. "Peculiar, that."

"Exactly, dear Watson."

"Oh, no you don't, young lady," he grumbled. "I'm not your sidekick. I'm your boss."

"True."

"And former landlord."

Kit bumped his shoulder. "And friend?"

He gave her a look, but then his unshaven, wrinkled

face spilt into a grin. "Mm, that, too. But not sidekick and never assistant."

"No, more like a trusted sounding board."

His thick eyebrows lowered in thought for a moment, then he resurfaced. "Yes, I'm all right with that one."

"Awesome. Right, my next move is to seek out the other suspects and try to get a feel for them." Kit closed her eyes against the sharp sunlight, wishing her glasses had those lenses that turned into sunglasses. What were they called? Transition lenses? "I just need to find time between work, helping Rachel and Shannon, Aimee's phone calls, getting my exercise in, and this ridiculous farce with hiding my relationship status from Maximillian."

Rajesh huffed. "That ruddy plant pot!"

Kit choked on a breath. "I won't say I don't agree with you, but we should probably be careful with the name calling."

"I don't mind that he has a mind full of dust and sprinkles, Katherine," he admonished. "We're librarians. Half of the authors we love and admire were peculiar and were called as mad as a box of frogs. Blooming hell, my doctor keeps suggesting *I* try antidepressants." He glared at a passing duck. "No, what irks me about Maximillian is that he's not mentally ill. He's selfish, jumbled, and theatrical. And he shouldn't stand in the way of your relationship."

Kit went back to patting Phyllis, who rolled over to show her balding, soft belly.

"Well, everyone else did when Laura and I started dating. Back then he was still in hiding in his house, so I suppose he's making up for it now. I still can't believe he didn't hear about our relationship back at the time of the scandal."

Rajesh held up three sausage-like fingers. "One: like you said, he's a recluse. Two: he listens to no one. Three: since no one likes him, including his children who scrounge off him, no one tells him anything."

Kit pondered Maximillian and realised that if anyone had mentioned to him that Laura was involved with someone, he'd probably have forgotten it right away because it wasn't interesting to him. Kit was about to say that to Rajesh when heavy boots stomped somewhere near their bench. The sound stood out, considering it was June and everyone wore light, summer shoes.

There was one person in Greengage who defied any season or temperature, Kit thought. One person who wore a knitted hat nearly pulled over her eyes, a big coat, and heavy-duty boots year-round.

Mrs Mabel Baxter. A pensioner and battle axe who, together with her friend, the sweet and funny Ethel Rosenthal, had decided to partially adopt Kit. Something she found equal amounts amusing and infuriating.

Now, Mabel was headed right for them, like a guided missile in a grey knitted hat.

"Is it too late to hide?" Rajesh muttered. This was one older lady that not even he dared to romance.

The weight of Mabel's intense staring and stomping made them both stand up. Kit had once read a book where a forceful, older, and broadly built woman was described as "entering the room like a galleon at full sail." That quote popped into Kit's head when she shielded her eyes and squinted at Mabel. People around the square moved aside when she passed, not only because she'd knock them over if they got close but also because she'd tell them off, and the way Mabel Baxter told you off was worse than being knocked over by her wool-clad, stocky body mass.

Rajesh had now, through some sort of magic trick, made himself and Phyllis vanish. He and the dog were most likely hiding behind some of the trees, leaving Kit alone in the firing line. Kit was pondering his treachery when Mabel's booming voice shattered her train of thought.

"You smell like gin."

"What?" Kit started. "Well, I haven't been drinking. I'm not really a daytime drinker. Hello, by the way."

"Yes. Hello." Mabel sniffed the air. "I think it's your cologne or whatever you call it. Smells like gin."

This wasn't the first time Kit's signature perfume, Voyage d'Hermès, had gotten comments. She didn't care. It was as much her as her leather jacket and faded Converse. She tried for a genial look and put her hands in her pockets. "Ah, right, I think it's meant to smell like cardamom and citrus."

"Gin," Mabel grunted.

Kit gave up on geniality. She was starting to get that *ants in her bra* feeling again. "If you say so. I'm sorry about my smell. Was there anything else, Mabel?"

Those wrinkled lips pursed. "Of course there was, girl. I didn't traipse all the way to the main square to tell you that you smell of gin."

Kit wondered how long she, Laura, and other thirtysomething women would be called "girl" on Greengage. "I see."

"Precisely," Mabel said, standing even more ramrod straight.

A few quiet moments passed while Kit waited for more information.

Mabel merely glared.

Kit began rocking back and forth on her heels. "Right, um, so…?"

"Don't 'um' and 'ah.' You're an intelligent girl. Use your words."

"Thanks for noticing! However, I was 'umm-ing' to give you a chance to continue."

Mabel squinted. "Continue? What are you trying to say, mainlander?"

"Did you want to tell me something? Or did you just want to see me because you missed me?"

Kit hadn't been able to resist teasing Mabel with that last comment, but she had done it with a big, friendly smile. Unfortunately, that didn't help.

Mabel's frown deepened into chasms of disapproval. "I. Am. Waiting. For. Ethel."

Kit stepped back. "Oh."

"She's the one who needs to tell you something. She's late, though. As always."

"I'm not late," a small, cheerful voice said to their side. "Only slower than you, you old steam locomotive!"

Kit leaned in to give Ethel Rosenthal a kiss on the cheek, smiling at the smell of lavender and talcum powder. Mabel was still huffing at the steam train comment, making it seem more and more appropriate, so Kit focused on Ethel. "How are you?"

"Oh, I can't complain. You see, *I* am not in a pickle with a sweetheart who pretends to be my friend and nothing more to spare her uncle's feelings," Ethel said.

Kit sighed. "Ah, you've spoken to Laura?"

"I didn't need to. All of Greengage knows what's going on. Well, everyone but Maximillian. Which is not surprising, considering it's doubtful if Maximillian Howard knows who's prime minister or what year it is. Or if he is wearing socks."

"Probably true. Anyway, Mabel, says you wanted to tell me something?"

"Yes, dear! Rajesh mentioned you are finally helping Alice Caine with her missing book?"

"I am, yeah."

"Excellent," Ethel said. "He also said that you didn't know why someone would want to steal that particular Jules Verne book."

"That's right," Kit said, eagerness upping her pulse.

"When he said it, something rang a faint bell in my mind. Except, the bell wasn't making itself clear until this morning." Ethel lowered her voice as if imparting a secret. "I remembered talking to Alice about books and their themes. She mentioned *Journey to the Centre of the Earth* having a minor theme of hiding things within books. In the case of that book, which I feel has not stood the test of time, it's a cypher."

Kit's pulse picked up. "Okay."

"And then," Ethel's milky blue eyes grew wide, "Alice said that *Journey to the Centre of the Earth*'s theme was why she chose it to hide her will in it."

"Hide her will?" Kit squeaked.

"Yes! She said she was planning to take it to the bank when her arthritis had subsided enough to let her walk there. Meanwhile, she kept it in that book so that her family wouldn't snoop." Ethel paused to shake her head with woe. "She's not trusted them for years, which should tell you all you need to know about them as Alice is usually a trusting soul."

Kit's mind was hurtling in several directions, like a cat on catnip chasing imaginary mice. A will! That was an excellent reason for stealing the book. Who would do such a thing, though? A person's will is such an important and personal thing. She remembered Anthony keeping the missing key a secret and Phillip's lack of care for his mother's autonomy.

Yes, maybe them? If so, was it one of them acting alone? Surely they weren't working together if Anthony felt such sibling rivalry as Rajesh claimed? Maybe one of them was in cahoots with Jackie, but if so, which one? Her husband or her brother-in-law and possible lover?

Kit gave herself a mental slap. *Slow down, woman. You're making assumptions. Ask more questions.*

"Ethel, do you know what was in the will? For example, who would stand to benefit the most?"

"No, afraid not, dear."

Kit's shoulders slumped. "Oh."

Ethel tapped a crooked, wrinkled finger against her lip. "I may not know for certain, but I can always venture a guess. When you've lived for as long as I have, and have a habit of watching people, you tend to become quite good at these sorts of things."

Mabel snorted with derision, but Kit ignored her. "Sure, take a stab at it. Goodness knows I have no clues myself."

"Well, first of all, you might want to trust Alice's instincts, bubelah. She knows these people better than anyone, and she's a good judge of character."

Kit smiled at being called the term of endearment before replying, "Alice thinks it might be Phillip since he really wants her to stop digging in this."

"I bet she has other reasons, too," Mabel muttered. "That man is arrogant and condescending."

Ethel nodded but didn't look convinced. "I must say,

though, both Phillip and Anthony are quite well-off, so they don't need their inheritance. Perhaps Jacqueline or little Caitlin took the will to see if they benefited directly or only through Phillip?"

Kit chewed the inside of her cheek. "I guess that's possible."

"Then there is the unfortunate Liam," Ethel said. "That lad always had a knack for getting into trouble. He's just turned twenty, and he already seems to have given up on himself. Such a shame."

"Do you think he could have taken the book with the will?" Kit asked.

Ethel tapped her finger on her lip again. "Perhaps. Somehow, though, I doubt it was for his own benefit if he is the culprit."

"Why do you say that?"

"Yes, why?" Mabel echoed. "The straw-headed boy is a delinquent."

"No real reason. Instinct, I suppose. A feeling you get when you're around a person long enough. If we're being honest, I think instinct is what's driving Alice to think the main suspects should be her darling sons."

"I said that she thought it was Phillip," Kit amended. "Not both sons."

Ethel shrugged her bony shoulders. "Whatever you can suspect Phillip of, you can usually suspect his little brother of as well. Anthony always wanted what his brother had. He also tended to do what his brother had done before, even if it got him into trouble."

"Sometimes I'm happy I'm an only child," Kit said, her mind wandering to what Laura's nuisance of a brother was currently up to. How could he even afford to go to Monaco, never mind get arrested there?

Being arrested surely cost a pretty penny in a place like that.

"That can get lonely, though, can't it, bubelah? It can leave marks in your heart that you must carry with you into your adult relationships?" Ethel said with that knowing, kind smile of hers.

Kit's cheeks burned. "Yes, I suppose it can."

Ethel put a hand on her forearm. "I shall tell you another thing: what you said about Mabel earlier is true. She *has* missed you, and so have I."

Out of the corner of her eye, Kit saw Mabel suddenly become fascinated with the ground and her big boots.

"We must all take tea soon," Ethel urged. "I'll buy you a crumpet, you're looking thin."

"I'll scoff it down with glee," Kit promised. "You always know what's best for me. Last Christmas and Hanukkah proved that."[2]

Ethel looked pleased. "Well, you're far away from family and friends. We must look after you, especially now that Laura is otherwise engaged."

"We should be off. It's far too hot," Mabel sniped.

Kit leaned closer to Ethel. "If I told her it'd be cooler if she took off her boots, woollen coat, and that hat, would she bite my head off?"

Ethel gave a conspiratorial wink. "She'd most likely tell you to go boil your head. It was her favourite expression when we were younger."

"Ha! Of course it was. I'll let you make your getaway without any suggestions then."

Ethel grinned. "Clever girl."

Kit kissed Ethel's cheek again and got a pat on the shoulder before the wispy woman wafted away in the wake of her steam-locomotive best friend.

As if summoned by magic, Rajesh popped out from behind a statue. "You know what's next, don't you?"

Kit eyed him with suspicion. "No… What?"

"Time for a walk over to Widow Caine's cottage to talk about that will she hid."

Kit snapped her fingers. "Of course! Make Phyllis stop eating that begonia and we'll go right away."

A short while later, they arrived on Nettle Road. A nearby lawnmower sounded like it was on its last leg. Competing with its noise was a song by Pink blasting out from an open window nearby. Kit hummed along to it as they knocked on Alice's quaintly three-ledged, sage-green door.

"Lots of noise around. No wonder her windows are shut tight," Rajesh noted.

Kit nodded in reply.

Despite the heat, Alice's windows were closed and the curtains drawn. In fact, the whole cottage seemed dark and quiet. When Alice finally answered the door, she was dishevelled and blinked at the sunlight.

"Kit! Rajesh! Dear me, I'm afraid you caught me having a bit of a kip."

Kit gave her a broad smile. "Great idea! I love a good nap. I'm sorry to wake you, but we have something important to talk to you about, and I know you don't always answer the phone."

"Of course. Come on in," Alice said and stepped aside. "I'm sorry that I am so awful at answering the telephone. It's just that these days it's often someone trying to fool me into handing over my pension or to sign up for something I don't need."

"Fair enough," Kit said. "Answering the phone to people I don't know makes me a bit socially anxious at times, so I get your reluctance. Besides, this might be easier to talk about face to face."

They were shown into the living room, where they took a seat after declining drinks and snacks. Phyllis plonked her considerable weight on top of their feet and began snoring as only old dogs can.

"We're not going to take up too much of your time, Alice," Kit said. "It's just that I was talking to Ethel Rosenthal, and she recalls you saying that you'd put your will in that missing Jules Verne book. Is that right?"

Alice was worrying at the hem of her cardigan. Wasn't it too warm today for a cardigan? And were the buttons done up incorrectly?

"My will?" she murmured. "In the book? In *Journey to the Centre of the Earth*?"

Rajesh leaned back. "That's what we were told."

Alice was quiet for a moment. "The will. Yes, it was in there. Hm. Yes, it was, wasn't it? It's not anymore, of course." Her voice sounded hoarse and uncertain.

Suddenly it struck Kit: Alice was still half asleep. Their hostess drifted over to a wooden box on a side table. Rajesh and Kit watched her take out a small pair of scissors and cut a thread sticking out from her cardigan's hem. All this was done with slow, sluggish movements and the occasional stifled yawn.

"I'd ask to come back later if I were you," Rajesh said in Kit's ear. "When you're our age, it takes a long time to wake up after a sleep."

"Good idea," Kit whispered back. "Um, Alice?" she asked in a louder voice.

"Yes, dear?"

Kit heaved the snoring Phyllis off her feet. "I've remembered that I have an errand to run. Would it be possible for us to discuss this later? Perhaps even with your family present?"

"Hm?" Alice blinked at her a few times. "Yes. Naturally. My family. That would be a good idea. Then you could draw your own conclusions about them all. I'll find out when they're free and then ring you to let you know when you should come by."

"Sounds great," Kit said, getting up from the plush sofa.

Alice smothered another yawn. "I would imagine it will be after dinner some evening, since Phillip and Jackie often dine with acquaintances of theirs." She stared into space. "I'll serve some nibbles and drinks, I think. Yes. It'll be lovely."

"I'm sure it will," Kit said.

They said their farewells and Alice saw them out. When she'd closed the door behind them, Kit dragged her feet out to the pavement.

"Are you all right?" Rajesh asked while patting Phyllis' head.

"Huh?" Kit turned to him. "Yeah, I'm fine. It's just that seeing Alice so out of it made me wonder about her memory and state of mind. Should we trust her completely regarding that book and the will that was apparently in it?"

Rajesh frowned. "I don't think you can judge her memory or her mind from the fact that she was struggling to wake up from a nap on a hot day. She's no spring chicken."

"No, I guess not." Kit linked her arm with his. "Anyway, let's get on with our day."

"Only if it includes ice cream."

"Brilliant idea, young Master Singh! A cheeky ice cream is bang on what we need."

"Oi, I don't like this modern obsession with the word 'cheeky,' Katherine. I object to being called 'young Master Singh' even more."

Kit laughed. "Fine, I'll make it up to you by buying you an ice cream."

"Agreed. But only if it's a Mr Whippy and has a flake in it. And that we find Phyllis some nice, cold water."

"It's a deal," Kit said as she led him towards more ice cream-filled pastures.

Chapter Ten

BARBIE BALLOON

At six on Wednesday night, the day's bouts of summer rains had finally stopped, but the leaden sky appeared ready to tear open again. Those fat clouds promised a shower right on your head if you looked at them funny.

Sheltering from said clouds was one reason Laura currently had Kit backed up against the glass of an old-fashioned phone booth. Another was that they'd been walking hand in hand through town and somehow begun reminiscing about the first time they made love. A third one was that this phone booth was out of the way and completely devoid of Maximillian Howard.

Kit was aware that the glass and red metal were all that kept her, and her profoundly amorous girlfriend, away from public sight. They were on a street which back in the island's heyday must've been a busy side road, despite now being all barred-up storefronts and one single charity shop hanging on for dear life. As the charity place was closed, no one was around. So that was fine, right? Still.

Should Laura be kissing her like this in public?

Should Laura be running her hands up Kit's hips and sides like that?

Oh! She definitely shouldn't be grabbing on to *certain attributes* like that.

"Babe, slow down," Kit panted, although her treacherous hands seemed to be pulling Laura closer.

In her ear, Laura whimpered. "I'm sorry, dearest. I'll stop."

"No, don't you dare stop! Just slow down a bit."

"I'm trying. It's just so hard because you're so sexy. Your perfect, fit body feels so good, and goodness, how I've missed touching you." Laura sighed, her hot breath caressing Kit's ear and cheek in a way which made her wonder if her knees had been replaced with marshmallows. Laura whispered, "A few more seconds, and then we'll return to decent behaviour. For now, I need a little more of you."

Kit couldn't argue with that. She needed Laura, too. In fact, she ached for the physical reminders of their love, even if a pay phone was digging into her side. Wait, was that the phone? Things were getting far too intimate. Then Laura moaned and Kit forgot all about phones, or whatever it was, poking into inappropriate places.

"Yes. A few moments more," Kit said and took firm grip of her girlfriend's bum.

Laura nibbled at her ear, and Kit whimpered.

Laura pushed their hips and breasts against each other, and Kit moaned.

Laura's right hand slid between them, and Kit... yelped!

She wasn't yelping at what Laura was doing but at a sudden appearance on the other side of the fogged-up glass. It was a pink helium balloon with a Barbie doll's face on it. Holding it was a small, elderly man with a moustache.

Charlie Baxter, of wheelbarrow fame,[1] knocked on the glass and shouted, "Hello? I say, are you all right in there? This glass is rather steamed-up. Are you stuck, sir or madam?"

Laura turned the colour of a piece of chalk that's been in prison for the past decade. Though she was the one who had instigated this steamy situation, she was also what some would call a good girl with a constant worry about what people thought of her. Not to mention that she was a pillar of society and a recognised role model for Greengage's youngsters. This somewhat clashed with running your hands and mouth all over the local librarian in a cramped public space.

Kit rubbed Laura's upper arm consolingly as she replied, "Hi, Charlie. We're fine. We, uh… I needed to make a call, but my glasses were foggy, so Laura came in here to help me dial."

It sounded feeble to Kit, but Charlie, like so many other Greengagers, wasn't much for logic on the best of days. He waved and then chirped, "Ah, hello, Kit! Good evening, Laura. Splendid. I'm glad you're not in a spot of bother. Look here, I bought a balloon."

"I can see that. Barbie. Unexpected choice," Kit said and cleared her throat. She was trying to sound normal but was aware of her beating heart, her equally pulsing crotch, and the auburn-haired beauty in her embrace who clearly wanted to sink through the ground.

"I'd say the whole balloon is unexpected, what?" He boomed. "Imagine me with a balloon! It's a birthday gift for my neighbour, Mrs Shaw's niece."

Kit took a deep breath. "Great! I'm sure she'll love it."

"Oh, rather! Anyway, I should leave you to make your phone call. Pip-pip."

"Pip… uh… pip." Kit said, once again doubting if Greengage existed in the same time or space as the rest of the world.

Laura put her hand over her eyes and giggled.

Kit started adjusting her T-shirt, which was all out of place. "What? Are you laughing at us getting caught? Or, well, semi-caught?"

"No. The balloon. He said it was for Mrs Shaw's niece?"

"Yes."

"Jessica Shaw is sixteen! Not young enough to want a Barbie balloon or old enough to laugh at it in an ironic way. Dear Charlie hasn't made as good a choice as he believes. I would have told him, but I was too panicked."

Kit leaned her head back onto the phone booth's wall. "Sixteen? Oh, and *Pip-pip*? Honestly. This island. These people."

Laura's face fell.

Kit gripped her shoulders. "Babe? What's wrong?"

She was quiet a while longer before asking, "Is it too much for you? Greengage, I mean. Do you want to move?"

Kit grabbed her shoulders. "Honey, no! I love the amusement factor and how sweet and wholesome it is here most of the time. I've never seen anywhere this gloriously weird. Plus, it grows the most charming women." Kit let her hands slide down from Laura's shoulders to her plentiful chest. "Grows them *very* nicely."

Laura quirked an eyebrow at her. "While I appreciate being on this side of the objectification, I thought we were meant to stop that? Heaven only knows who might walk past next."

Kit retracted her hands, taking her time with it, because those hands *really* wanted to stay put. "You're right, as always."

They shared a quick kiss.

Laura watched Kit from under her long eyelashes. "I was being serious, though, dearest. If you ever want to leave, return to London or something, then you have to let me know. I want you to feel at home and be happy. Completely and utterly happy."

"I want to stay here," Kit stated, leaving no room for doubt.

Laura beamed. There was really no one else in the world who could embody that expression. When she was happy or relieved, Laura Howard *beamed*. It left Kit breathless. She kissed Laura again.

Of course she wanted to stay. Not only because she'd grown to love the bizarre island and its six thousand interesting inhabitants, but because Greengage was in Laura's blood. After all, her Howard Hall, with the attached Gage Farm, was the crown jewel of the island. Laura's ancestors were some of the first people to settle here, and she seemed to know every person who lived here now. Furthermore, there was the fact that Laura loved this place, with all of her big heart. Kit wouldn't take Laura away from Greengage for any reason other than physical safety. Even if the lack of exotic food, city culture, and sensible people could be a bother.

Then Laura kissed her, deeper this time. Kit's senses filled with Laura's mouth, the warm, velvet feel of it and the ghosting taste of the red wine they'd drunk with dinner. It would be easy to lose herself in this again and end up making love to Laura right here and now.

Then the memory of a big pink balloon and a moustachioed little man popped into her head, and she pulled away from Laura. "Maybe we should leave before I tear your clothes off."

Laura gave a shy, flattered sort of smile. "Yes. This dress was made for me by a London tailor who's not only retired but far too expensive for me these days."

Laura stepped back, and Kit tried to compose herself by asking questions. "Oh, really? When?"

"Hm. Must be around eleven years ago."

"Eleven? But we're both thirty-one. Did you get this when you were twenty?"

Laura smoothed down said dress. "Yes. That's good tailoring for you. It can leave room for when you fill out through the years due to too many jam-drenched waffles."

"At least if you fill out in all the right places."

"Behave," Laura said with a smirk that was ordering Kit to do the opposite.

She reached out to touch Laura, but she danced away and opened the door to let herself out of the phone booth. Kit followed, heart bubbling over with affection.

Outside, the heavy, wet air still felt refreshing compared to the air in the booth.

They returned to the walk they'd been taking before that phone booth lured them in, now heading up the hill to Howard Hall and Kit's cottage.

As they strolled in comfortable silence, Kit thought about Laura's dress. Back in London, the rich people she'd seen had often been businessmen and women, third-generation bankers, and foreign oligarchs.

However, the landed gentry tended to be just that: out

on the land. They had their manor houses, halls, and old seats out in the countryside, most of them crumbling by what she'd heard. They often seemed to have more titles and family history than ready cash.

Someone like Laura, modest as her ancestry was compared to old families with actual titles on the mainland, would be more likely to have boots made by a shoemaker and a dress that some old tailor had sewn, and keep them all until they wore out or didn't fit. The upper middle class, the stockbrokers, CEOs, solicitors, and so on, were more likely to buy expensive designer brands and change their outfits every season.

The rich are bloody confusing.

"Where are you with the book affair?" Laura asked, interrupting Kit's musings.

"Alice has arranged for me and the suspects, I mean her family, to sit down and chat over drinks. Then we can get to the bottom of the will-hidden-in-the-book thing I told you about."

"Excellent. Will you want company?"

"I doubt your uncle would let you go alone, so it's best that you sit this one out, babe."

Laura sighed. "You're probably right. Speaking of him, I should get back to the Hall to babysit. I guess there'll be an evening of playing chess while he prattles on and I daydream about you."

Kit laughed. "About little old me, huh?"

"Mm-hm. About those cornflower blue eyes behind cute glasses, rosy cheeks, a stunning pair of long-fingered hands, and girlish curves supported by… mmm… lean muscles."

Kit withdrew her hand from Laura's so she could cross her arms over her chest in feigned annoyance. "Oh, so you're not going to daydream about anything else than how I look? Now who's objectifying who, mate?"

Laura playfully slapped her hip. "Don't 'mate' me."

"You don't want me to mate with you?"

Laura made a noise like a badger who's been stepped on.[2] "Kit! You know what I mean."

Kit was laughing too hard to answer. Instead she let herself be pulled into a kiss and embrace halfway up the hill. Here, she thought, they should be safe from Charlie Baxter and his Barbie balloon. Too bad the same couldn't be said for Maximillian. Oh well, spending time with Laura was always the best way to spend time. Even if it was without kissing. Or cuddling. Or wrapping her legs around Laura. Or, well, why not be honest?

Going at it like two rabbits after a plate of oysters and two pots of coffee.

Love was never straightforward on Greengage, but that made it all the sweeter.

Chapter Eleven

THE BIGGEST TOSSER

T he late evening's light had that warm tinge of summer eves, all honey and gold. It filtered through bleached-white net curtains and perfectly cleaned windows. Alice Caine was without a doubt houseproud.

Kit stood in Alice's little cottage, admiring the gorgeous, big bookshelves while ignoring the floral wallpaper in eye-bashing pinks and purples.

All the suspects were present. Well, except Liam Soames, who had been invited but claimed he was busy. Maybe he was. Or perhaps he didn't want to socialise with the Caines, since most of them looked down on him. Kit didn't know if Liam was an astute judge of character, but surely that sort of snobbery and rudeness would be obvious to anyone.

The Caine family, on the other hand, were all accounted for.

Phillip Caine's appearance was as stern and unpleasant as his manner on the phone. He and Jackie sat on either side of the mauve sofa. Kit had the feeling that the space between them was as much due to years of arguments as it was due to comfort. A round pillow with the words "Home Sweet Home" embroidered on it sat between them. However, that was probably not as telling of their marriage situation as the distance between them was.

A bit ironic, Kit thought. *Bet their home is anything but sweet.*

The only interaction Kit had seen between the pair was the occasional glare and sharp word. This stood in sharp contrast with the doting Jackie did on their daughter. She cuddled and coddled the girl as if she was a baby and not a teenager. It made you wonder how much of it was for Caitlin's sake and how much of it was Jackie needing the affection. Jacqueline Caine also had kind words to spare for her brother-in-law and even gifted him a smile or two, something which she didn't do for anyone else in the house, including Kit. This did nothing to dispel the gossip that Jackie and Anthony were having an affair. Nevertheless, Kit refused to make any assumptions on the basis of island gossip about a woman who was unhappy in her marriage seeking kindness from another family member. That might be naïve, especially for a Londoner, but Kit tried to give people the benefit of the doubt.

Speaking of Anthony, he was standing by the fireplace, fidgeting with a small porcelain elephant. He put it back on the shelf with a little too much force, and Kit jumped with worry about the porcelain cracking. It seemed to hold together, much as Anthony gave the impression of barely avoiding cracking under pressure.

With bleached blonde hair and clothes of an equally unnatural platinum colour, Caitlin was propped against the wall, typing away on her phone at the speed of light. Kit didn't blame her. This little gathering must have been boring for her, and she probably had friends she wanted to talk to. Kit tried to observe her, but, of course, saw no signs of the girl either being prone to stealing or feeling guilty about having taken a book. It had been a year since that book disappeared, and thirteen-going-on-fourteen-year-old Caitlin's life was no doubt filled with much more recent and juicy drama.

Alice Caine was in the kitchen, preparing drinks and snacks. Earlier, she had offered to whip up a pitcher of Pimm's and serve the cheeseboard she had prepared. At that point, Phillip had banged his fist on the armrest of the sofa and griped that this was too much for a regular Tuesday evening, especially as he planned to leave soon. Jackie had added that it was a school night for Caitlin and then glowered at her jewel-encrusted watch as if she wanted to have left ten minutes ago. Alice had thus simpli-fied the treats down to glasses of sherry and port, served with some crackers, and Kit had tried not to pout. Big summer-sweet glasses of Pimm's and a full cheeseboard sounded like a lot more fun, even if she'd have to exercise like mad to counteract the calories.

Kit was still standing there, casting glances at the Caine family, when Phillip rubbed one of his thick eyebrows and growled. Actually growled. His face was a picture of annoyance.[1]

"You'll pardon my restlessness, Ms Sorel," he said, leaving no room for negotiation. "But I simply cannot see why Mother thought we all needed to meet to discuss trifles such as missing books with someone who, no offence, is a complete stranger to us. I told you the other night, this is all codswallop."

Kit gave a slight shrug. "And as I told you, your mum is worried because things were moved around the house and something went missing. That would be disconcerting for anyone, but especially for someone who is elderly and lives alone. I think it's natural that she wants some answers."

"I could see that if there were signs of a break-in or something valuable stolen," Jackie said in a posh voice with a tinge of her native Scottish accent. "In this case, though, we don't know anyone has actually been in here. Perhaps the book merely fell down behind the bookshelf? Or someone borrowed it when they visited and never told Alice?"

Phillip waved his hand in the direction of his wife as if he wanted to waft away her words. "What does it matter anyway?" he snarled. "I can buy Mother ten copies of the missing book, ones that are in better condition than the ratty, old, dog-eared copy she lost."

Kit's gaze shot to him. "You remember the condition of the book that went missing? Did you ever read it?"

His upper lip twitched. "Do you mean *Journey to the Centre of the Earth* in general or that exact copy?"

Alice tottered in slowly, carrying a tray of tiny, high-stemmed glasses. Three contained pale amber liquid and two held blood-red port. Kit tried to not be annoyed at that it was assumed the women would want the sweet sherry and the men got the strong port, especially as she did in fact want the sherry tonight. She picked up a glass, briefly marvelling that the spirit's colour matched the evening sun's before answering Phillip.

"I meant that exact copy. The one you described as... 'ratty, old, dog-eared,' was it?"

He squirmed. "That was an educated guess. All Mother's books tend to be old, careworn copies. Oh, and obviously no port for me. I'm driving."

"Of course. Silly me," Alice said, placing the tray on

the coffee table. She smiled at Kit. "He's right about my books being old. I like buying books second-hand. It feels like I'm adopting them, saving them from the rubbish bin, as it were."

"Agreed," Kit said, returning the smile.

Alice glanced around until her gaze set on her grand-daughter. "Caitlin, dear, I'll go fetch the crackers and some water for your father. I'll get you a drink at the same time. What would you like?"

The fact that this fragile woman in her seventies was waiting hand and foot on her family without any assistance hit Kit. "Maybe Caitlin could fetch a drink for herself and pick up the crackers and water when she's in the kitchen? I'd like you to be here for this, Alice."

The last bit wasn't quite true as she was more here to observe Caitlin than chat with Alice, but it was either that or Kit would have to help her, meaning that she would miss out on her reason for this visit: watching and questioning the suspects.

To Kit's surprise, everyone looked appalled at the suggestion. Alice's eyes widened, and she quickly said, "No! There's no need for Caitlin to wander around on her own." She took a breath, smoothed down her skirt, and then in a calmer tone added, "You are all my guests. Naturally, I will fetch the refreshments."

Caitlin was blushing a shade of red you rarely saw on anything else but a mailbox. "I'll have a Sprite if you've got some."

"I think there are a few cans left since your last visit, dear. I shall pour you some in a nice glass," Alice said.

Kit couldn't help but notice the relief in the other three adults in the room. Either this kid was a menace when it came to pouring drinks or there was some truth to the rumour of her stealing things. Or maybe that was a bit of a reach. Perhaps there had just been an incident in the past where Caitlin had snuck herself some sherry while alone in the kitchen.

Alice trundled off to get the Sprite, water, and crackers, so Kit turned back to Phillip. "Where were we? Right, the missing copy of *Journey to the Centre of the Earth*. So, you never borrowed it?"

A muscle bounced in Phillip's cheek. "No."

There was a moment of silent, challenging eye contact. Kit leaned back against the wall, trying to seem nonchalant. "Okay, um. You're absolutely sure?"

Phillip gave her a burning stare which probably served him well in the air force. Through gritted teeth he said, "Obviously I'm bloody sure, you silly woman!"

The way that he sat back on the sofa suggested that he thought he'd ended the discussion with fear-inducing rage and a sprinkling of misogyny. Kit tried to not smile pityingly at this misconception. "I see," she said, unmoved. "I was just wondering if you might've known if there was something in it? A slip of paper or something?"

"What? Of course not," he barked.

Alice came back in with two highball glasses and a plate of crackers. "Are we back to that, Kit? The idea that something was written in the book or left in it?"

Kit surveyed her. *Has Alice forgotten our chat about the will? Or is she acting for the benefit of the present company?*

"I think it's likely," she replied. "There had to be some worth to the book, and if it wasn't a special edition or a particularly uniquely bound book, the only worth I can imagine it having is as a container for something else."

Kit didn't mention Aimee's idea of the book being a cypher. She was sure that Ethel's mention of the will was the ticket here. It had to be! She needed to prompt Alice's memory without putting words in her mouth. After all, perhaps Alice never put the will in the book but only talked to Ethel about doing it.

Kit weighed her words carefully. "Perhaps there was an important document hidden in there?"

Alice stopped mid-movement. The lines around her eyes deepened as she squinted towards her bookshelf. "Wait. Hidden? *Journey to the Centre of the Earth*..." Her forehead furrowed, making the wrinkles collide with each other. "There is a hidden message in the Icelandic book the professor finds in that novel, isn't there?"

"Yep," Kit said hopefully.

"Yes," Alice said under her breath. "That was why I hid it there. We spoke about this when you woke me up from my nap, didn't we? I remember. I hid my—"

The grandfather clock in the corner chimed nine. This seemed to drain the last drop of patience from Wing Commander Caine. He smacked his hands against his solid thighs.

"This is a waste of my time! I told you that we only had time to stop for a minute, Mother. I'm sure Anthony has more time to lounge about since he was fired. However, Jackie, Caitlin, and I are leaving."

"You can't stay long enough to let your mother finish her sentence?" Kit asked.

In one sharp movement, he was on his feet and standing to his full height. She had to admit that he looked terrifying, even though he wasn't the biggest or fittest bloke she'd ever stood up to. At his age and with his back injury, if he did get violent, she could probably hold her own or at least get away without too much issue. Not that she expected things to go that far. Phillip cared too much about society's expectations, and about seeming in control of himself, for that.

He fixed his piercing eyes on her. "Don't be impertinent. I told you to drop this matter. Instead you have made it worse."

"Phillip, calm down," Jackie said, with no real feeling in the words.

He kept his gaze on Kit. "I am calm, despite this monumental waste of time. I wish you wouldn't help my mother make a molehill into a mountain and fill her head with conspiracies when all that's happened is that a tattered book has been misplaced." He took a step closer to her, and she made a point to sip her sherry in the most unfazed way possible. "Ms Sorel, if you want to keep my mother safe and avoid a robbery, you should make her take back Liam Soames' key. However, if all you want to do is interrogate important people about a bloody book, then you should have your head examined and stay out of my precious free time."

Precious free time? He's not in the RAF anymore, Kit thought but said nothing.

Looking annoyed that he hadn't goaded a reply from her, he stormed off with pounding steps.

Jacqueline rose with much more poise. In no rush, she drank the last of her sherry, picked up her handbag, and elegantly hung it on her thin shoulder. Then she trained her false-lashed and black-lined eyes on Kit. "While Phillip was a bit rude just then and should have stayed longer, he's right. This is pointless and will only end up frightening dear Alice. Furthermore, it makes us all feel like suspects in some sad, second-rate detective story."

Kit was thinking of how to reply, but Jackie hadn't finished. She tilted her head to the left in an affected gesture of sympathy. "I'm sure this is all very exciting to you and that you need something to do on this quiet island, but this is real life. No one has time to worry about a missing book. It was nice meeting you, Ms Sorel."

Jackie click-clacked over to Alice on her high heels and gave her mother-in-law an air kiss near each cheek. Then she turned to give Anthony a slow nod and what looked like a flirty smirk, before linking her arm with Caitlin's. Caitlin downed her drink, left the glass on a side table with a subtle burp, and grimaced at Kit. They left without a word, slamming the door with a deafening thud.

Alice was left wringing her hands and looking from Anthony to Kit. "They're... very busy, Kit. Especially Phillip, who is so stressed and in rather a lot of pain with his back. Please forgive him."

"He certainly seems stressed," Kit muttered before having the last of her sherry.

Anthony put his unfinished port on the mantelpiece and sniffed. "I must say, while my brother is dramatic, he does have a point. No offence, but I've got to be frank." He broke off to clean his glasses on his sleeve with rapid movements. Kit, knowing the pains of wearing glasses and trying to clean them on the wrong material, saw that he was only smearing them further. "Mummy, I believe the book has been misplaced or that there's some other obvious and harmless explanation. I fail to see why we need a librarian to look into that. In fact, this is all quite stressful at a time when many of your family members are adjusting to new circumstances."

Kit put her hand in her pocket so he wouldn't see her clench it into a fist. She tried to catch his eye. "Do you mean like the loss of your job? Or Phillip's back injury?" She considered mentioning the cheating rumours and the talk about Caitlin stealing but wasn't prepared to sink that low. Not until she knew there was more to them than vicious rumours.

Anthony didn't appear furious or even put out. He had the appearance of a mannequin, his face blank and his body stiff. The likeness was heightened by his perfectly pressed suit trousers and starched white shirt. He was as silent as a mannequin, too.

Next to them, Alice put a hand to her brow, which snapped Anthony out of his frozen state. "Mummy is tired. That's enough for tonight."

He pointed to the door and then hovered a hand about half an inch from Kit's back, as if loath to touch her but still wanting to usher her out. She was about to jump away from him and give him a piece of her mind when she noted how pale and stricken Alice was. Anthony was staring at Kit as if it was her fault. For a moment the mood in the room made her doubts creep back in. Maybe she was making a big deal out of nothing. Perhaps she was egging an old lady on to see danger and mysteries where there was nothing but a misplaced book.

Either way, Alice was clearly done for the day. Bringing up the will now would only upset her even more. Besides, it'd be of little use to have the chat about it now since only Anthony remained in a fit state to answer.

"Fine. We'll call it a night for now," Kit said. She gave Alice a quick hug and thanked her for the refreshments.

As she walked out with Anthony, leaving the quiet house and its oppressive mood behind, she thought back to the Post-It note from the library and the Caine family's overly aggressive behaviour. How could she, even for a second, have thought there was nothing strange going on here? She set her jaw and debated how to ask Anthony about the will as soon as they were out of Alice's earshot.

Any approach she picked would've been good, if only she'd gotten the chance. The moment they were outside, Anthony spun towards her and sniped, "Haven't you wasted our time enough by now, you blasted, meddling outsider?" Then he darted to his car and sped away before Kit could digest what he said.

Ugh. Isn't he charming? No wonder Alice suspects one of her sons of suspect behaviour, she thought as she began walking home.

Above her, the sky was darkening enough to show off a huge, full, butter-yellow moon. It was so bright it outshone the pale stars, making it look lonely in that big sky. Kit wished Laura were there for a romantic walk together. She got out the phone to call her. Even if Maximillian was there, they could at least discuss the evening's Caine interactions and how they affected the case. Perhaps, they could even make plans to meet up soon.

After two rings there was a reply. Kit hadn't noticed that her whole body was tense until she heard Laura's voice greet her. She felt herself relax from top to toe.

"Hey, baby," Kit said. "You doing okay?"

"I'm fine, dearest. How are you? How did it go tonight?"

Kit adjusted her glasses. "It was... dramatic. Hey, do you wanna play 'Which of the Caine Brothers is the Biggest Tosser' with me?"

Laura giggled. "Of course. Tell me everything."

And so Kit did.

Chapter Twelve

THIS ONE HAS SEX IN IT

I t was only ten past six, but Kit had already managed to come home from work and scoff down one of the left-over veggie-and-hummus wraps from the fridge. She had Rajesh locking up the library that evening to thank for all of her extra time. Sadly, as he was getting older and increasingly aware that Kit was the junior librarian, she was the one locking up most of the time these days.

Anyway, the workday was over, dinner had been sorted, and now the pot of chilli-chai tea Kit had just brewed awaited her. A new book waited for her, too; it was about the mother of a gifted child falling in love with the child's teacher. A dose of sweet, Sapphic romance was exactly what she needed right now. She poured the tea, breathing in the scents of chilli and chai mingling with her wood-scented candle.[1] She sat down on the sofa, sipped the tea with a delighted sigh, and chose her favourite font and page colour on her e-reader before starting to read.

The doorbell rang.

Bloody hell.

She lowered the e-reader, grunted, and considered

ignoring it. The doorbell rang again, and she knew she had to be an adult and answer it.

"I'm coming," she shouted. When the e-reader and the mug of tea were safely placed on her coffee table, she hurried to the offending door. Outside was the one visitor Kit would happily allow to ruin her reading experience, Laura. Kit's chest and belly filled with drunk butterflies.

"Wow! Hey, babe! Why didn't you use your key? I'm—"

Kit's words were cut off by the sight of Maximillian muscling in front of his niece with an unlabelled glass jar held out as an offering.

"Susan!" he roared. "We have a sample of the new gooseberry jam. Invite us in and rustle up some scones or toasted bread or something. We must try this little beauty immediately!"

"Uh, sure, come in."

He did so, and after him came Laura, gorgeous as ever but unusually sheepish. She whispered, "That's why I didn't use the key, my love. I wanted to give you some warning before I sprang my uncle on you."

"A text, an email, or even an actual phone call could've been a good warning," Kit said with a smile.

"I know," Laura groaned. "I'm so sorry, but he's on me like a hawk and never stops talking. It makes it very hard to get anything done or to have a moment to think things through. Besides, this visit was an impulse of his. He decided we needed a non-Howard to try the jam."

Kit scratched her head. "Babe, I don't have scones or any white bread. He doesn't strike me as the type who likes wholegrain bread."

"Please don't worry about that, I'm sure we'll find something." Laura paused to look towards the kitchen.

"I'm afraid the racket we hear is him going through your cabinets. We might want to stop him before he creates a mess."

Kit halted to get her tea and then headed for the kitchen where the astronomical pain in her bum was currently rummaging through everything, searching for something to slather jam on. Kit wished he'd stick it on his own face.

§

Ten minutes later they were eating the last of the jam-drenched wholegrain bread. Maximillian did occasionally grumble something that sounded like "seeds." Nevertheless, he hadn't complained.

The fact that he was so busy with the bread and quiet assessment of the jam left Kit and Laura to sneak glances and play the "get as many innuendos and hidden flirtations into a chat about jam" game, which they had now invented. The game kept escalating.

Laura batted her long lashes. "Don't you find the jam has a hint of almost feminine spice and a savoury tang in the taste? It reminds me of some other naughty treat. I just can't put my finger on it right now."

Whoa. She clearly needs to get laid as much as I do.

Kit surveyed her last bite of bread with jam dripping over the edge and onto her hand. "Yeah, I see your point, Laura. It does remind me of *that,* and all that inviting, sticky, sweet juice oozing out to coat my fingers right now only adds to the comparison," Kit said, sure she'd gone too far with her last comment.

When she checked the reactions of the two Howards' at her cramped kitchen table, she noted with relief that

Maximillian was busy muttering about the fruit content while Laura… well, Laura was giving her the sort of look which made them end up fooling around in phone booths, that look now raked all the way from Kit's socks, via her tight jeans and even tighter T-shirt, up to her mouth. Kit swallowed hard and tried to fight the rising heat.

Thank goodness Maximillian was occupied with poking one of the berries in the jam to miss what was without a doubt the most wicked and sexual glance Kit had ever been blessed to receive. No wonder she was suddenly burning up, with a slight buzz between her legs.

In the potent silence, Laura oh so slowly slid the back of her fingers over her lips, across her jawline, and down her swan neck, making Kit have to fidget with how she sat.

Laura cleared her throat. "Uncle Maximillian, did you remember to tell Imelda that you can't have carrots or parsnips anymore, since they make your ears hot?"

He swallowed his mouthful with a look of confusion. "Imelda. Is that the cook?"

No, it's the towel rack, you numpty. She's worked for your family for over thirty years, learn her name, Kit thought, all patience waning as her need for Laura grew.

"Yes, that's her," his incredibly patient niece said. "You might want to hurry."

Kit fidgeted again, unable to get the wet, hot, aching mess between her legs comfortable. She could have sworn she had a fever.

"Hurry?" Maximillian queried. "Oh yes, before she leaves, you mean? Of course. Blasted woman. Putting carrots in everything. I'll tell her to cease this madness forthwith."

Kit wasn't surprised that he left without saying good-bye. That was common practise with him. She was however flabbergasted by that he grabbed her scarf with a Star Wars motif off the coat rack as he did so.

When the door closed behind him, Laura said in a thick voice, "I'll make sure he brings the scarf back. He has no idea that he took it or why he did so."

Kit was about to say that didn't matter when Laura added, "Oh, and he'll be gone for a long time. Imelda went home hours ago, but he'll still look all over for her. I tried this trick yesterday when I needed a chat with the employees."

"Sneaky little vixen," Kit said with a wink.

"Needs must and all that," Laura said, blushing from either shame or sexual tension. Knowing her, it was probably both.

Kit smiled. "Good for you, honey."

Their eyes connected, the intensity of it sending sparks through Kit. There was still arousal in the air, but now that they were alone, the mood had turned more romantic. More careful. Almost as if they were new lovers again. Had it been so long that they had grown a little shy of each other? Kit's heart was beating so fast. When had it started racing like that?

"You know," Laura said hoarsely, "that scented candle is quite strong. Mind if we go upstairs to get away from it?"

"Not at all, lead the way."

As Laura left the room, Kit blew out the offending candle, even though she was sure it wasn't Laura's real reason for going upstairs.

She watched Laura walk up the uneven wooden stairs and take in the two rooms on either side of it. One of them was a boxroom that Kit used as storage space and the other was Kit's bedroom. Laura sashayed into the bedroom in a way which made Kit suspect she knew that her girlfriend was watching every step and sway. The moonlight mixed with streetlight from outside the window, painting gold into Laura's auburn curls.

She turned and smiled—no, *beamed*—at Kit. "Finally alone."

"Finally alone," Kit echoed in breathy tones.

Laura paced around, shooting shy glances at her and dragging out the moment of tentative coyness between them. It had a tinge of magic and Kit wanted it to never end, but at the same time, she was going crazy with the anticipation. Or rather, with the need.

She had never known love could run this deep. All of her earlier relationships paled in comparison to the one she had with Laura. This overwhelming fascination and affection had been woven into every part of her, from heart to soul to crotch, so that she couldn't imagine who she'd be if she didn't love Laura anymore.

Laura stopped by the full-length mirror and ran her hands over her wide hips. "Do you think I've put on weight?"

Kit switched on the light on her bedside table, used to this question. She always answered honestly and added that, whatever weight Laura currently was, it suited her. Which was true. Everything suited this woman. It was unfair but amazing.

With the room now illuminated, Kit replied, "I'm not sure. Take your clothes off, and I'll have a good look."

"Kit!"

"What? How else can I give you an honest answer?"

Laura bit her red-tinted lip. "Well, I suppose that is why I'm here."

"Oh yeah?" Kit's heartbeat picked up even more. She moved closer and followed up with, "You didn't just come here to test the jam?"

Laura's hazel eyes darkened. "You know what I came for."

"Mm. 'Came' being a very well-chosen word, beautiful," Kit whispered. She didn't manage to make it sound like that rich, boozy, flirty purr Laura's voice always held, but it still did the trick. Without a word of reply, Laura stepped out of her shoes and unzipped her dress, throwing it over a chair.

There she stood, in the glory of only her underwear in the dim glow of the room. The swell of her chest heaved with rapid breath, and those much-adored eyes showed desire, love, and vulnerability. She was more beautiful than any creature had any right to be.

Kit's knees buckled so that she nearly lost her balance. Laura reached for her, and they collided without grace or thought.

Finally. No Maximillian. No Charlie Baxter. No interfering Greengagers in general. And no one was in a public phone booth or a cramped broom closet.

It was just two women in love, now kissing, grabbing, caressing, and undressing each other like starving people reaching for food. And bloody hell, did Laura taste good. Her mouth, her skin, her… everything. She tasted like all Kit had ever needed or wanted. She was high off the scent of Laura's hair and the feel of her hands.

Soon Kit was so light-headed with arousal and forgetting to breathe that she had to lay down. Laura took the opportunity to remove Kit's remaining clothes and her glasses and kiss her from top to toe.

Kit squirmed under her. They didn't have time for foreplay! She had waited too long. She needed Laura in a much more immediate way.

The sneaking around had been fun and so was this stolen moment, but Kit had no patience left. She couldn't wait, couldn't even think anymore. She needed something thoroughly physical. If this woman wasn't inside her within the next fifteen seconds, Kit was going to sue the whole bloody island!

"Laura, I can't do this slow and sweet. I need you to… well, sort of just get on with it and shag me silly, please. And unusually for me, I'm talking penetration."

Kit wasn't sure what reply she'd expected to that. A laugh? A witty, sexy retort? A turned-off grimace? What she got was a look of such animal lust that she actually gasped. Clearly, Laura was beyond rational thought and foreplay, too.

There was no talk about fifteen seconds. Kit was being truly and thoroughly ravished by Laura Howard the very next moment.

After that, followed an hour of some of the best sex Kit had ever had.

Not because it was thought-through, nicely orchestrated, or very skilled—in fact, they kept bumping their noses when kissing and rolling around while trying to decide whose turn it was to be on top—but because it was so sorely needed. Both their bodies showed it. Kit couldn't remember being so quickly re-aroused after orgasm since she was a teenager. Nor could she remember that Laura's moans had been quite this addictive. Or loud. Or bloody perfect.

By the time Kit found herself sweaty, satisfied, and soaked, with her cheek resting against Laura's crotch, she knew that they'd waited far too long to do that.

"You," she said, "are the best lover I have ever known."

"I feel the same about you. Although, I wonder," Laura panted back, "if there's such a thing as a great lover. Or if it has more to do with being in sync with your partner?" She had to pause for a ragged breath. "For example, if you like it rough and your partner does, too, you would both find the other a good lover, right?"

Kit placed a kiss on Laura's pubic bone, the auburn curls covering it tickling her mouth. "Wow, that last climax made you all philosophical. Do you mean that it's all subjective? Depending on what you want in bed?"

Laura sucked in another panting breath. "Yes, I think so. That and that it takes two to tango. You both need to be on the same page, enjoy the same thing, and be under the same circumstances. I mean, if you're in a hurry and your partner is taking their time—the intercourse, kiss, whatever it is—might not be very successful."

"You're very clever," Kit said, placing another kiss into those damp curls.

Laura made a sound somewhere between a sigh and a snort. "That would be surprising, considering you just shagged my brains out."

Kit sniggered, more than a little proud, and crawled up Laura's body until they were face to face for a kiss. She was about to ask if Laura thought they'd manage an encore after a break for some tea and a sandwich.

Sadly, she never got that far.

From downstairs came a creak and an almighty thud.

Kit sat up and quickly put her glasses on. *That was my front door. Bloody hell, didn't I lock it?*

A male voice coughing rang out and then came the words, "Laura? Susan—I mean Kit? Are you upstairs?"

Great. Now he learns my name.

Laura yelped before gathering herself to call back, "Yes, Uncle Maximillian. We're…" She gave Kit a pleading look.

Kit scanned the room for an excuse. "We're changing Laura's bra," she settled on. "She spilled jam into her cleavage, and it ruined the bra. I'm lending her one of mine right now."

Kit's heart and brain were going a mile a minute, and both were cursing her. She usually came up with better excuses than that. Considering their builds, there was no way even Maximillian would buy that she had the same bra size as Laura. Not to mention that he must have heard how weird they sounded. Kit was fully aware that her voice was at the junction of *freaking out* and *dying of embarrassment*. Any second now she'd hear his steps up the stairs. Should they hide? Rush to get dressed? Emigrate?

"Really? Well, jam accidents can be disastrous. Come down when you're ready," he called back.

"I'll be there soon," Laura squeaked.

She grabbed Kit and mouthed "thank you" before leaping into the bathroom. Kit stood in the doorway, watching her with affection that pushed most of the embarrassment aside.

In substantial panic, Laura cleaned off her most indecent parts and shouted, "Almost done," at least twice during the procedure.

"Calm down. You seem suspicious," Kit whispered.

"No rush," Maximillian bellowed. Then there was the unmistakable sound of creaking wood as he stepped closer to the stairs. "You know, the cook was nowhere to be found. I searched everywhere! Finally, I left a note in the kitchen saying no more parsnips and carrots due to their bad effect on ears."

Kit wrapped herself in the duvet and checked on Laura, who was now washing her mouth and so unable to reply. There was another groan from the old floorboards.

Please don't come up. She's so close to being done!

"Good solution! Laura will be down in a moment. Have a seat," Kit called down. She was relieved to hear his steps creak away from the steps again. She gathered Laura's clothes and put them on the bed.

A second later, Laura ran out and got dressed at a speed which must have been some sort of record. She kissed Kit goodbye with a promise to call later and then flew downstairs to collect her uncle.

When the door had shut behind them, Kit had a quick shower, even though it begrudged her to wash Laura's scent off her skin. Then she dressed and sat down in the kitchen. With Laura gone, she needed something else to do with her evening off. She considered her abandoned book or going for a run. Or a walk, considering her wobbly post-coital legs.

Still, it felt as if there was something else she should be doing. A restlessness niggled at her and told her she'd forgotten something important. Then the thought doused her like a bucket of ice water—*I should be asking Alice about her will!*

Yes, that must be it! Kit shoved her Converse on her feet with a half-arsed tying of the laces. She rushed out, down the hill and towards Nettle Road without even missing her leather jacket.

Chapter Thirteen

SNAIL MURDERERS AND SPILLING TEA

K it should've tied her laces better. She had tripped twice and become the unwilling murderer of one snail and one kid's chalk drawing since the start of Nettle Road. She felt guilty but had little time to dwell on that. The Caine brothers, with their lily-white hands and arrogant manners, weren't going to keep her from getting to the bottom of this hidden will business anymore.

Finally, she arrived and was rapping her knuckles against the quaint, old door. That was when her brain caught up, reminding her of her abandoned jacket as well as what forgotten thing had actually been niggling her: talking to Shannon on Rachel's behalf. She slammed her fist into her thigh. What kind of a friend was she? Well, it was too late to change course now; she'd already knocked.

Alice creaked the door open, and when she saw who it was, her face lit up. "Good evening, Kit! Fancy seeing you. I was worried that the boys had scared you off for good."

"Oh, I've had big-city, homophobic bullies after me in my day. I don't scare that easily anymore."

Alice's eyes went wide. "I'm horrified to hear that but

glad you don't find my boys too intimidating. Come on in, dear."

"Thanks, I hope it's not too late for a visit?"

"Oh, no, not at all. Still, I'll get some refreshments to keep us alert."

When they were both seated on the plush sofa with cups of tea and a plate of Garibaldis between them,[1] they picked up the conversation where they had been interrupted last night.

"We were talking about what had been hidden in *Journey to the Centre of the Earth*," Kit said, putting her cup back on its saucer.

"Of course. Yes, I remember. That was when Phillip was so awfully rude and downright unpleasant. I do apologise for him and promise that he's all bark and no bite."

"He's a grown man, he should apologise for his own bad behaviour."

"I know, but still…" She ran her hand over her white curls. "My late husband and I raised him better than that. Although sometimes I worry we might have spoiled the boys. Why else would they have turned from such sweet children to the sort of men I might suspect of meddling with my belongings? How can they be so horrid to someone like you, who only wants to help?"

Kit wasn't sure what answer would give this woman comfort. In the end she had to settle for, "Who can say? Great parents sometimes have… less great kids. Anyway, no need for an apology. Let's just get to the bottom of all of this. Do you feel up to talking about what was hidden in the book?"

Alice put her cup and saucer on the table, smoothed down her skirt, and matter-of-factly said, "my will."

"Right, that's what Ethel told me. I only wanted to

prompt you to make sure that she was remembering correctly."

Alice Caine gave her a knowing smirk. "And that *I* was remembering correctly?"

Kit squirmed. "Well, yes, that, too. I don't want to be ageist, but we all forget things. Especially things that happened a year ago and probably didn't seem all that important at the time."

"My will has always been important to me. The only reason I forgot it was in the book was that it was only there for a day or so."

"Ah, and then it went missing?"

Alice started. "No, dear! Then it was placed in the bank with my jewellery and other things I keep in a safety deposit box there."

Kit's heart sank. "Really? That wasn't why the book was stolen, then."

Alice turned her face to the window, suddenly pensive. "The boys took the will to the bank for me. Phillip said that it wasn't safe to keep it in the house. For the life of me, I can't remember where they got the will from, though."

"Wait… So, they could have stolen the book, found the will, and then maybe changed it and dropped it off the bank?"

"No. The will is exactly as it should be. I checked it about a month ago to make sure I had included my quite new collection of porcelain elephants."

Kit sat forward, knocking the table so that tea spilled into her saucer. "Okay, but you don't know where Phillip and Anthony found the will?"

Alice was still looking out the window, as if searching for

the answer outside. "Hm. No, I can't remember. Oh, isn't that silly? I was just trying to prove to you that being older doesn't mean I'm forgetful, and now I, well, I can't remember."

She seemed so disappointed and angry at herself that it stung Kit's heart. "As I said, it was a year ago, and clearly wasn't remarkable at the time. I bet I'd have forgotten as well. Don't worry about it."

"So silly of me." Alice shook her head, then her gaze returned to Kit. "Anyway, neither of my boys should have a problem with the will."

"No? Why not?" Kit asked before finishing what tea hadn't spilled out of her cup earlier.

Alice picked her cup up as well. "Because I've given them both everything they wanted. Through the years, they have both expressed the wish that eighty percent of my money should go to Phillip and his family, while the remaining twenty percent and this cottage would go to Anthony."

"And that's what your will says?"

"Yes. It does include one more thing: a triple-strand freshwater pearl necklace I got as a wedding gift. Phillip and Anthony agreed it should be sold and the money split evenly between the two of them. No quarrels or uncertainties there either."

"Huh," Kit said, putting her cup down with a feeling of dejection. "You're sure they're happy about all of this? And aware of every detail?"

"Yes, that I am certain of. Both the boys and Jackie were there when the will was written up and signed by me and my solicitor. Even Caitlin was there, as I recall, since she had just been picked up from school."

Kit ran a hand through her hair. "Okay, so there

would be no reason for any of them to steal the will? Or be curious about what was in it?"

"None that I can think of, dear."

Kit's mind was racing. Could this be the work of Liam Soames after all? Maybe he had hoped that the past years of helping Alice would lead to him being named in the will? Maybe he had stolen it to check? But if that were true, why hadn't he acted out when he learned he wasn't in the will? Perhaps he had in some way? After all, Kit knew little to nothing about him or his behaviour. Also, were those flowers on the light fixture up there? Who would want decorated light fixtures? [2]

Low blood sugar is making you go off topic. Take a biscuit and then get back to Liam!

Picking up a Garibaldi, Kit asked, "Would you say that Liam has been more friendly lately? Perhaps, I don't know, sucking up?"

With a shrewd look, Alice replied, "So you think it was Liam who borrowed the will and, when he found out he wasn't in it, attempted to charm his way into it?"

Kit swallowed a mouthful of biscuit and tried for a disarming smile. "Perhaps?"

"I haven't noticed any difference in his behaviour. What's more, despite my sons seeing him as some mastermind criminal, Liam is a straightforward boy. You can read him like a book, pardon the pun. I think I would know if he was plotting to get into my will by either charm or deceit."

"Okay." Kit pushed her glasses up her nose. "What about Rachel?"

"What about dear Rachel?"

"I hear she helped assemble and fill these bookshelves. Is there any way she could've borrowed the book?"

Alice shook her head with vigour. "If she had, she would have told us when you started looking into this. She's the most honest person I know. Furthermore, she has no reason to take the book with or without a will in it."

"Even though she's remotely related to you and might expect to be left something?"

"Rachel is not in the will. She knows that and wouldn't expect anything else. Should I refill your cup?"

"Oh, no, thanks. Why wouldn't Rach expect to be in the will?"

Alice put the teapot down. "We both know that Rachel isn't greedy or fussed about material things. She wants nothing from anyone except a chat and a laugh."

Kit had to admit that there was point to that. Rachel would gladly starve as long as everyone around her was happy and provided for.

"Moreover, Rachel has plenty of other relatives she might inherit from one day," Alice elaborated. "Not to mention that I helped pay her rent when she was temporarily out of work as a young woman. No, she wouldn't *want* to be in my will."

"You're right," Kit admitted. "I suppose that only leaves Liam for me to talk to about the will."

"I suppose so." Alice paused. "You know, I'm not so naïve that I don't know that Liam has done things he shouldn't have."

Kit only nodded as she now had a mouthful of biscuit. She hadn't realised how hungry that *quality time* with Laura had made her.

"With all this in mind, Kit, I feel it's important that I tell you how kind Liam is to me and how many times I have had to comfort him when he's been dealt a bad blow or someone has shown prejudice against him. He has struggled and made mistakes. Nonetheless, he's a good boy and should be given a chance."

"Sure. I see what you're saying, and I promise that I always try to not be prejudiced against people." Alice didn't look convinced, so Kit expanded, "I know, easier said than done. But being gay means that I know how it feels when people have preconceived notions about you, so I try to avoid having them myself. I'll treat Liam exactly like I did your sons the first time I met them."

Here's hoping Liam won't turn out to be condescending, rude, or threatening like them, she added in her mind.

Alice sat back with an air of contentment. "Good. You can speak to Liam while I have another jab at trying to remember anything else about the will or the book. Now, finish your Garibaldi."

Kit all too happily obeyed.

As she was walking home from Nettle Road, Kit got a text from Aimee that sucked her into a lengthy chat about the bookshelf mystery and Aimee's work life. They were six texts into the conversation before the topic turned to Kit missing Laura.

Kit was stepping around a cat washing itself in the middle of a pavement when Aimee wrote:

I don't get why you're not at Howard Hall every night. Sure, old Maxi-boy being there means that you can't put the moves on Laura, but at least you can spend time together. Chat or watch telly or something?

Kit's shoulders drooped while she texted back:

Maximillian doesn't like the TV being on, it hurts his eyes. Meanwhile, chatting with him around hurts my brain. I sometimes go over there and we all sit on our phone or read books. Once we played cards. I don't like being there too often because I worry I'll accidentally kiss Laura. Or kill her uncle.

She walked on while waiting for Aimee's reply. Her common sense berated her for whingeing about something this silly when there were plenty of couples out there who didn't see each other for weeks or even months.

With a start she realised that perhaps this was the sort of relationship Jackie and Phillip had before he had to take early retirement. Was it grating on their relationship that they were now spending so much more time together? If so, was it grating enough for Jackie to start thinking about what would happen when he passed away and how much of Alice's money she'd get?

Kit brushed away the melodramatic notion and focused on the text that now came in from Aimee, changing the topic from Kit's love life to the more immediate issue of little George having just dropped Aimee's toothbrush into the toilet. He was blaming it all on the stuffed fox that Kit had sent them, which was now named Flop.

Kit hit the button to call Aimee. She needed a blow-by-blow description of this.

Chapter Fourteen

WHO KILLED THE GLORIOUS BADGER?

I t was a Sunday. This meant the library was closed, Laura wasn't in the office for once,[1] and Josh could leave the pub since they had the weekend staff in. In short, today was a good day for Kit to get her socialising done. After a long lie-in followed by a big breakfast with an equally big book for company, of course. One must follow the rules of Sundays and be lazy.

When the clock struck eleven-thirty she fished out a pair of shorts and her thinnest tank top and got ready for what the radio was calling the hottest day of the year.

Soon she was on her way up to Howard Hall for lunch. Despite the short walk from her old workman's cottage up to its mother building, the heat exhausted her. She even stopped to fan her tank top over her sweaty chest and damp bra. She thought back to the day she'd run all the way up to Howard Hall in the rain because she had found out that Laura—the amazing woman she'd been having a one-sided crush on—was in fact crushing back and ready to talk about it. That day she'd arrived in a complete mess at that big, imposing door and been met by

Tom who had griped to Laura that Kit could be attractive if she didn't have glasses and wasn't such a wet mess. She smiled as she realised that she would be arriving as a hot mess now, and that Laura would find her as perfect as she always did. How did she get this lucky?

She let herself in through Howard Hall's huge door, grimacing at the heat lodged in its wood. This weather was downright un-British.

Inside she could hear Maximillian screeching something about parsnips. Kit loved this house, but why was there so often someone in it to annoy her? If it wasn't Laura's overcritical Aunt Sybil, or the sleazy Tom, it was this mad-as-a-hatter uncle. Kit had to admit that, out of the three of them, Maximillian was actually the best. At least he had good intentions.

A female voice hushed Maximillian. Kit couldn't make out the words, but she recognised that warm voice which a year later left Kit as breathless as it had the first time she heard it. She picked up her pace towards the sound and had to stop herself from calling out "baby" or "honey" or something else sappy and loving. Instead she called Laura's name and was answered by, "We're in here, Kit."

She followed the words to the minute library. Maximillian was holding up a badminton racket and saying, "Lunch can wait. First tell me why this was in the games room?"

"Because that's where we keep rackets, mallets, balls, and things related to sports and games," Laura said with a patient smile. "Where do you think the rackets should live? Not in here, I hope? I don't think the books would like it."

Kit coughed for attention. When she spotted her, Laura held out her arms and Kit rushed straight into them. She worried about if the hug was platonic enough but saw that Maximillian was busy inspecting the racket in his hand, so she pulled Laura close and breathed in the floral scent of her perfume.

"I missed you," Laura whispered in her ear.

"Same," Kit said as she pulled away.

Maximillian held the racket high in greeting. "Susan!"

"Kit," Laura and Kit corrected at the same time.

His eyebrows shot up. "What? Yes, certainly. Back to the matter at hand."

Kit and Laura eyed him expectantly, but he didn't carry on. Instead he leaned on his racket, puffed out a breath which made his cottony comb-over move, and looked as if he were waiting for them to speak.

Laura rolled her shoulders, and Kit heard a pop of tension. "What exactly *is* the matter at hand, Uncle Maximillian?"

"Why do you ask that, dear girl? You know very well that I wish to give Sus—I mean Kit—a new creation."

Kit's stomach turned. "If this is another dead, stuffed animal, please don't."

"What? Why should I abstain from gifting you this glorious badger that I have had the great luck to come upon?"

Kit adjusted her glasses. Then she did it again while shifting her footing. There must be a way to explain to him why most people wouldn't want gifts like these, glorious as the badger in question might be.

"The thing is, Maximillian, I'm not a fan of hunting or killing animals for anything but food. I only wear a leather jacket because it's cowhide. I'm likely to have already bought the cow's meat for my burgers and would hate to see the leather be wasted."

It made sense in her head but a small part of her reconsidered her choice to eat meat and wear leather when she realised how distressing she found thinking about this stuffed badger to be. It was quite different when the dead animal was sitting on your shelf staring at you with glass eyes. Wait, did they have glass eyes? Surely they couldn't be the animal's real eyes? Wouldn't they dry out or something? Great, now she was nauseous, and lunch had dropped off her priority list.

Despite her words, Maximillian was beaming at her. For the first time, Kit could actually see that he was related to Laura, because *beaming* was the only way to describe the way his face lit up in that bright Howard smile. It was astonishing how much that single piece of family resemblance made Kit like him more.

Still beaming and leaning sideways against his badminton racket, Maximillian said, "I haven't killed the glorious badger."

Kit tried for the same patient tone that Laura always used. "No, I'm sure you haven't, but someone clearly shot it."

"Another badger," he said with a knowledgeable nod.

Laura held up a hand. "Wait, another badger shot it?"

"No, dear girl. Don't be silly. Badgers don't have hunting licences and therefore cannot own weapons. I think they would struggle to carry a rifle anyway, due to their build and tiny hands." He pointed his racket at her. "Moreover, shooting an animal makes it harder to stuff it. It creates a terrible mess, you know. And a big hole."

Kit rubbed her forehead. "Yeah. Sure. Of course. Can we please get back to the badger? How did it die?"

"I am not certain as I wasn't present at the time of death," Maximillian said with a grave expression. "However, my taxidermist seemed convinced it had been killed by another badger. Perhaps there were claw marks? Tufts of foreign fur? Or the vision of an enemy male left in its deceased eyes?"

There was so much crazy in that statement that Kit wasn't sure where to start. "Ooookay. So, the salient point here is that no human killed it, right?"

"That's correct, yes." Maximillian tapped his racket pensively against his thigh. "In fact, all my conserved animals have died from natural causes. Hm. Perhaps the deaths were on occasion somewhat unnatural in method and means, but the magnificent creatures were never killed for sport or to be stuffed."

Kit was unsure when she'd last been so relieved. She also wasn't sure if this was the strangest Greengage conversation she'd been part of this week.

"I see. Thanks," she said, because what else was there to say?

"Jolly good! I shall go fetch it for you," Maximillian said and hurried off.

While he was out of the room, Kit and Laura shared a long-suffering glance. The steps in the distance sounded like he was running. Then there was a clank, much like a badminton racket being dropped by someone excited and distracted.

Laura sighed while running a finger under her eye and picking away a crumb of mascara with a weary gesture. "I'm sorry, dearest. I suppose you can always send it to Aimee like before?"

"Sure. A brilliant badger is sure to be icing on the cake of her new collection."

"You mean a *glorious* badger," Laura corrected.

Kit took her hand. "Please tell me we haven't reached

the point in time when you'll become as much of a plant pot as your uncle is, honey. I'm not ready for there to be two of you."

"If I have to keep spending this much time away from you, I might become even loopier," Laura said. "Oh, by the way, I left the Star Wars scarf that Maximillian accidentally stole out on the coat rack. Don't forget to pick it up later."

"Thanks. So, he's finished with it, has he?"

"He claims to never have seen it until I went into his room and fished it out of the pocket of his mackintosh. He believes the maid put it there."

Kit blinked a few times. "He thinks there's a maid?"

"Yes."

"Figures. We all know what these imaginary maids are like. They can't help stealing and hiding Star Wars scarves in people's rain coats."

"It's a nuisance."

"Like your uncle."

"Gods, yes."

Maximillian skipped in and handed Kit a wooden plank that held up a loaf of grey and white fur culminating in a face with a very surprised look. If this animal had been killed by another badger, Kit was willing to bet it hadn't seen it coming. Perhaps it was a badger it knew and thought wasn't a threat? Maybe it was its sibling or something? Oh, perhaps it was its lover!

She bit her tongue. She was becoming as invested in this dead badger story as Maximillian. All she had to do was accept the fur-loaf and then post it to Aimee. Where the hell she was putting these things in her small apartment, Kit had no idea.

"Thanks," she mumbled and took the surprised badger corpse.

"Don't mention it, Susan," he boomed. "I knew you would appreciate it. You are a woman of taste, after all."

Kit was desperately trying not to make eye contact with the dead badger. "Mm-hm."

"Right. Are we ready for lunch?" Laura asked.

Instead of an answer, there was a strange sound. It was like those noises sheep make. Kit wasn't sure but thought they were called bleats. However, it sounded more strangled than sheep did on TV.

Maximillian's ruddy face broke out into a wide grin. "Aha! That is the call of a fawn searching for its mother. I rather thought it would make a suitable ring signal for my phone." The sound rang out again. He patted his waistcoat pocket where the phone must be and added, "Charming, isn't it?"

Another bleat came from the phone.

Laura stared at him. "Very nice. However, if that's a ring signal, perhaps you should answer your phone?"

"What? Splendid idea! Clever girl," Maximillian said and fished out an ancient mobile phone from his waistcoat. He stared at the caller ID with dismay. "It's that daughter of mine. I thought I asked my offspring to leave me alone while I healed. Those helpless and selfish rats, they never let me grieve or get any peace. I should have disowned them when they were babies."

Laura's head snapped back at the unnecessarily cruel comment. "Still, it might be urgent. Perhaps you should answer it?"

"Yes, suppose I must," he growled.

He left the room while answering the phone.

The second he was out of earshot Laura grabbed Kit's

hand and pulled her into her embrace. "His calls last forever. Especially when speaking to his children, since they're as likely to babble on and come up with random topics of conversation as he is."

Kit wrapped her arms around her. "You mean we have a moment to ourselves?"

"Yes, dearest."

"Thank goodness," Kit breathed before moving in to kiss her, lingering longer and using more tongue than prudent considering they could hear Maximillian in the other room. Then she broke away to rest her warm forehead against Laura's much cooler one. "How have you been, baby?"

"Not great," Laura whispered. "I mentioned romance this morning to Uncle Maximillian, to see if he's any better on that front."

"And?" Kit whispered back eagerly.

"And he screamed, threw a piece of bacon at the wall, and then cried for an hour."

"Right." Kit clicked her tongue. "He's not ready for our relationship then."

"No. To make things worse, I've been going mad from missing you." Laura sighed. "I mean, I know that I've seen you and spoken to on the phone as much as usual, but it's not the same."

"No, you don't realise how much you miss being romantic and physical until you can't do it for a while. Perhaps this was a good thing after all."

Kit could feel Laura furrowing her brow. "What do you mean?"

"I mean that I appreciate some things more than I did before. Like being able to do this…" She closed the space between their mouths and kissed Laura again with all the tenderness of someone who has found the most precious person in the world and wants nothing more than for them to feel as utterly adored as they are.

She wasn't sure, but she thought she felt Laura shiver. She was, however, sure that she felt Laura's hands slide down her back to cup her bum as the kiss intensified. After a long while they broke apart, and Laura rubbed her nose against Kit's in an Eskimo kiss.

"I never knew I could love someone like this," she whispered against Kit's lips.

"I feel the same way," Kit whispered back.

They stood there, still and entangled for a while, feeling the other's warm breath on their lips. Laura rocked them a little, the tiniest sway making it feel as if they were secretly dancing.

There was a quiet reverence in that moment, an unexpected one for a mere stolen kiss with a clueless uncle a room away. Still, that was one of the many reasons Kit loved Laura: she could make a commonplace moment into something almost magical. Or perhaps it was their love that did that. Either way, this was worth all the messing around and the sacrifices that came with dating Greengage's favourite daughter.

As Kit marvelled at the beautiful hazel eyes fixed on hers, she felt the shift from sweet romance into something more adult as Laura's hands on her bum changed from a gentle cupping to a possessive grip and their bodies, especially their pelvises and breasts, were pushed tighter together.

"When my uncle moves out, I'll need the two of us to spend the next few weeks under the same roof. I don't care if it's here or in your cottage, I need to be with you every second possible," Laura said. Her warm voice made the words sound like a prayer, but the cadence of speech sounded a lot like when she was in boss mode in the office.

Kit tilted her head so she could run the tip of her tongue across Laura's plump lips. "I love it when you make demands. That sounds perfect. However, don't forget about the holiday and the sexy lingerie you promised me."

"Of course not," Laura growled and tightened her grip.

"Oh wow, getting a bit rough there, my love," Kit said, not complaining at all.

At a speed which belied his age and size, Maximillian popped back into the room. "Can you believe it? The foolish girl quit her part time job as an online blogger or whatever they call themselves! That was her only source of income other than scrounging off me." With his back to them, he slammed his phone down on an end table. "Mindboggling. What sort of job does she think she can get, locked up in a house on this island? None, because she expects me to give her a full-time allowance now. What does she think this is? 1922?"

Kit and Laura were still locked together. His back was still turned. The moment froze, and so did the three people in the room: Maximillian because there had been an unhealthy cracking sound from his phone when he banged it on the table; the two lovers because they had once again been caught in a compromising situation.

Laura whipped her head around in panic and then fastened her gaze on that damn broom closet out in the hallway.

"Nuh-uh. No you don't! I'm not going in there again," Kit hissed. "In fact, I'm going home for lunch because I can't stay here without kissing you again."

Laura hung her head. "Yes, you've got a point."

Kit subtly extricated herself from the embrace. "Call me if you get a second to yourself, honey. I love you."

"I love you, too," came the whispered reply.

Kit went over to pat Maximillian on the back, saying that the phone was probably fine, and then said goodbye to the Howards.

As she left for her own quiet cottage, pride and joy blossomed in her chest as she remembered the flush on Laura's full cheeks, knowing that only a part of it was because they were nearly caught. Most of it had been love and arousal.

Laura missed her and was as devoted to her as she was to Laura. Next time they were alone, wow, there'd be fireworks.

That afternoon Josh was finally coming by with his Pilates DVD for their promised workout. In preparation, Kit had moved the sofa out of the way, rolled out her exercise mat on the floor, and placed two towels, two water bottles, and two sugar-free protein bars on the table. She'd even done some stretching and jumping jacks to warm up. She was ready for whatever fresh hell this Pilates thingy could turn out to be. Thinking about Josh brought her thoughts back to his co-workers, and she realized she still hadn't spoken to Shannon about why she was mad at Rachel.

Shit, I'm such an arse! Well, time's moved on. Surely they must have sorted it out by now?

Kit called Shannon's mobile. She'd get the lay of the land, and if her help was still needed, she'd book in a chat over some tea with Shannon. There was no answer. Kit was about to leave a voicemail when there was a knock on her door. However, it was a loud and violent one, not the sort of knock you expected from a friend dropping by for some exercise.

Kit hung up the phone and ran to the door.

Chapter Fifteen

SEXY AS FUDGE

W ith a knock like that, Kit was sure something was on fire. Or that she was about to be arrested. Or worse than those things put together, that something had happened to Laura.

Luckily, there was no paramedic, police officer, or fire-fighter outside in the afternoon heat but only Josh, carrying a mat and wearing a muscle-fit T-shirt with tight shorts. However, it was a Josh whose expression showed every sign of having recently outrun the devil. Or at least several very fast and threatening minor demons.

"Whoa, you nearly knocked my door off the hinges. You okay, Josh?"

"I'm late!"

Kit checked her watch. "Uh, yes, by two minutes."

"What? No. By an hour and two minutes! I'm so, so, so sorry!"

He pointed to his arm where a large digital wristwatch, which looked more advanced than Kit's laptop, hung loose.

Kit checked her fitness watch and then her phone for a second source. "Nope. Two minutes."

He jumped forward and craned his neck to see her phone display. "You've got to be joking. Bollocking hell! He's done it again."

"Who? And what have they done?"

Josh fastened the gigantic timepiece on his wrist. "Clark. He likes to play with my watch. This is the second time he's accidentally changed the time on it." He ran his hand through his lush but sweaty hair. "Last time he set it back six hours and slobbered all over it, so I noticed right away. This time, I've been running around like a headless chicken since this morning."

"The joy of having kids, huh? Well, you can now come in and do Pilates like a chicken with its head intact, knowing that you are perfectly on time."

He blew out a breath so long that it all but knocked Kit over, but he came in anyway while muttering, "This better give me back my superb physique. I'm not having this stress ulcer and heatstroke for nothing."

An hour later, with every muscle stretched, every beat of pulse upped, and every single fibre of their abs contracted, their Pilates session was completed.

Kit sat drinking deep from her water bottle while Josh lay in a puddle on the floor, saying that exercise must be a punishment made up by homophobes.

Kit chuckled into her water bottle, and he glared up at her. "No really, I didn't used to mind working out. Can I blame being this shattered now on having a kid? Or do biological mums who have to lose pregnancy weight have the monopoly on that?"

"Like you said at the pub," Kit towelled down the back of her neck, "you're either working like a dog or spending all your time with that little boy. No wonder this knackered you."

He leaned up on his elbows. "Thanks, mate. I'm glad to have a reason to be this out of shape."

"Oh, come off it, you're not that unfit. Besides, at least it means the workout did its job. They're meant to leave you sweaty and exhausted."

Josh hummed his agreement while stretching his legs up towards him. "Anyway, Clark is worth getting out of shape for. He's becoming such a kind and fun little lad. I can't wait until he's older, and I can take him with me to do more stuff."

Kit started stretching to cool down, too. "Yeah, I suppose it's hard to get out of the house and stay active with a one-year-old in tow?"

Josh grimaced. "It is, but I should be able to do more than take walks with him. Stuff like baby yoga and baby Pilates exist on the mainland, if I only braved the ferry and a train ride, but I'm too tired and can't be arsed." His legs flopped back down to the floor. "Matt stays active and manages to include Clark, you know. He took him swimming the other day and even has Clark with him when he lifts his weights. *He's* a great dad."

Josh's face, normally so pleasant with its fine features and designer stubble, was a scowling mask of embarrassment. Or was that regret?

While thinking about her reply, Kit recalled how her own father was rarely around. When he was, he was often more interested in his mistresses than in what she was doing. Of course, that was still better than her mum who left after their divorce and barely spoke to Kit these days.

She stopped stretching. "You know what? We should make a habit out of these workouts, and next time, bring Clark. He can either flop about on the exercise mats with us or he can have a nap in the next room. You can simultaneously keep fit and spend time with Clark outside the house."

"Really?"

"Sure! Or I can come over to your flat. Think it over. Whatever you decide, don't beat yourself up so much. The fact that you're so worried about not doing enough with him and feeling guilty for resenting your parent-weight shows what a great dad you are."

"You think so?" he said, doubt lacing his voice. "I really want to get this right, Kit. I always wanted to be a dad, and more to the point, I wanted to be the sort of dad my child could be proud of. Someone who made them happy, safe, and who gave them every chance I never got."

"You will be. Or, I mean, you are."

He sat up and shook off some moroseness. "Anyway, love, I'll be the sort of dad who is dead from exhaustion if I don't get one of those protein bars and a big bucket of coffee before I go home to shower."

"Protein's on the table. I'll go put the kettle on."

"Kettle?" He whinged. "You mean you only have instant coffee?"

She pointed a finger at him. "Yep, and you'll bloody well have it without any coffee snob comments. This is a tea-drinking house. You're lucky to get any coffee at all."

He held up his hands in a placating way. "Sorry. Instant is fine."

She went into the kitchen to put the kettle on, and

Josh soon joined her. He swallowed down a big bite of protein bar before saying, "How are things going with the bookshelf mystery? Rumour has it that you haven't found the culprit yet?"

"The rumours are right," Kit grumbled.

He knitted his perfect brows. "Sorry to hear that. Where are you up to?"

During the tea- and coffee-making process, Kit told him all: everything from Alice's suspicions, to all the suspects, all the way up to the hidden will. She knew she could trust Josh, and what was more, he was a good listener. Unlike people like Aimee and Rajesh, he wasn't so eager to help that he ended up spouting theories before Kit had even finished. He simply listened with his head tilted and his hands cupping the milky coffee she had handed him.

"So that's where we stand now," she finished.

"I see. Quite the tangled mess there, love."

"You can say that again," Kit said, blowing on her hot tea.

He frowned. "I can see that it has you worried."

Kit peered into the russet liquid of her mug; its darkness matched her mood. "I like to help people and puzzle out how to fix stuff. That's why I agree to these things. Except… there's another side to it."

"I've known you long enough to hazard a guess. You don't like disappointing people?"

"Good guess. I hate it," Kit said with a wince. "I disappointed my mum when I was little and helped my dad hide his affairs from her. It was the first time I learned to meddle and to solve people's problems, and it lost me her love."

Josh clicked his tongue. "Sounds like her love was easy

to lose if she didn't forgive a child, who didn't know any better, for helping its father?"

Kit grunted and turned away. "Never mind all that. My point is that I can't stand disappointing people, and I'm failing with this bookshelf mystery. I can't fix this, so I'll have to let that sweet old lady down."

"Isn't it a little early to assume you're failing?"

"I don't know. I thought this whole business would be simple and straightforward. I figured this would take a few days before turning out to be a friend searching for a recipe book and forgetting to tell Alice, that sort of thing."

"Except now it's been weeks and you haven't got a neat explanation to hand her on a flowery plate?"

"Exactly. It sucks." She paused. "Wait, why a flowery one?"

He shrugged. "Rachel says Alice loves flowery patterns."

"Blimey, the fact that everyone on this island knows everything about everyone is scary," she said, returning to her tea.

They drank in silence for a moment. Kit made herself nibble her protein bar, more to fuel her muscles after the workout then due to an appetite. She was too worried to be hungry.

Josh patted her arm. "You know, earlier you told me not to be so hard on myself. You should take that advice, too. You'll figure out who did it. Hey, what about Liam?"

Kit took another listless bite. "Yeah, talking to him is next on my list. What do you know about him?"

"Liam has always been a troublemaker, but I think his heart is in the right place. Of course, I might be seeing him through rose-coloured glasses since he's got that misunderstood, bad-boy vibe and is sexy as fu—um… as fudge."

Kit's downheartedness poured off her like rain off a pair of wellies. "He's sexy as fudge, huh? Well, at least me and my lesbian libido won't be swayed. We stick to…" She tried to think of another sort of sweets. "I don't know, love hearts."

He put a hand to his chest and gasped. "Love hearts? Are you using my childhood's wholesome sweets as some sort of euphemism here?"

Kit considered this. "I actually don't know what's euphemisms and what's plain rambling anymore. My brain is knackered after the Pilates and this book mystery. I need an easy, normal day at work tomorrow to clear my head. After that, I'll go see this sexy-as-fudge bloke and see what he knows."

"Do. If nothing else, I hear he's a good handyman, so if you need anything fixed around here, hire him."

"Uh-huh." Kit crossed her arms over her chest. "So you and Matt can come over to ogle him?"

"No! Well, I mean, if you need some extra handymen, we can perhaps swing by to help out."

"Ha! Funny that you didn't feel the need to do that when Shannon was helping me lay new flooring after New Year's."

He gave a good-natured chuckle. "If you have Shannon here, you don't need extra handymen. Take it from someone who works with her."

"Fair enough." Kit adjusted her glasses and looked away. "So… Thanks, um, for listening."

"Don't mention it," he said kindly. "I feel the same way about chatting and listening to people as you do about fixing their problems. It's kind of what I do. Matt is the same, actually."

Josh put his mug down and headed for the door. "Anyway," he said. "I better hurry home and have a hot shower to relax these muscles. They're not used to working that hard." He stretched and whimpered. Then his face brightened. "After that, it's my turn to give Clark a bath and read him his bedtime story. Thanks for the coffee."

"Thanks for the workout." Kit handed him his Pilates DVD. "Don't forget this, mate."

He took it. "Cheers. Good luck with Liam tomorrow!"

He put his shoes on, blew her a theatrical kiss, and left.

In Josh's wake, the doubts and worries about the bookshelf mystery came creeping back. The cottage was so still and empty. The silence of her home felt heavier now that Kit couldn't get Laura to pop over and fill it in the blink of an eye.

"Only one thing to do," she mumbled to the quiet room. "Ring Aimee and hear a bunch of mainland gossip and be told what miracle little George has achieved today."

First, though, she needed a shower and then some more tea. After all, most things could be solved with tea.

Chapter Sixteen

SHIT LIES ABOUT MANURE

The weather, with all its clouds and dampness, was as dreary as you'd expect of a Monday afternoon. *Terribly clichéd of it,* Kit thought. Despite this she had a new spark of energy. Josh had been right; she shouldn't assume she had failed with the bookshelf case yet.

Since Rajesh was closing up, Kit was able to go straight from the library to Nettle Road. This time she wasn't heading to Alice's cottage but to the far less picturesque two-bedroom, semi-detached house next to it. The home of Liam Soames.

Kit checked her phone for any new texts. She had asked Rachel to duck out from the pub for a little while and help her with Liam. This was partly to ask Rachel if Kit's help was still needed with Shannon, and partly because if Liam really did have a crush on her, Rachel's presence might make him more talkative and helpful. Also, she knew what he looked like. Kit didn't fancy walking around asking every young bloke in sight if he happened to be Liam.

There was no text yet, but as Kit stood staring at the

screen in wait, she felt fingers spider up her side and heard Rachel sniggering.

"Evenin', detective! Laura said you were ticklish."

Kit quashed a laugh and stood back to avoid another tickling attempt. "Oi! God, you're almost as much trouble as Aimee."

"Aww! Since I like Aimee, I'm taking that as a compliment. How is she and that little cutie of hers?"

"They're good. Aimee likes her job and George thinks Southampton is—in his words—'pretty and squishy.' No one knows what that means."

"That's great to hear!"

"Yep. What about you? How are you tonight?"

"Good now that I'm out of the pub. Shannon is still giving me the silent treatment. Actually, no. She is talking to me now, but it's all terribly polite and cold. It's driving me bonkers."

Kit pushed her glasses up, then did it again before she could stop the tic. "Rach, I'm so bloody sorry I haven't spoken to Shannon yet!"

"It's okay. I knew you were busy with the Maximillian thing and the bookshelf case.

"Phew," she said and wiped her brow, making Rachel laugh. "To be honest, I'm surprised this hasn't sorted itself out by now."

"I'm sure it would if she'd talk to me," Rachel said. "Although, in a way, I think the silence is good. If it was something serious enough to end our relationship, she would've said something by now. Still, it's not like her to sulk like this."

Kit put an arm around Rachel's shoulders. "I'll talk to her. Soon, I promise. Right now, though, we need to chat to Liam. Is that okay?"

In a flash, Rachel looked as happy-go-lucky as ever, making Kit wonder how much of it was an act every day.

"Sure," she said while tucking flyaway strands back into her messy bun. "Let's go talk to him. He's a decent bloke, he's just… surly and has a chip on his shoulder."

"Thanks for the warning."

Kit was about to knock on the door when it was flung open, revealing a young man a little taller than Kit. He had a pained look, accentuated by the ash-blond hair which fell into his eyes. He had delicate features and a slender but fit build. He made Kit think of Ryan Gosling. Or maybe James Dean?

He slouched against the doorframe and squinted at them from under lashes, as if posing for a picture.

Wow. This guy's trying too hard. Does he think we're here from some teen magazine to interview him about his star sign and his favourite colour?

"Rach," he said with what was probably meant to be a smouldering look. "I haven't seen you for a while."

"No," she replied cheerily. "I think the last time was when we raked up the leaves from under Alice's elm. I'm glad you cut that tree down. It shed like a cat before summer."

"Yeah, it was sick, too. It had to go. I had to take care of it."

"Mm-hm. Anyway, this is my friend Kit. She's the one who's helping Alice figure out who messed with her shelves and stole a book."

"I know," he said. "Alice talks about it a lot. It really bothers her that one of her poncy sons has messed with her stuff."

"Hi. Nice to meet you," Kit said, quickly deciding that

this guy wouldn't want a handshake. "So, you think it was either Anthony or Phillip who nicked the book?"

He leaned even closer against the doorframe. "Yep. I mean, who else could it be? Unless it was that bratty, thieving cow."

Rachel cleared her throat and fidgeted with the spaghetti strap of her tank top. Kit tried not to let her dislike of his choice of words show as she asked, "Do you mean Caitlin Caine?"

"Uh-huh. The golden princess who can do no wrong, even if she steals your lighter and then refuses to give it back." He scoffed and peered up at the overcast sky. "When I told her dad that she had my best lighter, he said I was lying to try to get her into trouble. Like, why would I give a shit about her? I just wanted my bloody lighter back."

"So you suspect Phillip, Anthony, or Caitlin?" Kit clarified.

"Well, yeah, unless some outsider snuck in. Or Alice just lost the book, but that doesn't sound like her."

Kit wondered if they were ever going to be invited in. At the moment Liam had one foot in his house and one foot out in the drive, blocking the doorway with his slouch. His body language didn't exactly scream hospitality, so she suppressed the idea of the cup of tea she was gasping for.

"What about Jacqueline Caine?" she asked.

"Jackie?" His sullen face cracked into a wolfish grin. "Nah, she's all right. She wouldn't go nicking things. Or, well, if she did, she'd tell *me*."

There was a definite air of smugness wafting off him, much like his cheap body spray. If he thought he was being subtle, he was wrong. Either there was something going on between him and Jackie, or at least he was sure she wanted there to be.

Or, wait, perhaps he's trying to make me to think that?

Kit bored her gaze into his. "All right. Do you happen to know anything about Alice's will?"

"Her will?" He sucked his teeth. "Does she need one of them? Doesn't everything she owns pass down to those wankers she calls sons when she goes six feet under?"

Kit tried to tell if he was lying, but it was hard to see anything beyond that bad-attitude facade he kept up.

"Are you at any point going to let us in, Liam?" Rachel asked.

He pulled himself out of his slouch. "Nah, I wasn't planning on it. I need to go out. Gotta get some…" He hesitated. "Um, manure, for when I'm helping Alice with the changes to her garden."

From the disappointed sigh that Rachel let out, Kit could tell that her friend believed him as little as she did.

He reached out a hand and brushed something invisible off Rachel's bare shoulder. "I mean, you could come with me if you fancied?"

Rachel gave him a look so withering that it made him take three steps back inside before she answered, "No, Liam, you go ahead and deal with your own shit… I mean, manure."

He smiled like a little boy caught doing something naughty. "Okay, yeah, sure. Anyway, I'm sorry I couldn't help." He nodded towards Kit. "I like Alice, okay? She's real decent, and she gave me a job when no one else would. I'd help her if I could, but I don't know anything about this."

Kit squinted at him. Perhaps it was paranoia, or the fact that she really wanted a cup of tea. Either way, she was sure Liam knew more than he was saying. Sadly, she was also sure that he wasn't going to tell her anything.

"Right, well, thanks for talking to me. I'm sure I'll have more questions for you later, if that's okay?"

He looked about as enthusiastic as a dog on the way to the vet but still nodded.

Assuming that was all she was getting, Kit waved and said, "We'll leave you to go get your manure. Just be aware that all the shops selling that sort of stuff on Greengage would've closed an hour ago. So, you know, you might want a better excuse for getting rid of people."

She gave him a wide smile and held her arm out to Rachel, indicating that she could go first. They walked away from the open door and the stunned youth standing in it.

"Nice one," Rachel said with a snigger.

"Not as nice as the ten quesadillas I intend to scoff down at your pub."

Rachel bumped her shoulder against Kit's. "Ha, I'd like to see you try fitting them in that tiny belly."

Kit smiled at her. "You know, while I eat, I'm going to have to properly ask you about the missing book. Just so I can tell the people involved with this that I did actually ask you."

"No need to wait until we're eating, I can answer now. You mentioned this before, and I was about to say that I know nothing about it when Laura interrupted us. If I did, I would've told you."

"Yeah, I assumed that was the case," Kit said, weariness making her voice flat. "I was just hoping there'd be something. You helped fill those shelves. Anything you can tell me about that at least?"

Rachel slowed her pace and watched the sky as she

pondered. "Well, the books were arranged alphabetically. As a librarian, you'll appreciate that."

Kit pretended to shiver. "Yes! Most people just place books on their shelves willy-nilly. Or by colours or size."

Rachel laughed. "I suppose so. Anyway, Alice said that was how she noticed the books had been moved: a Wharton book showed up next to a Dickens."

"Yes, she told me that, too."

"Did she also tell you that no one but she and I knew that the books were arranged alphabetically?"

Kit clicked her tongue. "No, she didn't. Hm. Thank you, but I don't know if there's anything I can use there."

"Only that no one would have known that she'd see any moved books right away, I guess?" Rachel shrugged. "Anyway, now you know all that I know."

"What about Alice's will? Any insights on that?"

"Nope. Why do you keep asking everyone about her will?"

"It was hidden in the book for a while. It's in the bank now. Still, I think it might have something to do with the disappearance of the book."

Rachel's eyeliner-framed eyes widened. "Oh, I see. Well, I'm afraid I'm as little use to you regarding the will as to the book."

"No probs. Thanks for answering my questions."

"Of course. Anything to help. Now that we covered that," she linked her arm with Kit's, "dinner time can be devoted to something much more important."

"Talking to Shannon?" Kit asked.

"No, she's got the night off, so the pub will be drama-free. I meant *your* love life and what Laura's uncle is doing to it."

Kit groaned and leaned her head onto Rachel's

shoulder as they walked. "In that case I'm going to need a stonking big glass of Diet Pepsi and vodka with my quesadillas."

"It'll be on the house, little miss detective," Rachel said with sympathy. And perhaps the faintest hint of amusement.

Chapter Seventeen

A VERY HOWARD BIRTHDAY BASH

K it sat on a foldable chair on Greengage's main square, watching her girlfriend work the crowd. As always, Laura shone with the beauty of her good-natured personality and that warm smile. The sun above tried to keep up, but Kit was proud to see that it was failing.

It was nice to see Laura smiling today of all days, considering it was her birthday. Less nice was that Kit was sure the smile was for her guests.

"Oi, lovely birthday lady!" she said, poking Laura's thigh as she walked by.

Laura stopped, quirked one of those auburn eyebrows and then made a big deal of adjusting her skirt, even though Kit's prodding hadn't moved the garment in the slightest.

"Do you mind?" Laura said before returning her eyebrow to the starting position.

"Sorry, baby. I needed to get your attention," Kit said with as much love as she could fit into the words. "We haven't spoken all day. On my birthday it was just you and me and that picnic on the beach. On yours, all of

Greengage seems to be involved and demanding your time."

Laura scanned the crowd. "Not all of Greengage, dearest. I estimate that about two hundred people are here right now. Still, folks will come and go. That's why I decided to have the celebration here on the square and not up at Howard Hall."

"I'm sorry, but I still don't get why you'd celebrate your birthday by having a big-arsed tent with refreshments for the whole island. It must've cost a fortune."

"It's a marquee, my love, not a tent. Besides, I'm not feeding everyone. It's first-come, first-served. If we run out of cake or the Gage Farm juice and cider, the celebration is over. Then you, me, and a chosen few will go back to Howard Hall for cocktails and dinner. Later tonight, it'll be—"

Kit crossed her arms over her chest with a smirk. "Go on. I dare you to say, 'you and me' when you know Maximillian will be hanging over us like a raincloud."

"It will be *a more quiet affair*, was what I was going to say," Laura said, not looking at Kit, but smiling and nodding to a man on the other side of the square who was waving at her.

"Uh-huh. Are you at least having fun, honey? You haven't had time to sit down for ages."

"Having fun? I'm," Laura seemed to be searching for an answer written on her shoes, "feeling content and relieved, I suppose."

"Relieved?"

"Yes. Relieved that everything is going to plan, and everyone seems to be having fun. We have enough refreshments, the brass band has promised to play at least twice during the event, and the weather held out."

Laura paused to shake hands with a woman around their age who interrupted to say happy birthday. When the woman left, Laura picked up again. "Also, I'm relieved that people can't say that the Howards used to treat the island to big birthday bashes but stopped to have all the fun for themselves behind my back." She stopped again, this time to do a 360-degree turn and scan the entire square. "Granted, this is nothing compared to the parties my parents and the generations before them had for their birthdays, but at least I can relax knowing that everyone will see that I made an attempt and that I didn't snub anyone."

Concern for her girlfriend niggled on Kit. "So, 'relieved' is as close as you're going to get to 'having fun,', then?"

Laura lifted her chin and avoided eye contact. "I don't see why you're being so confrontational about this."

"Babe, I'm not being confrontational," she said gently. "I only want to make sure that you have a good time on your birthday. You know, making sure that you think about yourself for once."

She worried that there was a hint of wanting Laura to spend time with her too, but she quashed that thought. Her worry for Laura was greater than her own need.

Laura blinked at her. "A Howard birthday belongs to the island as much as to the person having the birthday. That's the way it's always been. Anyway, I *am* thinking about myself in a way. Like I said, I'd feel horrible if I knew that people were complaining behind my back."

"In my experience, shitty people will talk behind your back and bitch about pretty much everything anyway. However, if this party makes you feel better, it's the right thing to do."

"I'm glad you see that. As an outsider, I know a lot of this doesn't make sense to you, but Greengage always had two leading families, the Howards and the Stevensons. We represented the island. That came with benefits, but also with responsibilities." She paused to reach down and push Kit's glasses up for her, stroking her face as she did so. "We may not live in that sort of society anymore, but some things remain. Besides, it makes me happy to see people having a good time. It also makes me happy to see so many smiling faces wishing me a happy birthday. It's nice to share an important day with Greengagers. They're important to me."

"Fine, weirdo. Do it your way," Kit said with a wink.

Laura huffed at the word *weirdo* but didn't comment.

Kit reached out to officially smooth down Laura's skirt but unofficially get to touch Laura's leg. It was a tiny, hesitant moment of skin to skin, but Kit needed it. Her hand lingered for a heartbeat, and Laura inched closer to show that the touch was welcomed.

"Look at it this way, my dearest Londoner. If I marry you one day, you'll be a Howard, and the island will probably expect you to throw a birthday bash like this one."

Kit pulled her hand back as if she'd been burned. "What? Bollocks. No one would expect an introverted, city-dwelling librarian to do that, would they?"

Laura didn't answer but gave an enigmatic smirk, adjusted Kit's shirt collar, and then walked away with a taunting sway to her hips.

Bugger me, but it'd be worth the nightmare to get to be married to that woman, Kit thought.

Laura only made it about four steps before Ethel stopped her to wish her a happy birthday. Kit overheard her recalling when Laura had turned five and had pink bows in her hair, which got eaten by one of the petting zoo's goats.

Kit leaned back a little, enjoying a light breeze and the sun on her face. The realisation that Maximillian's, and his kids', hatred of crowds meant they wouldn't show up here warmed her almost as much. She leaned back further and heard the foldable chair give an ominous creek. She eased up on the lean with an embarrassed look around. That was when she spotted Liam.

He was one of the few people who hadn't dressed up. In fact, Kit doubted he had even combed his hair, though perhaps that was one of those hairdos that was meant to look unkempt but actually took lots of work and hair products. He seemed like the type who'd put a lot of effort into making it look as if he hadn't put any effort in. She watched him load up three glasses of cider and then empty them one by one. When done, he placed his hand over his mouth to cover a loud burp and then sauntered off towards the bandstand where the brass band were unpacking their instruments.

Kit got up. After all, as the birthday girl's partner it made sense that she would check on the band. If she happened to have a quick chat with Liam about the missing book and the will, to see if he was more talkative after all that cider, who could complain?

She arrived at the bandstand just in time to hand the trombone player the handkerchief he'd dropped. The trombonist thanked her, and she put on her biggest customer service smile and said, "No problem. Thanks for playing for us today."

When she turned back to where Liam had been standing, he was gone. She spun around, trying to catch a glimpse of that ash-blond hair and the black Imagine Dragons T-shirt he was wearing. Nothing.

A voice which could probably give the trombone a run for its money boomed, "What are you gawking at?"

Kit didn't have to turn to recognise the owner of the voice. "Hello, Mabel, I was looking for Liam Soames. He was just here, and now he's vanished. I think he made a run for it to avoid me and my questions about the missing book," she said distractedly.

"Don't be silly, girl. That slattern of a lad rushed off to do what he always does at big public events," she lowered her voice, "have what the Scottish used to call Houghma-gandy [1] with one of the married women. This time, I wager it was Jacqueline Caine."

Kit spun to face her. "Jackie? Really? Are you sure?"

Mabel sniffed. "I should say so, considering I saw the two of them cooing like lovebirds at the east entrance to the square about ten minutes ago. No doubt they were planning when to sneak off together."

Kit chewed her lower lip. "Huh. Thanks for telling me."

With the speed of a whip, Mabel's hand flew out to tap on the trumpet held in the nearest musician's hand. "You! As the trumpeter, you must be the person I need to speak to about volume."

The reedy trumpet player shuffled back. "Mrs Baxter. How nice to see you."

"Yes, yes," Mabel said with a dismissive grimace. "That's all very polite. About the volume…"

The trumpeter swallowed. "Yes?"

"As a service to your community you must play quieter, except for the parts which we struggle to hear." She waved her hand in the air as if swatting away a fly.

"You know which ones I mean, I'm sure. They must have taught you about this in toot-toot school."

The trumpet player, who was now very pale, croaked out, "Toot-toot school?"

Kit put a hand on Mabel's arm. "Uh, perhaps you should go over to the cider bowls. I think I saw Charlie causing a fuss over there. I know you'll want to keep an eye on him so he doesn't sully the good Baxter name."

Mabel drew herself up and steamed off without a word. Kit hoped Charlie would excuse her for getting him in trouble with his powerhouse of a relative, but, in all fairness, he probably *was* causing a fuss somewhere. He was also more used to dealing with Mabel than these poor musicians.

"Thanks," the trumpet player breathed.

"Don't mention it. Just follow her orders and remember what you learned in toot-toot school," Kit said.

While they were both laughing, Kit could hear a posh voice with a Scottish lilt saying, "You look ever so handsome in that roll neck."

It took her a second to place the voice as belonging to Jacqueline Caine.

"Excuse me," Kit said to the musician and hurried off to locate Jackie. It only took a moment as she stood right behind the bandstand. Her hand was on the shoulder of— Kit squinted to see in the bright sunlight—Anthony Caine!

She stopped in her tracks. What did this mean? She tapped her fingers against her thigh. It meant Jackie hadn't left with Liam. It also meant that she was flirting with Anthony, since she now let the hand on the shoulder caress down Anthony's chest and stay there. Kit peered closer to see how he'd react and saw him correct his glasses with a cocky grin. He said something which Kit couldn't make out.

He's not nearly as loud as Jackie. Probably because he isn't half as drunk as her. Man, she can barely stand. She must've had more than cider.

Jackie jolted and took out a phone which was clearly vibrating. "Ugh, it's your brother," she slurred.

Anthony tensed and began staring around the area. "I should go before he comes looking for you. You know how he tends to get the wrong idea."

Jackie gave a shrill laugh. "Aye, but I also know how it pleases you that I fancy you more than him. Poor little Anthony. Always the second child. Always looking to be chosen first. Why not stay here and let him see that I prefer you?"

He glowered at her with disgust. "I don't know what you mean by all this nonsense. It must be the alcohol talking. You reek of it. Perhaps you should check yourself back into that clinic, Jackie. I'm going home. These modern Howard affairs are a farce."

He marched off, leaving Jackie there stumbling in her towering high heels. She was giggling to herself, but there was no amusement in it. It sounded more like desperation to Kit. Suddenly she felt like she was watching something private. Shame burning her cheeks, she walked back to the crowds on the other side of the bandstand.

She took in the happy families and all the pets playing on the grass. Anything to cheer herself up and stop her from brooding about the bookshelf mystery and this messed-up family. Perhaps Phillip was right: searching for the book had made her pry into their lives too much. She ignored that thought by watching two big blonde girls spraying each other with water pistols on the other side of the square. Leslie Stevenson, Aunt Sybil's main nemesis, came over to try to calm them. Or maybe egg them on, which would be more in line with her personality.[2]

Kit never found out which one it was as, right then, gentle hands were placed on her lower back and fanned out to clasp each side of her waist.

"Only a few more hours, dearest," Laura whispered in her ear. "Then it'll be dinner for five or six. Then a quiet night of drinks, reading, and generally cosying up in armchairs for you, me, and Uncle Maximillian."

Kit felt her smile go from ear to ear. "And when he leaves the room to do a wee or to refill the brandy bottle? What then, babe?"

"Then I'll expect you to put your book down and get ready for some quick but intense groping and/or cuddling," she answered before placing a kiss in Kit's hair.

Kit put her hands over Laura's and tightened the embrace. "Oh, I'll be ready, birthday girl."

There they stood in their own quiet corner of the hubbub, neither of them breaking the embrace—Laura at the back, holding Kit tight and gently snuffling her nose through her pixie cut; Kit leaning into it and thinking of ways to get Maximillian to leave Howard Hall that night. Maybe she could get Aimee to call him and tell him he'd win a lifetime supply of taxidermy stuff if he went to the Himalayas right away? Now there was a thought.

Chapter Eighteen

SKULKING AND HOW THEY MET

A couple of days later, Kit was in the library, pondering if the man she'd seen skulking outside the library on her lunch break was Anthony Caine. He had been some distance away, but still… walks like a duck, talks like a duck. Or was it quacks? And was it a duck or a hen?

Idioms were soon forgotten as she'd spotted someone else now. This time there was no doubt who it was. From the corner of her eye, as she served a mum and her well-behaved kid, Kit saw Shannon lurking in the sci-fi section. Why was everyone skulking around today? More to the point, why was *she* skulking around *there*? Shannon wasn't into sci-fi or books. Unless Rach had asked her to go find some books in which women took their clothes off. Or more likely, took each other's clothes off. Kit's librarian brain started reeling off sci-fi books with female sex scenes before she could stop herself. Obviously, Shannon wasn't here for a book.

When the mum and kid left with a pram full of books,

Kit strode over to the skulking pub owner. "Oh, hey! I thought that was you. You all right?"

"I'm fine, thanks, Kit. You?"

"Yep, work is pretty quiet as you can see. I'm savouring it as we have 'baby rhyme time' in an hour. This place is going to be manic."

Shannon smiled. "Sounds like I came at the right time then."

"You did." Kit braced herself against the bookshelf. "In fact, you saved me the effort of figuring out how to approach you about something."

"Oh yeah?" Shannon's surprised tone was belied by her wary body language and jerky movements. They both knew why she was there, and they both knew where this conversation was going.

Kit cleared her throat. "Look, I won't beat about the bush. There's a ginger extrovert milling about in a state of depression because the woman she loves won't talk to her. That's the obvious topic of conversation here, right?"

Shannon's handsome face scrolled through the full range of human emotion before she emitted a faint "yes."

"Rach adores you, you know."

"Yes, she does, and I adore her even more. That doesn't mean that she won't annoy the living daylights out of me on occasion. Or that she doesn't hurt me sometimes."

"Ah. Well, that sounds like something you might want to talk about?"

Shannon squinted her eyes closed. "It is. I'm… not sure I'm ready, though. I've been struggling with this for a while."

"I know. It's okay. There's no hurry." Kit adjusted her glasses, trying to think of something to say until Shannon was ready. "How did the two of you meet, anyway?"

She opened her eyes, and her whole posture relaxed. "It was about seven years ago, at a charity cricket match that my mum organised to raise funds for a rundown nursery."

"Rach played cricket? I've heard her say sports are for people who can't dance."

Shannon chuckled. "Oh, she wasn't playing. She was manning the drinks stand, handing out glasses of weak squash and cups of water." Shannon's gaze moved to the window, turning wistful. "I'd seen her around. She's hard to miss with that wild, red hair, her enthusiastic charm, and those come-hither-eyes. But I never gave her much attention. She was so much younger, so popular, and a total stunner."

"What changed?"

"That cricket match was awful. It was cold and wet out. Everyone got muddy and more or less drenched by the persistent drizzle."

"Yikes."

"Exactly. Still, the day went from nightmare to dream when I saw Rach tip her head back and laugh at a young woman's comments before saying, 'I'm not going to hit on you just because I'm into women. You're not nice enough, Julie. Sod off.' Or something to that effect."

They both chuckled before Shannon continued, "Not only had she told off a homophobic ex-friend without offending anyone—she has a way of being breezy like that —but," she ran her hand over her short afro while searching for words, "this gorgeous goddess was *gay*. Openly gay. Here on Greengage! Josh and Matt were the only non-straight people I knew here other than me at the time."

Kit whistled. "I see why she suddenly popped up on your radar."

"Yep. That was when I allowed myself to look at her without the bitter assumption of 'Why bother, I can never have her,' and mate, my heart nearly pounded itself out of my ribcage."

"Aww."

"Don't get sappy on me, Kit. It's just that she was so exuberant and cheeky. Plus, she was kind and helpful even when she didn't have to be. She was always laughing, always dancing, and always seeing the silver lining. She was like unadulterated sunshine poured into a sexy twenty-four-year-old woman."

"So you spoke to her?"

"No, no, not at all," Shannon muttered. "She might like women, but I still saw myself as too old and too dull for her. Not everyone who's gay likes someone as butch as me either."

"Hang on, you do know that you're both cool and hot, right?"

"Nice of you to say so, Kit, but don't interrupt the story."

"Fine, sorry! Anyway, now it's common knowledge that butch women are Rach's weakness."

Shannon's sudden grin was as smug as it was heartfelt. "Yep, but back then I didn't know that. Nor did I know if I only liked her because she was charming and gay. I decided to wait."

Kit lounged against a shelf and rested her chin on her fist. "Okay. Then what?"

"Then my team won the match. We all went into the changing room to shower off the mud, sweat, and rain. Man, every muscle in my body was stiff."

"I get that. Move on to the romance part."

Shannon rolled her eyes. "Calm down, I'm getting to it. Over the other women's chatting and showering, I heard someone in one of the booths shouting, 'This shower feels so good I want to shag it!' at the top of her lungs."

Kit sniggered. "Let me guess—Rach, and she didn't say 'shag' but something worse."

"Oh, she used the f-word as usual, all right. Even though she hadn't played, she'd decided to wash the rain off and warm up. Kit... the moans and pleasured whimpers she emitted in that damn shower booth, not caring who heard her or what they thought." Shannon laughed quietly and shook her head to herself. "I dropped my towel on the bench as it hit me: I *had* to get to know this woman, even if it was only as a friend."

"So, what then? Tell me more!"

"After we'd all showered and changed, people started to head for home. I stayed behind and took the risk. I told Rach that I was impressed by how she'd handled No-Homo Julie. I threw in that I was never that good at dealing with that sort of thing."

"Ah, to send out the signal that you were a fellow sapphic."

"Sapphic?" Shannon looked like she was trying to remember something long ago forgotten.

"Yeah," Kit said. "It's one of the terms we can use for women who are into women. To avoid excluding the women-loving women who aren't lesbians, like Laura who's just come out as bisexual."

"Right! I knew I'd heard it. Sorry, I'm not as young as the rest of you, so I grew up with fewer words to describe people. I get confused. But I'm trying to learn and be respectful."

Kit smiled to show she wasn't trying to preach. "That's all you can ask of someone."

"I like to think so," Shannon said with a smile of her own. "Actually, Rach wasn't sure if she was into all genders or just women when she was younger. That's why she wasn't out as a lesbian until she was twenty-four and telling No-Homo Julie off on the cricket grounds. Hence why I hadn't heard the rumours about a new gay on the island."

"So now you had something to chat about," Kit said, eager to hear the rest of the story.

"Yep. We stood under the awning of the ladies' changing rooms and talked for almost an hour, despite the cold," Shannon said with a sentimental chuckle. "I told her how I'd only dated women on the mainland and thought no one else here was a lesbian—I mean, sapphic. She talked about how the blokes on the island refused to believe that a feminine, flirty woman like her could be gay and how she hated that. Time flew."

Kit moved closer. "Then?"

"She got cold. I gave her my jacket. She said she liked the way it smelled. You know, normal flirting."

Kit squashed a squeal. "I love this romantic stuff! Then what?"

Shannon looked embarrassed by the attention all of a sudden. "I drove her home, and we talked more. It was only the next day she admitted that she'd driven to the match. She hadn't needed a lift after all but wanted more time with me. About a week later, we were a couple."

"That's so sweet! You're great together, and in my opinion," she gave Shannon a careful glance, "you've always been the most stable couple on Greengage."

Shannon ran a hand over her face. "And now you want to know what's changed. Meaning I can no longer stay away from the topic of why I've been strange around Rachel?"

"I do want to know, yes. She says you're still acting angry by being distant. You know, weirdly polite and not romantic or intimate at all. She's freaking out about what she's done."

"I know." Shannon groaned. "I shouldn't torment her like this. It's just that I don't know how to talk to her about it. We've always had such perfect communication, but this has hit right in my weak spot."

"Which is?"

"My insecurities, I suppose."

Kit put an arm around Shannon's shoulder but removed it when the other woman tensed. "Mate, we all have insecurities and things that are hard to talk about. Especially in regards to the person we love. Maybe it would be easier to discuss it with me?"

"I'm not sure I should tell you." Shannon hesitated. "Or anyone else."

"Come on. Go oooon." Kit pushed her elbow. "Tell me. I'll keep it a secret if you want."

"Fine. I'll tell you." Shannon closed her eyes, as if to protect them from the words about to come out of her mouth. "It all happened on that night when Rach got so terribly drunk."

Kit checked that the library was still quiet and then rested back against the shelf. This story was probably going to be long and would need all of her attention.

Chapter Nineteen

SUGARED CANDLESTICKS, AN HEIRESS, AND SKUNKS

The first of July had introduced itself with the fanfare of a thunderstorm lasting most of the night, leaving the morning air heavy and thick like treacle. It was a Sunday, so Kit was heading to Howard Hall to try for some quality time with Laura. Sadly, when she used her key to let herself in, she ran into the wrong Howard.

Maximillian stood staring at a mahogany table as if it confused him. Kit gave a discreet cough to ensure she didn't scare him. He spun around until he could locate the source of the cough. This took a good thirty seconds more than it would most people. "Ah, Susan. Back from your travels, I see. How are you? How was Bulgaria?"

With great restraint, Kit managed not to whine or roll her eyes. The situation would be funny if she wasn't so tired of trying to explain who she was and what she did.

"Bulgaria was brilliant!" she improvised. "Some pretty landscapes out there with all those purple trees. I rode an antelope and ate sugared candlesticks, you know, their national dish."

It was a childish outburst of sarcasm, and she fully

expected negative consequences. However, Maximillian merely smiled at her and said, "Jolly good! Now help me move Great-Uncle Godwin's table. It should be facing the window."

Kit gaped. He either hadn't been listening, or he was really so away with the fairies that he had no concept of the complete nonsense she'd just spouted at him. Either way, she had no idea what to say now. Especially not as trying to put the large table Maximillian was pointing to —Great-Uncle Godwin's or not—so that it faced the window would mean blocking the only door into the room.

She decided to distract him before he wrecked another part of this beautiful, old house that meant so much to Laura. Taking his arm, she led him away from the room. "Why don't we leave that for later? I'm sure we have lots to discuss. By the way, where's Laura?"

"Oh, the dear girl went down to the kitchen. I think she said she was going to discuss the week's menu with… someone."

"Probably the chef, Mrs Smith."

"Who's a metal smith?" he said, busy checking his phone.

"Never mind," Kit said, patting the thick arm linked with hers. "We'll head down there then."

He put his phone back in his jacket pocket, tripping over a threshold. "Splendid idea, Susan."

"Kit," she said mechanically.

He knitted his white, bushy eyebrows. "Pardon? A kit? What kit? As in a set of clothing or as in the progeny of a fox?" Those immense eyebrows of his squished together even closer. "Or wait, are not the young of skunks, beavers, and badgers also called kits?"

"Kit as in *me*," she explained. "It's my name."

Maximillian gave her a bored look as soon as it was clear this wasn't a chat about animals and then moved his gaze to a nearby window. "This weather is appalling. That thunderstorm last night kept me awake."

That answered the question of what was at the root of his behaviour, especially the Susan/Kit issue. It wasn't due to confusion or some form of memory loss. He simply wasn't listening and didn't care what her name was. Rajesh had been right, all this git cared about was himself.

It's sad that Laura makes sacrifices for someone who doesn't even bother to listen. If he were my uncle, I'd have told him to go snuggle an angry porcupine.

They walked on in silence until they got to the basement stairs leading down to the kitchen. "Speaking of skunks," Maximillian said, returning to the discussion about which animals had kits. "I wanted to show you a website that Laura helped me find. On it are several taxidermy collectors showing off their latest purchases. There was a particularly attractive skunk that I believe you might appreciate."

"Maximillian."

"Yes?"

She squeezed his arm, maybe a little harder than needed, until he faced her. "I want you to listen very closely to me now. I. Don't. Want. Any. Stuffed. Animals."

He froze and searched her face. "Oh? Well. As you wish," he said with a displeased sniff.

Kit was torn between the joy of not having to accept any more animals and the guilt of having upset Laura's uncle, something they'd been trying so hard not to do. It made her think. They were trying so hard to keep him happy after his heartbreak, but had anyone come straight out and asked how he was feeling? Maybe he had healed?

She squared her shoulders and steeled herself. "Maximillian, I hope you don't think I'm sticking my nose in where it doesn't belong here, but I was wondering how you were doing?"

"Doing?"

"Yes, Laura said that—"

He interrupted her by adjusting his collar. "This jacket itches. I wish there was better tweed to buy on Greengage."

"Stay with me here, Maximillian. Laura told me that you moved in because your relationship ended, and you needed a change. I just wanted to see if you're on the mend?"

His arm, still linked with hers, grew rigid. "No. I am exactly as miserable as when she told me she loved another." He stopped on the first step, and his voice grew shaky. "Women always break your heart. They crush your self-esteem and shatter the calm that you need to live your life. They leave you lost and alone."

Kit threw a sideways glance at the man next to her, the man who'd had such bad luck with love. The man who lived as a hermit, despite being part of the most esteemed family on the island. The man who locked himself away with only his kids for company, even though he couldn't stand them. Yes, he was selfish, and yes, a lot of his vagueness was for effect. Still, he was *broken*. Perhaps Laura was right to have spent these past weeks allowing him to get away with whatever he needed to feel better.

Maximillian straightened and retracted his arm from hers. "Although, as a woman yourself, I'm sure you have no inkling of the damage you do. All you ladies care about is getting your own way."

Kit felt her sympathy drip off her and down into the floorboards.

"I know exactly how it hurts to be left by a woman you love," she muttered.

He carried on walking down the stairs. "What's that, Susan?"

"Nothing. I was going to say that perhaps you shouldn't be so harsh towards women when a woman, your niece to be exact, has shown you such generosity and kindness lately."

She was expecting him to not have heard her or for him to miss the point.

"Laura is the best of us Howards," he said quietly. "Her behaviour proves that."

The surprise nearly made Kit swallow her tongue. "Uh, yes. Her behaviour mirrors her big heart."

"Yes, unlike my offspring and her useless brother, Laura is thoughtful and sensible. Have you heard what Tom has gone and done now?"

"You mean being locked up?"

"Not anymore, he was released on bail. It was paid by some rich woman in Monaco."

"What, he's snagged himself an heiress or something?"

"Not quite," Maximillian mumbled, focusing on the uneven stairs below his feet. "I understand that the lady in question made her fortune by marrying rich men and then divorcing them."

"More of a gold digger than an heiress, gotcha. Do you think she's trying to get Tom's money? Should someone tell her that he doesn't have any?"

"Well, he might have duped her into thinking that the

Howards have money, omitting that our fortune, shrunken as it has become, is locked into Gage Farm. And in my case, also the businesses I'm a silent partner in."

"Ha, I guess they're two gold diggers trying to dig out each other's gold. Still, maybe Tom has fallen in love with her? Either way, I hope they'll get married and go live off her inheritance somewhere, so Laura doesn't have to support Tom anymore."

"Mm. This topic is dull. Did you know that skunks are omnivorous? They eat anything from berries to frogs, even honeybees!"

He babbled on about skunks without needing her to reply, and just like that, the most sensible conversation Kit had ever had with Maximillian had derailed. They were downstairs now, so soon Laura and Mrs Smith would help manoeuvre this wonky conversation.

Still, some things had been uncovered. Living here hadn't made Maximillian any happier. Kit knew for a fact that she wasn't happy with the situation, and that Laura felt the same way. There had to be a way to fix that. After all, fixing tricky situations was what Kit was known for, even if she yet had to fix the issue with Alice Caine's missing book.

She bit her lip and put her brain into overdrive as she ushered the jabbering Maximillian into the kitchen.

Chapter Twenty

TOP SHELF AND OTHER DISASTERS

Pub 42 was busy on this Monday evening. This meant it took a long time before Rachel could join Kit and Laura at their table. Shannon was behind the bar at the moment, serving a group of blokes who looked like they might be celebrating some sports win. Kit wasn't sure. Was there a football thing going on? Rugby, maybe? Either way, she and Laura weren't here for that. They'd come to talk to Rach about Shannon.

Pleasantries and small talk handled, Rachel sat forward and wrung her hands. "Tell me, what did I say or do to make Shannon behave like this?"

Laura sat forward as well, seeming both curious and worried.

Kit put her beer down. "You sure you want me to tell you?"

"Of course I bloody am," Rachel said.

Kit blew out a breath. "Fine, but it's not pretty."

"Tell me already. I'm dying here."

"Okay," Kit said. "That night when you were dead drunk, you were right to assume you had done something.

You did. However, you were also right when you suggested that you had said something."

"All the blunders then, huh? Great. What was my first mistake?"

"You came home singing Julia Michael's 'Pink' more than nine times in a row but changing every 'he' in the text to 'Shannon' and loudly playing air drums to it."

"That's not too bad," Laura said.

"No. I started with the cute thing to ease us into it," Kit admitted.

Rachel groaned.

Wanting to put her out of her misery, Kit carried on. "Then you threw up on Shannon's favourite shoes."

Rachel groaned louder.

"Then you refused to apologise and said that it wasn't the booze making you throw up, but the meatloaf Shannon had made earlier that night. You claimed it had tasted underdone and poisoned you."

Rachel buried her face in her hands.

Kit knew there was no point in stopping now. "Then—"

"What? There's more?" Laura asked.

"Yep," Kit said. "Everything so far I'm sure could've been handled with a chat the next day. Possibly with a lover's quarrel and lots of apologies from Rach, but it wouldn't have led to this long, infected silence and weirdness, would it?"

"No," Rachel replied in her stead. "I must've said or done something even worse. I have to admit that Shannon doesn't go quiet when she's furious. That's reserved for when she's hurt. What did I do?"

Kit ran her finger around the rim of her beer glass,

wondering how to approach this. "You know her concerns about being so much older than you?"

"Mm-hm," Rachel whispered, suddenly pale as milk.

"Like that it makes her worry that you secretly want to date a woman your own age? Possibly someone who's more extroverted and femme like you?"

"Yes," Rach said in a strangled voice.

"Okay, so does the name Sophie Morley mean anything to you?"

Rachel's mouth popped open, but she didn't answer.

Laura filled in by saying, "I know her! She went to school with us, didn't she, Rach? She's a year younger than us. Blonde. Tall. Works at the ferry office?"

"Yes, she comes here all the time and usually hangs out at the bar with me," Rachel said, grabbing a fistful of her hair as if she wanted to yank it out. "She was buying me drinks that night when I got so sloshed. Oh, god. What about her?"

Kit pushed her glasses up her nose. "Shannon told me that after you'd finished throwing up all over the hallway that night, you talked a lot about her."

"I did?"

"Yep, you were saying how you'd talked about TV shows and movies you both watched when you were little. Also, about the music you loved then and people you knew from school. Basically, how much you had in common since you were the same age."

"I don't like where this is going," Laura said, giving Rachel a sour glance.

"Neither did Shannon," Kit confirmed. "Because after you raved on and on about how much you had in common and how great it was to spend the evening with

Sophie, you said that she's gorgeous and—I quote—that 'her arse is top shelf'."

Rachel screeched and face-planted onto the table.

Laura turned to Kit. "Wait. 'Top shelf?' What does that mean?"

"High-class or superior, I suppose. I think it comes from alcohol being the best stuff if it's kept on the top shelf at a bar?"

From the surface of the table they heard Rach repeat the words 'top shelf' over and over again in a voice packed with regret.

It struck Kit that now yet another part of her life was connected to the word shelf or shelving. One: shelving books was part of her job. Two: Laura had asked if they could shelve their relationship while Maximillian was around. Three: Alice's bookshelf had been meddled with. And now, here was the issue of Rach's drunken babbling about an attractive woman's arse being "top shelf" hurting her insecure girlfriend.

Life is weird and full of coincidences, she thought.

Rachel sat up again. "I do like talking about things we eighties and nineties kids remember, but I do that with anyone my age, including you two. It doesn't take away from how much I adore dating older women with all their knowledge, strength, and humble confidence. I love that Shannon is older than me."

"Well, she still worries about it," Kit pointed out. "So much so that she feared that if you talked about that evening, you might realise that Drunk You was right and that you wanted a younger, curvier woman."

Laura gave Rachel a disappointed look. "I have to say, who can blame her after your 'top shelf' comment?"

Rachel put a hand over her eyes. "I remember ranting

about Sophie's looks and her amazing arse, but I meant it as in that I'm jealous of her body and especially her much rounder, thick bum. I'm not bloody attracted to her. She's not my type. Shannon is."

"You should probably be telling *her* that, sweetheart," Laura said. "Because it seems as if Shannon isn't sure."

Rachel stood so quickly that she almost knocked her chair to the floor. "I will! I have to explain that I absolutely don't fancy Sophie. I mean, she's not even butch! And she wears pink slippers out in public!"

"Go tell her," Kit cheered. "When you do, you might want to say sorry for throwing up in the hallway and on Shannon's favourite shoes, without apology or regret."

Laura winced. "Yes, and for blaming that on Shannon's cooking."

"Bloody hell." Rachel reeled. "Yes, I need to apologise for all of that. Also, I'll buy her new shoes. And, um, I don't know… Crucify myself as an apology? Where the hell should I start?"

Kit locked eyes with her. "Rach…You start by telling her that you'll never leave her for someone else. You start by telling her that she's perfect for you and everything you could ever want."

Rachel swallowed, nodded reverentially, and then ran towards the bar so fast she almost upended tables and chairs. She shouted to the blokes being served by Shannon that this round was on the house because she had to talk to the bartender in private.

Then, she fell to her knees in front of Shannon and howled, "If you will talk to me, that is? I don't blame you if you don't, babe. Kit told me what I said and did that night, but I promise I have explanations for all of it."

Shannon looked around, aware that the whole pub

was staring at them. "Okay, sweetheart. Stand up, and we'll go talk about this in the kitchen."

When the door had closed behind them, Laura leaned closer to Kit. "Do you think Rachel can fix this mess?"

"I think Shannon is absolutely mad about Rach and that the feeling is mutual. So yes, with apologies, explanations, time, and some of that generous communication they usually pride themselves on, they'll be fine."

Laura gave her a quick kiss on the lips. "Well then, that's one problem you have seen to. Now you can focus on the missing book."

Then she went back to sipping her gin and tonic, leaving Kit to think that she had one more issue to solve. The one where Maximillian was not only putting a dampener on their romance but also taking advantage of Laura's kindness. The worst part was that Kit couldn't see a way of fixing the situation without hurting him or asking Laura to go against her nature and conscience. Should she even try to fix this? Perhaps she should give it more time. After Maximillian felt better, they could come clean to him.

She drank her beer, hoping that a solution might be found at the bottom of her pint glass. If not, at least she'd have an excuse to get a refill.

Chapter Twenty-One

GOSSIP AND A QUIVERING MOUSTACHE

Kit was having lunch at Tea Gage, the greasy spoon that liked to put on airs and pretend it was a posh cafe. Sadly, while the artwork and fancy tables looked the part, the food disputed any such ambition. There had been nice, posh paninis last year, but the mainland bakery who made them hiked their prices up. Kit was now grimacing at the stale white toast which was soaking up the grease from her scrambled eggs. At least it had come with Gage Farm greengage jam. Kit smeared some on the unsoaked toast and took a bite. The welcoming sweetness of it filled her mouth, leaving a hint of crisp tartness lingering on her tongue afterwards.

It amazed her city-dweller mind that she'd been on the island with these greengages when they were still growing. No doubt she'd seen them on the trees while taking walks with Laura, before the perfect green ovals had been picked and mushed into this tiny pot of jam.

She blew on her steaming tea and found her place in her book. It was the library's copy of Jules Verne's *Journey to the Centre of the Earth*. If this story was going to stay so important for the mystery, she should probably reread it, although the current description of different kinds of stones and minerals was putting her off a bit. At the age of thirty-one, Kit had shrinking patience for books that bored her.

She was about to skim a bit about sedimentary deposits when the bell above the door chimed and in came two women in their fifties. Kit glanced up at them simply because these days it fascinated her to see people on the island that she didn't know. Greengage had about six thousand residents and yet she seemed to run into the same peculiar but lovable cast of characters. However, her fascination faded fast. While the women were strangers, they were talking about someone with whom Kit was very well acquainted.

"Well, it would be that annoying, fussy, heirloom Charlie Baxter, wouldn't it? He always manages to be in the middle of some sort of scandal," the first woman was saying.

Her friend gave her a reproachful look. "It's not his fault that someone tried to steal his cufflinks."

The first woman sniffed. "No, but it is his fault that he's making a meal out of it and causing a scene. Besides, no need to say *someone*. We all know it was that spoiled Caitlin Caine. Anyway, do you want to eat here or not?"

They marched past Kit, so she never heard the answer, not that she cared about that. She took another bite of jam-drenched toast, chewing it while she thought about the important part of that conversation.

Not only Charlie popping up in island gossip, but Caitlin Caine as well! Huh.

She put the book down and instead scooped up as

much scrambled egg as her fork could hold, suddenly eating faster.

Wonder what happened with his cufflinks. Knowing Greengage, it's probably something bizarre. Still, none of my business. It's just another weird coincidence that I heard about it.

She ate some more egg, washing it down with her black tea. Then she felt the corners of her mouth pull into a smile as the decision formed.

Be it a coincidence, be it gossip, be it something I shouldn't be worrying about on my lunch break, Charlie counts as a friend and Caitlin stealing stuff relates to what I'm helping Alice with. I have a reason to snoop—I mean, look into it.

If there was one thing Greengage had taught her, it was that her flaw of being nosy could be used for good. Besides, no one was perfect, and there were worse vices than snooping.

She shovelled a final forkful of egg into her mouth, drained her tea fast enough to burn her throat, and put the book in her rucksack. She waved goodbye to the owners and the place's stink of grease and baked beans.

Checking her watch, she was thrilled to see that she'd have just enough lunch hour left to go see Charlie.[1]

When she got to the edge of the high street, she saw Charlie's bachelor pad of a terraced house. He was pacing outside it, bowler hat on and moustache quivering. He was arguing with someone even shorter than himself. Kit peered round him and saw the platinum hair of Caitlin Caine. So, she was still at the supposed scene of the crime.

If that was what had happened here. You never could trust gossip, though here on Greengage, you couldn't trust logical deduction either.

Kit got closer and shouted, "Hey, Charlie! You all right?"

"No, Kit, I am most certainly not. This miscreant was in my house trying to convince me to sell her my old Jaeger-LeCoultre watch." His pitch was rising as he spoke, and so was the colour in his wrinkled cheeks. "I went upstairs to fetch it and heard her rooting around downstairs. When I returned, she was cupping my favourite cufflinks into her thieving little hand!"

He was pointing at Caitlin, whose gaze was fixed on her posh, bejewelled sandals.

Charlie's moustache twitched as he screeched, "Well, urchin! Do you have anything to say?"

"Yes," she said.

"No, you haven't," he shot back.

They all stared at each other in silence for a moment. What did you say to that?

"But you asked! And I do. I can explain everything," Caitlin finally said with incredulity.

"No, you can't," Charlie carried on, now the colour of a tomato with sunstroke.

"I can," Caitlin said, now with confusion.

He shook his head violently. "No, you can't."

It was all very serious, so Kit wasn't at all amused by the interaction. No, of course not. Not even by Charlie hopping from foot to foot and getting louder and redder by the moment. Or Caitlin's puzzled face. Not amused at all. Well, not outwardly, at least.

Kit put a hand on Charlie's shoulder, easily done considering his height. "I understand why you're upset, but for your heart's sake, try to calm down, Charlie. Will you let me see if I can help?"

She waited for his nod of approval before turning to the youngest member of the Caine family. "Caitlin, please tell us why you had those cufflinks."

The teenager stared back down at her sandals. "I was only looking, all right? My dad says that cufflinks should've been buried with the Victorians, but I like old shit like that. You know, stuff with history that's been cared for. That's why I wanted to see the stupid, old watch I came there for."

Kit tried to catch the girl's eye. "So, you weren't going to take the cufflinks?"

Caitlin kicked the pavement. "No. I only wanted to check them out. See how, like, heavy they were. I've been trying to explain that!" She whinged and fidgeted with her bleach-frizzed hair. "Ugh. I'm sorry, okay? I've been bored this week and trying to find stuff to do and look at."

Charlie's moustache shuddered again. "It is a nuisance that children are not in school over summer. Especially if they are going to spend all that time stealing from the elderly."

"I don't steal shit, okay?" Caitlin roared. "People keep saying that because they're jealous that my family has money. I mean, it's not like I need to steal. My dad would buy me anything I wanted."

Kit wondered if she should point out that there were many reasons to steal. Hell, the fact that Caitlin's parents gave her everything she could wish for, and thereby robbed her of any chance to long for things, could be a reason why she was trying to obtain things on her own. Or it could be causing her to act out, in this case by stealing. Still, Kit had no experience with teens, wasn't a social worker, and in general had no idea of what she was talking about, so perhaps it was best to keep quiet. This girl needed to talk to someone, though.

"Speaking of your father, I called him, you know," Charlie said. "He's on his way. He shan't be happy when he hears about this."

"He's never happy," Caitlin muttered, her arms over her chest and a blush creeping from her neck up to her cheeks. When she noticed Kit watching her, she scowled and seemed about to cry. Everything in her body language screamed that she wanted to be alone.

Kit gave her a moment to collect herself by taking her glasses off and polishing them. She couldn't understand why, if Caitlin's parents were so willing to spend money on her, they didn't instead spend *time* with her. Surely then they'd see that the stealing was a warning sign? Maybe Caitlin needed something useful to do with her time or just some attention. Perhaps she was lonely. Who could say? Again, Kit wished someone would take this girl under her wing. She just didn't think it should be her; Kit had always been bad at talking to teenagers and she wasn't really role model material.

As she watched Charlie pace while keeping an eye out for Phillip's car, she heard the unmistakable sound of sandals slapping against pavement.

Caitlin had run off.

"Damn," Kit said under her breath.

Charlie was next to her, hopping on one spot so that his perfectly polished wing-tipped brogues tapped a frantic drumbeat. "Yes and also 'curses' and 'damnation' and… and… well, bugger it all!" He rushed off inside.

"Wait, where are you going, Charlie?"

"To call the police! I don't care if nothing was stolen.

This is all wrong, and I don't know what else to do," he all but squeaked.

Kit watched him scurry into his house. He might not know what to do. Kit, however, did. "Man, I hate running," she muttered.

Then she took off sprinting in the direction Caitlin had vanished.

Chapter Twenty-Two

THE INEVITABLE CHASE SCENE

K it might hate running, but the lack of a gym on the island and her therefore enforced evening runs had prepared her for this moment. By the time Caitlin was bent over and wheezing on the roadside outside of the city centre, Kit was still going strong. In fact, she'd caught up with Caitlin much quicker than either of them had expected.

Kit stopped in front of her. "Hey, are you okay?"

"No, I'm a thieving idiot who doesn't even low-key cover her tracks," Caitlin panted with a hollow laugh.

"Well, since we're being honest… I think you wanted to be found out."

Caitlin glared at her. "What? Why the fu—"

Kit cut her off before the profanity was completed. "Look, no matter what you wanted, here we are. Oh, and running off really did you no favours. Why don't we go back and talk to Charlie?"

Caitlin stood and wiped her forehead. "No. He called my dad, who will be disappointed with me again." She hesitated. "When Dad's disappointed, he won't talk to me or even look at me. Or let me go out to see my friends, not that they *want* to see me." She kicked a pebble.

Kit watched the stone roll away, trying to figure out what to say. She wished Laura were here; she was so much better with people. Or maybe Rach? Kit let her gaze travel back to Caitlin. Perhaps she didn't need to talk to another woman since she had her mum and her gran. Maybe she'd listen more to a man, like a father figure? Did gender matter in these things?

"I'm sure you just need to talk to your friends. They'll be happy to see you. And maybe if I help explain to your dad, he won't be so disappointed?"

"Doubt it. He thinks you're an idiot. No offence."

Kit chuckled. "None taken. He's not really a hero of mine either."

"He's shit. So why do I…" Caitlin sighed. "Why do I always want his approval? It's the only reason I work hard to get good grades, and why I compete with everyone in my class."

Kit thought she heard a car in the distance, but didn't want to interrupt Caitlin as she added, "And that makes them hate me. That and my shitty habit of nicking their stuff."

"So, you *do* take things then?" Kit asked, hoping she was being sensitive enough.

"Yeah. I suppose."

"Um, okay. Are they expensive things or just anything that's around?"

"Are you trying to figure out if I'm a klepto? Mum thinks I am. I don't know, sometimes I take stuff because the owner made it too easy, so they don't deserve to have those things. Sometimes I don't even realise I'm doing it."

Caitlin stuffed her hands in her pockets. "The book was different."

Kit jolted. "The book? Do you mean your gran's copy of *Journey to the Centre of the Earth*?"

"Yeah." Caitlin appeared to age five years in a second. "I didn't nick it because I wanted it. Or, you know, just as a reflex. I mean, this time I was actually asked to take something. I was *helping*."

Kit's ears had been right; a car was approaching. Now, at the most inopportune time, Wing Commander Caine's white BMW pulled up next to them.

He wound down the window. "Caitlin! Get in this car right now."

"But Dad, I…"

"Not another word. Don't tell this woman anything. Just get in."

With sluggish movements, Caitlin obeyed.

Phillip turned his piercing gaze to Kit. "And you will either find yourself a useful existence on this island, one that doesn't include bothering citizens, or you'll go back to wherever the hell you came from!" He bared his teeth before adding, "Is that understood?"

He didn't wait around for an answer, but instead drove off at a dangerous speed.

"I guess that was a rhetorical question," Kit muttered at the back of the speeding car.

So, Caitlin had stolen the book, but it wasn't due to her habit of taking things. If she was to be believed, she'd taken it for someone else. Someone who had used a thirteen-year-old's need to matter and to be noticed to steal for them.

Kit set her jaw. Now she was even more determined to find out who the culprit was. *Now…* that word brought her back to the present and what time it was. Her lunch hour had ended twelve minutes ago.

"Shit! Rajesh is going to make me clean the kitchen drain again. And then flay me. Or maybe the other way around."

There was only one thing to do. She'd have to bloody run again.

Chapter Twenty-Three

LUCKILY, BOB/KIPP TUMBLES IN

I t was unbelievable. They were alone. Kit was able to walk through the orchards, the one with the greengage trees to be exact, with her girlfriend without being bothered by a certain uncle, any of Greengage's strange inhabitants, or even the bookshelf mystery.

Laura's hand was warm and soft in hers. There was a plaster on her right thumb where she had a paper cut, one which she somehow had gotten cherry jam into when demonstrating their wares to a new buyer this morning. Kit felt that plaster, and her heart warmed at her usually so elegant girlfriend's clumsiness.

The sun shone through the lush, vivid leaves above them, making Kit squint up at the trees, which were filled with greengages in every shade of yellow and green. She reached up to squeeze one.

"They're not ripe yet, right?"

Distractedly, Laura said, "No, they'll be ripening for another two to three months since we pick them in early autumn." She knitted her brows. "Sorry, I'm still digesting what you told me about yesterday's events. Caitlin took the book?"

"Yep."

"But not to keep it?"

"Nope, she took it for someone else."

Kit dodged a branch. She preferred the orchards with taller trees. They didn't make so many attempts to smack you in the face.

"I see. It's a shame Phillip interrupted her. To be honest, I'm surprised he didn't catch up with you earlier. He's determined to make sure you don't investigate this case."

"Yeah. I wonder if it's because he's trying to protect Caitlin. Or does he really just want to be left alone? Or does he, you know…" Kit ducked under another branch.

"Have something to hide?"

"Exactly." Kit's blissful calm had disappeared, her brain back in crime-solving mode.

Once again, she pondered the role she was moving into. The island's mystery solver. Did she have the time and energy for that? Well, she certainly had the nosiness for it, but still, it was a lot to take on.

"That," Laura paused as if unsure, "well, that is not the only thing on your mind lately, is it? The book mystery, I mean. You've been quiet. Around me." Laura stopped and ran her hand absentmindedly over the bark of the nearest tree. "It hasn't been as extreme as the way Shannon behaved with Rachel, but I can tell that something is wrong. I haven't mentioned it before because I assume," she winced, "that it's my fault. Or Uncle Maximillian's. All depending on if you blame him for his behaviour or me for encouraging it, I suppose."

Kit stopped as well. She felt giddy with relief. Finally, a

chance to bring up the shelved-romance issue. "Since you ask, I'll be honest. I need more time with you. Alone. It doesn't have to be sexual or romantic, I just want it to be you and me without any interference or worrying about what we might say."

"Mm."

"I love you, and I don't want to hide it anymore."

"I know," Laura said quietly.

The words that had been buried in Kit's mind kept spilling out. "I promised to be patient and not complain about this, but it's been *a month and half,* and when I spoke to Maximillian, he said he wasn't feeling any better. Who knows how long he'll stay! It's time to ask him to shove off." Kit rubbed the overheated back of her neck. "Babe, sometimes I wish you were less, I don't know, obliging."

She stopped the flow of words. Laura's normally pale skin had gone chalk white. Kit's heart skipped a beat.

Shit. Why did I say that? Didn't last Christmas teach me not to whinge about Laura's helpfulness? She must be disappointed.

Kit kicked a branch in her path.

No, not disappointed. Hurt. Because I want her to change. Even worse, if she does what I asked and throw Maximillian out, she'll suffer because I made her do something that goes against the core of her personality. I'm a pillock.

Laura began walking again with slow heavy steps. "It goes without saying that I see your point, Kit."

"I- I didn't mean to order you to do something or to change you," Kit stuttered. "Or to act in a way that makes you uncomfortable. I only—"

Kit was interrupted by a man falling down the slope

next to them and rolling into the orchard, barely squeezing past two rows of trees and avoiding hitting them. His tumbling mess of limbs came to a stop at their feet. He shook himself off and stared at Laura with wild eyes.

"Your uncle!" he panted.

Laura brushed dirt off his shirtfront. "Calm down. Take a breath." He obeyed. She nodded and said, "Good. Now tell me."

"Your uncle's been locked in your office for the last hour. I went to check on him and found him on the phone."

Laura grabbed his shoulder. "You let him use the phone?"

"He's a Howard. This is Gage Farm. As he likes to point out, this place is his… what's the term he uses?"

"Birthright," Laura intoned.

The man, Kit was pretty sure his name was Bob or maybe Kipp, gulped in a breath. "Yes, anyway. He was on the phone, and on the desk in front of him was your client list."

"What?" Laura shrieked.

"Yes," Bob or Kipp said with a wince. "I asked what he was doing, and he put his hand over the receiver and explained that he was calling all Gage Farm clients to inform them of our immediate raise in prices."

"WHAT!?"

Bob/Kipp's wince deepened. "Yes. Almost doubling the prices. He refused to stop when I asked him. Also, he said he was working alphabetically, and when I left, he was on the Es. Meaning that he'll soon get to—"

"Farradays," Laura breathed.

"Who are they again?" Kit asked.

Laura faced her, fear making her left eye twitch. "A chain of pubs all over the Midlands and the borders of Wales. They're our biggest client! Kit, I must run. We'll have to continue this discussion later."

As Laura and Bob/Kipp rushed up the slope and towards the office, Kit shouted after her, "I love you!"

She hoped that the fact that Laura didn't turn and reply was only because she hadn't heard her.

Chapter Twenty-Four

TAPPING HER

T he next day, Kit had closed up the library and was fiddling with the alarm system, which today had decided that the number four key didn't work, when her phone buzzed with an incoming text.

She squeaked with joy and relief when she saw it was from Laura. It read:

I'm sorry about yesterday and for missing our good-night call last night. I fell asleep at my desk after hours of figuring out which clients he phoned. He wasn't working alphabetically but randomly, so it's a huge job and won't be finished for a while.

Kit texted back:

That's fine! I'm glad the reason I haven't heard from you wasn't that you were too pissed off with me after our chat in the orchard. Do you think you can undo the damage Maximillian caused?

By the time the alarm had agreed to let her use the number four key and finish, a reply came in.

Hopefully. Many of our clients complained about that we had to raise prices at the start of the financial year. Hearing now that we were raising them, almost doubling them, again made many of them have a knee-jerk reaction to go elsewhere. So, as I said, I'll be busy with this for a while.

Kit had just finished reading that when another text from Laura came in.

In regards to me being upset with you, there was a lot to ponder and to discuss after that chat. Sadly, that will now have to wait. I'm aware that this is bad timing considering the argument was about me not having enough time for you. I promise we'll work something out. I love you. x

As fast as Kit's fingers could tap the screen, she typed out a reply:

We will. I'll do anything to make this relationship work. Even be called Susan until I die. I love you so much. xx

Kit inhaled a deep lungful of the warm evening air, feeling much lighter. They'd sort it out. Laura still loved her just as much. She could now focus on the next step in the bookshelf case.

During a lull after lunch, she'd been emailing Aimee. Neither of them were allowed to use their phones at work but both had to check their work emails, so that was a great way to bounce ideas off of each other. Aimee claimed that neither of the Caine siblings, or Jackie for that matter, would be happy to share their inheritance. How was it she'd put it? Something like:

They're selfish pricks. No way would they share. One of them stole the will to check how much they got. Then they placed the will in the bank and spent the past year scheming about how to get their hands on ALL the dosh. Trust me, they're plotting something evil!

It had taken Kit two emails to convince Aimee that this wasn't a thriller or a detective story where family members would start kidnapping or killing each other for money. Especially not as the sums involved, which would be huge for someone like her and Aimee, were a pittance for these people. As much as Kit disliked some of the Caines, she didn't think they'd venture past petty theft and heated arguments. Unkind as the thought was, she doubted they had the imagination to plan anything too nefarious, not to mention the nerve to go through with it. Besides, they all cared too much about what people thought of them to risk prison.

Aimee was right about one thing, though: the will had to be at the centre of this.

Kit pocketed the library keys and enjoyed the warm air. It was a nice night for a walk. It was an even nicer night to get some answers. She'd failed when trying to interrogate Phillip, Anthony, and Liam. Alice didn't know anything. Caitlin was being kept under wraps by her dad. That left Jacqueline "Jackie" Caine, and Kit knew she liked to have her pre-dinner tipple at Pub 42 right about now.

This time she wouldn't mess it up. She considered possible questions to ask Jackie while opening her ruck-sack to rifle through books, half-empty hand creams, tissue packs, protein bar wrappers, and old receipts until she found her Voyage d'Hermès. She sprayed the perfume on her pulse points, pulled up her skinny black jeans, smoothed down her hair, and slung her rucksack over one shoulder. She was ready for battle.

She marched to the pub, thinking about the burger she was going to inhale as she did her questioning. She might not be Sherlock Holmes, but at least she could multitask.

Next to her, Mrs Carlton walked past with her pregnant terrier. Kit noted their energy and stamina. Here was one to watch in the lady-and-dog-walking bets.

🐚

Kit was sat at the bar and halfway through her burger when Jackie entered Pub 42 as if every piece of floor her high heels touched was now her domain.

"Ay up, here's the Queen of Scotland," Matt said as he handed Kit another Diet Pepsi.

Kit watched Jackie approach the bar and stand next to

her to order a dry martini. Matt was right, there was something royal about the way she held herself. Although, it reminded Kit of Jackie's time in the theatre, as her demeanour looked even more put on than the vast amounts of make-up that adorned her face.

While waiting for her drink, Jackie cast a glance to her side and saw Kit.

"You."

"Me," Kit said with what she hoped was a charming smile.

Jackie looked amused. "Pardon a random question, but what blush do you use?"

Kit tried not to wince. Her pink cheeks had always been a source of embarrassment. "I'm afraid I don't. I only wear make-up to very posh events, and I don't go to many of those."

"I suppose you attend more of them now that you're dating Laura Howard." It was a statement, not a question, and Jackie left no space for a reply. "I know that was how it was for me. I went from having drinks with the cast and crew of Edinburgh theatres to all of a sudden being a Greengage swell, expected to uphold a certain…" She rubbed her fingertips together in the air as if trying to use friction to find the correct word.

"Style?" Kit supplied.

Jackie pursed her lips. "No. That wasn't it. Never mind."

Her martini was placed before her, and in an unlady-like gulp she swallowed down half of it with eyes closed tight. Kit tried not to gawk at what was probably a person self-medicating away an unhappy life.

"So, um, I'm glad we ran into each other. I wanted a quick chat," Kit ventured. She had a feeling that when that martini glass was emptied, Mrs Caine would be out the door without warning.

Jackie gave a mirthless laugh. "Of course you did. You either want to harass me like you did my daughter over that misunderstanding with Baxter's cufflinks or tap me for information regarding this missing book silliness." She raked her clever eyes over Kit, from her Converse up to the hair, which Kit now smoothed self-consciously. "Or perhaps, you've grown tired of Greengage's favourite daughter's self-righteous wholesomeness and want to… tap me in a different way."

Jackie's tone made the innuendo crystal clear. Kit didn't think it was used for the shock factor either; it appeared to be an actual invitation. The Kit from a few years ago would have considered it. This woman had a damaged beauty and the air of someone who could be saved by pure-hearted affection, someone who'd offer her the freedom to live life the way she wanted.

Except Kit didn't save women anymore, at least not by getting them into her bed and her heart. All she needed and wanted was Laura. Well, and more of the burger she'd abandoned for this chat.

"In the past, I'd have jumped at the chance to be with you. Now, however, I'm in love. And I never cheat. So, you were right the first time—I want to tap you for information."

Jackie sneered and took another gulp of her martini.

Kit quickly turned to the person behind the bar. Most of the time that was Rachel, but that night Matt had left his kitchen to play bartender. Kit hoped this meant Rach and Shannon were off in some corner having a chat. Maybe even a snog?

"Matt, could you get Mrs Caine here another martini?"

"Sure, I'll keep them coming," he said conspiratorially.

Jackie groaned. "Don't call me Mrs Caine. You make me feel old."

"Okay then, Jackie. Can I start by asking if you know anything about how Caitlin is involved with the missing book business?"

With a disdainful laugh, Jackie replied, "Do you really think that smiling prettily and buying me a drink will make me say something that might get my daughter in trouble? She's one of the best things in my life. If it wasn't for my children, the few attractive men on this island, and this pub's strong martinis, I don't know if I'd keep dredging on."

Matt raised his eyebrows at Kit while pushing a fresh martini over to Jackie. Kit ignored him. She had to get this chat right.

"That's quite bleak, Jackie, but I'm glad you love Caitlin so much. She clearly needs love and," Kit crossed her fingers this wouldn't backfire, "maybe someone to talk to? About her stealing and her loneliness, I mean."

Jackie slammed down the martini glass so hard Kit was surprised it didn't crack. "Are you actually sitting there telling me what my daughter needs? While hinting that I'm not providing her with it?"

"No, I only meant that I worry about her. She's a good kid but not a very happy one, and I think that shows in her addiction to taking things." Kit hesitated, rolling the next words around in her mouth before she took the risk of letting them out. "I also worry that someone used her coping mechanism of stealing to get their hands on that book. Caitlin told me she did take it, but that is was for someone else. That she was being helpful."

A myriad of emotions crossed Jackie's face. Kit thought she could spot worry, sadness, and anger. However, those feelings could mean many different things. They could mean she'd known that someone was using her daughter this way and felt guilty. Or that she hadn't realised the severity of it. Or that she didn't know. Those emotions could also mean that she was upset about being caught, if she had made Caitlin take the book.

"I've spoken to Alice, you know. I'm aware that you think this all boils down to the will," Jackie said in clipped tones. "I am also aware that you've been told that the will was very fair and that none of us Caines would contest it. So why don't you look further afield if you're so convinced that there's something immoral about this book going missing?"

"Further afield? Do you mean Liam? I know your husband and his brother believe Liam's out to rob or swindle Alice."

Jackie's head snapped up. "No, not him. Liam is only a misunderstood, young lad."

Her Scottish accent had been stronger in that last sentence. Was it the martinis having an effect? Or the fact that she'd been more emotional than one would predict from this numbed woman? Also, Kit noticed, that defence speech had been shorter than expected. Was she trying to be subtle?

"Okay, fine, not Liam. Who then?"

Jackie rubbed her thin eyebrow, leaving a little smudge which proved most of the brow had been painted on. "Look, I didn't mean you should go find some poor sap to make your new *suspect*." That last word had all the venom of a king cobra with a hangover. "The book has been misplaced, Ms Sorel. I'm sure it will show up at the bottom of Caitlin's wardrobe."

There was a beat of significant silence. Then, Jackie's hand clasped the edge of the bar. She tightened her grip until her knuckles whitened. "I mean, in Alice's wardrobe. Or under her sofa. Perhaps my dear mother-in-law never even had the book but has imagined it."

Matt put another martini in front of Jackie, who took it as if it were a lifeline and downed it in one long gulp. She stood and gave Kit a glare so malicious it nearly burned a hole in her head. "My husband was right, you *are* trouble. You're making our lives miserable for your own entertainment. Well, why don't you take up golf or knitting? Perhaps even head back to the mainland to one of your gay bars and bother your own people?"

Before Kit knew it, she was standing as well. "Whoa. Hold on, Jackie."

"No, I won't. Did I offend you? Such a shame. Now, listen to me." She pointed a red-nailed finger at Kit. "Even if the will was read and the book stolen, hell even if the bookshelves were tampered with and the alphabetical order disrupted or whatever, no serious crime has been committed. If it had, we would've called the police. Your snooping is unrequired." She grabbed her handbag. "Thank you for the drinks. Now stay away from me and my family, especially Caitlin."

Jackie swanned out with poise, showing little effect of three martinis downed so fast.

Kit watched her go, remembering how Alice had told Rachel that her family weren't aware that the books had been alphabetised before they were interfered with. Since this was hearsay from Rachel, Kit didn't know if it was true. She also didn't know if Alice had recently told Jackie about the alphabetising, but it was still interesting that Jackie knew about it and had mentioned it. She sat back down.

My burger must be stone cold by now, she thought with a pout.

Kit leaned her elbows on the bar. More than Jackie's defensive behaviour, the sudden rudeness, and the comment about alphabetized books, the words "at the bottom of Caitlin's wardrobe" kept spinning in her mind. Misspoken words or a slip-up?

Since you pay before your meal and don't usually tip in pubs, Kit could run off with only a quick wave in Matt's direction. That saved time was needed. She had to hurry into the Caines' house and check Caitlin's wardrobe before Jackie got there and moved the book.

Luckily, they'd both be on foot. Jackie would be hampered by her heels and her need to look sophisticated and controlled. However, to get there before Jackie and somehow get access to the wardrobe, Kit would have to be much faster.

She swore under her breath and once again broke out into a petulant run.

Chapter Twenty-Five

DON'T DIE TO DEATH!

The route between Pub 42 and the Caines' house ran through the town centre and out to the leafy, posher outer areas. As Kit sprinted, she intersected the road that led up the hill to Howard Hall. Therefore, it wasn't unexpected to see Laura's little Beetle come pottering along, but it still hit Kit like a blow to the stomach. She squinted to try to see Laura's face.

How upset is she?

The Beetle slowed, and Laura rolled her window down. "Hello."

"Hey," Kit panted, every feeling under the sun crowding into her chest.

"Is… is everything okay? You look like you've seen a ghost. In fact, you're running like said ghost is chasing you!"

"I'm okay," Kit panted. "I hate to ask this, particularly since we have relationship baggage to unpack, but could you quickly drive me to Jackie and Phillip Caine's house?"

Laura drummed her fingers on the steering wheel as she considered it. "I was on my way downtown for a surprise visit to schmooze a supplier. I can do that tomorrow, though. Sure, I'll drive you. Get in."

Kit didn't have to be asked twice. She put her seatbelt on and watched Laura tuck a big curl behind her ear before starting the car and driving off.

A long second later, she had to break the silence. "Is it okay if, um, do you mind if we save talking about my comments in the orchards for later? The clock is ticking on this."

Laura didn't take her eyes off the road. "If this is helping Alice, then we should shelve our relationship chat, yes."

Kit's sigh of relief was so loud it made Laura chuckle, which broke the ice somewhat.

"See, me being *obliging* can be a good thing," Laura teased.

"Shush, gorgeous, we're shelving that chat, remember?" Kit bantered back.

While she filled Laura in on the mission, they came to a tall, mock-Tudor villa. It was at the end of a long road of nice houses, which all seemed to hide in embarrassment at not having a massive, wrought-iron fence with the name "Caine" in big metal letters, a showy front garden, and a garage bigger than Kit's cottage.

Kit squinted through the windscreen up at the house, which was lit by surprising amounts of streetlights.

"It's amazing what some inheritance and an RAF officer's wage can buy," she muttered.

"It helps if your architect brother designs your home for you," Laura said, not unkindly. She was trying to park somewhere and having no luck.

"I meant the amount of lighting they have. The streetlights down on the high street barely function, but sure, the villa and garden are impressive too. Looks a bit out of place on the street of smaller houses, though."

Laura opened her mouth to answer, then closed it. Then she thought better of her decision and said, "I think that was intentional. On a road with more high-end houses, this place would look normal. Here it looks—"

"More like the swanky mansion I assume the good Wing Commander Caine has wet dreams about."

"Kit."

"What? It's true."

"In all fairness, I'm sure Jackie had something to do with that as well. Her theatre background has always made her tastes run towards the, shall we say, ostentatious."

Despite their hurry and the tension between them, Kit couldn't help being cheeky. "Babe, are you trying to say tacky?"

Laura squirmed in her seat while she parallel-parked. "No. I meant *ostentatious*. Now shush, I'm trying to park."

Kit dutifully kept quiet while Laura squeezed her car in between two pristine suburbitanks.[1] When the sound of the car engine had died away, she asked, "Any thoughts on how we can get into the house?"

"Can't we simply ring the doorbell?" Laura asked. "I'm not comfortable with breaking into people's houses. The Caines stealing a book from a family member might not be much of a crime, but us committing burglary certainly is."

"It's not burglary. Laura, I'm not a criminal. I only want to find that book for Alice."

"Can't we call the police and ask them to get it?"

"They're busy with loud drunks and domestic fights. If we tell them that there might be a missing book at the bottom of a teenager's wardrobe, they'll tell us to bugger off."

"I suppose so," Laura whispered. "And Alice didn't want the police involved."

Kit ran a hand through her hair. Of all the people she could bring along for this highly dubious quest, her conscientious girlfriend might've been the worst choice. Aimee, Rajesh, or even Rachel would've been halfway into the house by now.

And yet Laura now looked around and said, "No sign of Jackie. Getting a taxi around here is unlikely unless you have pre-booked, so she must still be walking over. Whatever we do, we should do it now before she arrives."

Kit grinned. "That's the spirit, honey! I promise that if we get in trouble or offend someone, I'll take the full blame and say you didn't know what I was doing."

"Like I'd let you do that," Laura said grimly. "Let's go before I change my mind."

She got out of the car, and Kit followed. Laura's hands trembled as she tried the gate and found it unlocked. She snuck in and started creeping about like a villain in a kid's show, all long steps and arms out to the side. She looked so comical that Kit had to fight the urge to giggle. Instead, she followed Laura while trying to formulate a plan.

"If I remember correctly from my last visit years ago," Laura whispered, "Caitlin's bedroom is on the second floor to your right."

Kit threw a glance up and saw a light on in that window. "Shit, she's home."

"She would be. Phillip has her under house arrest when she's not at school," Laura whispered, still walking like the ground was trying to eat her feet.

"Right."

Kit found herself happy that Laura was here. Firstly, because she was being adorable, and secondly because she knew the layout of the house. Google Maps had given Kit the address to this place but obviously not where to find Caitlin's bedroom.

Thirdly, everything was better when Laura Howard was around. Even if things were unsettled between them at the moment.

Kit nearly tripped over a root and traced it up to a tall tree. Laura could no doubt identify what kind of tree it was, but while Kit was rubbish with distinguishing flora and fauna, she always recognised something useful when she saw it. The tree wasn't far off from Caitlin's window. She gave it a cheerful pat and whispered, "Babe, if I climb this, do you think I can reach the window and open it from the outside?"

Laura stared at her, the disbelief in those hazel eyes obvious even in the dim light. "No. That window will be locked. There will be a teenager in there. They probably have some sort of advanced alarm system. Not to mention that this tree is too far away, so you'd have to throw yourself the last bit."

"Stop being a Negative Nellie," Kit hissed back. "I'm gonna climb up to get a better view at least. Hopefully Caitlin's napping. Wait, maybe she's not in the room but left the light on?"

Laura made a groan of doubt mixed with pity. "Slim chances, dearest."

"Better than no chances. Besides, like you said, Jackie could be here any moment. The time is now."

Kit examined the tree trunk. Growing up in a flat on the outskirts of Raynes Park, Greater London, there'd been few trees she was allowed to climb. However, Kit had been the monkey bars champion at her school's playground, so she began climbing with confidence. That soon waned when she found there were no handgrips. Weren't trees meant to be knobbly and full of branches? Why was this one so bloody smooth!? It didn't help her nerves that, when she wobbled, Laura squeaked like a mum when her toddler picks a flower full of wasps.

Still, Katherine "Kit" Sorel hated quitting. She engaged her muscles more and clumsily shimmied up, climbing higher by the second. Moving like this made her aware that her knickers felt weird. Had she had put them on the wrong way around this morning? Typical. When she finally reached her goal, it was impossible to avoid seeing how high up she was due to the light streaming out of Caitlin's window.

Kit avoided the urge to punch the tree trunk in rage. Caitlin was both awake and occupying her room. She was sprawled across a four-poster bed, typing on her phone.

What the hell do I do now? Knock and demand to search her room? She'd laugh in my face.

Kit changed her grip as she was sliding. Maybe she could get Laura to distract Caitlin so she left the room. Or perhaps Laura could throw some stones on a downstairs window? Maybe ring the landline phone, if they had one.

Yeah, Phillip Caine will still have one of those. Probably a posh one, placed next to a drinks table with expensive booze in carafes. I wonder if…

Kit's train of thought stopped as dead as if it was out of train tracks. In front of her loomed the face of a bored teenager, who was currently chewing gum and taking a picture of Kit with her iPhone. When she was done, she opened the window.

"Hey. Up a tree, huh? Right outside my room, too. I

can't decide if that's lit or creeptastic. Dad says you're stalking me. Are you? If so, are you gonna kill me, or do you want my autograph?"

"Caitlin. Be serious." Kit didn't know why she was whispering. "You know I'm only worried about you and want to help Alice clear this mess up."

Caitlin put the phone down and stopped chewing her gum. The bored facade made way for real concern. "You're not going to stop investigating, are you?"

"No. Not unless I fall out of this tree tonight and die to death!" Kit hissed in panic.

"Die to death? Don't you mean 'drop to your death' or something?" Caitlin said.

"Please don't do either" was heard from the bottom of the tree.

Caitlin peered down. "Who's there? Is it Rach? I know she's part of your squad 'cos Liam said she came with you to question him."

Kit had no time to reply as Laura piped up, "No, it's me, Laura Howard."

"Oh! Hi, Miss Howard!"

"Good evening, Caitlin. How are you?"

"Fine, considering I'm flippin' grounded. What about you? I hear your uncle's squatting in your house?"

"I'm well, thank you. And yes, he's staying with me for a while."

Kit shut her eyes against Greengagers and their small talk. "Right, if we're done with the chit-chat, can I climb down this bloody tree, before I fall, and be invited in, please?"

"God, chill! I'd let you in, but Dad says I can never talk to you again. Oh, and Mum is on her way home. I'm not allowed to talk to anyone until she's back."

"Caitlin, if you don't open that door, I'll attempt swinging from this tree, through the window, and into your room. I won't make it."

"No, she absolutely will not make it" was heard down near the tree roots.

Kit rolled her eyes at her girlfriend's lack of confidence but couldn't argue with it.

Caitlin chewed her pink-glossed lip. "I suppose I've got to let you in. Dad won't like the garden being full of dead librarians."

"Thanks," Kit said sardonically.

"Climb down, and I guess I'll go open the front door," Caitlin said, sounding as thrilled as someone accepting a glass of grey, lumpy milk.

❧

After Kit's descent down the tree—half climb and half fall —she'd been too frazzled to appreciate the interior of the house. Besides, it was too confusing to be appreciated. Phillip's starkness had squared off against Jackie's flamboyance. The starkness had won most of the battles, especially when it came to colour schemes.

Except in Caitlin's room, where the walls were painted magenta at the bottom and, over a blue dado rail, mint green. Suddenly, Kit re-evaluated trusting this girl.

"I suppose you're here to ask me to give you the book," Caitlin said, her voice dripping with weariness.

"Nope," Kit said. Quick as an oiled fox, she slipped past Caitlin to the poster-covered wardrobe. She flung it open and waded through schoolbooks and shoes, to Caitlin's complaining grunts, until she found *Journey to the Centre of the Earth*.

Kit stood with the book in her hand. She'd been wondering why Caitlin hadn't pushed her away from the wardrobe or at least shouted about the intrusion of her private space and property. Now she saw why. The relief was obvious on Caitlin's face.

At least until the front door was opened with such a crash that they heard it clear as day upstairs. Then Caitlin's eyes widened, and she whispered, "Mum's home."

Chapter Twenty-Six

ATTACK OF THE (DRUNKEN) MUMMY

A great number of thoughts went through Kit's mind during the time Jackie slammed the front door, stomped up the stairs, then threw open the door to Caitlin's room.

Sadly, none of the thoughts were useful. They mainly consisted of advice like: *Run! Hide! Pretend to be someone else!* And most unhelpful of all: *Did my fitness watch count my climb up that tree as part of my daily exercise target?*

Also, there was the muscle-memory guilt of being found in a girl's bedroom by said girl's mother. Kit hadn't felt that since she was a closeted teenager.

She chased these thoughts off with a bout of rightful wrath.

She was the advocate for truth.

The one stepping up to help despite threats and hard-to-climb trees.

The defender of Alice Caine's interests.

She was… possibly in over her head.

That last thought popped up when Jacqueline gave her a glare which not only made the hairs on the back of her neck stand up, but also made the hairs want to apologise for ever having been so insolent as to exist in Jackie's presence.

Kit, however, wasn't going to cower. Laura's hand rested against her lower back now in a silent expression of support, so Kit dredged her emotional larder and found a smile to plaster on her face. "Hello again, Jackie."

"Don't you *dare* hello me," Jackie hissed between panting breaths.

Kit buried that smile back where she'd found it. This was not going to be pleasant. "Are you all right, Jackie?" she asked. "It's quite the walk here from Pub 42. Especially if you're in a hurry."

"Oh, do keep quiet, you nosy, blasted nuisance!"

Jackie's shrill voice echoed in the small room. This was a true feat considering how the walls were covered in posters of various boy bands, whose pretty boys all looked a bit like butch women Kit had dated in the past.

But less attractive. These boys could do with taking clothes tips from those ladies.

"Are you listening to me?" Jackie snapped.

Kit pulled her gaze from the nearest poster. "Sure. I was keeping quiet, like you ordered me to. You see, I don't need to speak when I have this." She showed Jackie the book in her hand before adding, "It was right where you happened to suggest such a book being. At the bottom of your daughter's wardrobe."

Jackie swayed on her feet.

The other three women all stepped closer to her, but it was Laura who got there first. "Mrs Caine? Hi, it's me, Laura Howard. Would you like to sit down?"

"I…" Jackie trailed off. She swallowed, straightened her posture. She planted her feet and then, finally, cleared her throat. "I am going to fetch my phone and call the police. You've broken into my house."

"No, we haven't," Kit said. "Caitlin let us in. She's got better manners than you do." Kit tightened her grip on the book and clenched her other hand in her pocket. It was time for a gamble. "After letting us in, Caitlin told us everything about the theft of this book. And about the will. This doesn't look good, Jackie."

Jackie's posture fell again. "Everything? W-well, th-then you know that it was all Liam's fault! He used his charm to convince her. Caitlin was only twelve and a half back then, a mere child!" She grabbed the doorframe before adding, "To think I had to defend him when we were in the pub earlier. Even worse, can you imagine I used to sleep with that slutty, chavvy, little rotter!?"

Adorably, Laura covered Caitlin's ears with careful hands. The teenager moved away with a sigh and a muttered, "Mum. I didn't tell them that. They just tricked you."

Jackie, open-mouthed, looked from her daughter to Kit and then back again.

Caitlin plonked herself down on the bed, making the bedsprings groan. "I guess we might as well tell you now."

"Caitlin," Jackie warned.

"Mum! There's no point! They pretty much know everything already. Let's get this all over with."

Jackie lowered the hand she'd been raising and gave a curt nod.

Caitlin's tear-filled eyes fixed on Kit's. "Mum was telling the truth. Liam asked me to nick the book with a will in it. He'd tried to go through the books, two times actually, until he found the one with the will. Both times he got caught by Gran before he found it."

Kit groaned. "*That's* why the bookshelf was disturbed twice!"

"Yeah," Caitlin said in a small voice.

"After that, he asked you to get it," Laura stated. "That makes sense. Alice would let you wander around the house for longer without suspecting anything."

"Yeah, back then at least. Now everyone worries I'll steal everything," Caitlin said with an air of petulance.

"Why did Liam want the will?" Kit asked, wanting them to stay on subject.

Caitlin lowered her gaze. "He didn't explain, just made it seem like he wanted to read it for a laugh. Like a harmless dare or something."

Laura sat down on the bed next to Caitlin. "You know now that it was more than that, right?"

"Obviously! I'm not bloody daft," Caitlin snapped.

"No. Of course not," Laura said. "But you told Kit that you were only being helpful when you took it. I'm sure that was a lie to cover your tracks, but I had to ask. There's been so many lies, many of them told to you. It's time for the truth to come out completely, for all of us."

"With that in mind," Kit said, "are you sure Liam didn't tell you anything else about the will? For example, if he wanted it for himself or to give it to someone? Do you know how it later ended up in your dad's or your uncle's possession?"

Caitlin's gaze was fixed on her hands. "No. I feel silly now for not asking Liam about it. I only thought we were having fun. He even gave me a nice hairband as a reward for beating him in the game of getting the will." Her gaze shot to her bedside table where a rose-gold hairband was half-squished under a magazine. "Then when he'd had the book for a few days he gave it to me, without the will, and said that I should hide the book. That was when I started to think it was a bit dodgy."

From the corner of her eye, Kit saw Jackie leaning her head against the doorframe.

"Mum? Are you okay?" Caitlin asked.

"Yes, sweetheart, I only wish you would've confided in me," Jackie answered with a dejected slur to her words.

Caitlin returned to staring at her hands. "Well, I told you pretty soon. Like, right after Gran started asking questions about her books."

"Yes, you did. That was good. I wish we would've told Alice the truth, but that was when the subject of you," Jackie paused, seemingly choosing her words, "taking things was quite infected. Also, back then, I believed Liam was a harmless, misunderstood, silly boy who thought it'd be funny to look at someone's will. When the will turned up and I knew the book was safe, I forgot all about it."

Caitlin nodded. "Same. The next time I heard about the will was when Uncle Anthony said he had found it on Gran's coffee table."

"Exactly," Jackie said. "He claimed it had been laying around and that he was worried about its safekeeping. Alice mumbled that it must've fallen out of the book but when pressed became vague about the whole thing. She was tired that day, I recall, and stressed by her sons shouting at her for leaving her will unguarded."

"Then what happened?" Laura prompted.

"Anthony and Phillip took Alice to the bank where she has a safe deposit box. They double-checked that the will was in order and then put it in the box. I haven't heard anything about it during this past year, not until you brought it up."

"So, after Liam had the book and will for a few days,

the will turned up in Anthony's possession. Not Liam's?" Kit asked Jackie.

"Ms Sorel, I can see the difference between my ex-lover and my brother-in-law."

Kit quirked an eyebrow at her but said nothing.

"Don't you dare look at me like that," she growled. "I'm aware of the rumour regarding me sleeping with my brother-in-law. It's a lie. Anthony and I have always had a pact of flirting with each other to, I don't know, get some sort of petty revenge on Phillip. It's all smoke and no fire."

Caitlin groaned in disgust.

Kit took her glasses off to rub the bridge of her nose. "Okay. Well, Liam could've snuck the will onto the table so that Anthony honestly just found it there. Either way, it sounds like I need to talk to them both. Any tips on how to get them to open up?"

"One," Jackie said. "Start with Liam. A stone buried in concrete would be more likely to open up than Anthony."

Kit put her glasses back on. "I was worried you'd say that. I'm even more worried that you're right."

"We'll speak to Liam first," Laura said, pensiveness making her voice quiet. "He's a bit of a bad egg but has never been downright evil or cruel. If we push the fact that he has implicated Caitlin in this, I think we can guilt him into telling the truth."

Jackie squirmed a little. "There is something else you could use. I believe he still has… certain feelings for me. If nothing else, he feels bad about how things ended between us."

"*Certain feelings* is mum's way of saying Liam's still thirsty for her," Caitlin said in disgust. "But yeah, he's probably feeling guilty, too."

"Thirsty?" Laura asked.

"Fancies her," Kit muttered, feeling that this was pretty obvious from context.

"Oh. Right," Laura squeaked.

Kit stood in front of Laura so she could blush in peace. "Okay, ladies. Thanks for the suggestions and for finally being honest with me. We'll leave you alone now to chat about this."

"I'll walk you out," Caitlin said, lightning fast.

Jackie stayed behind, still leaning against her trusted doorframe, looking like she was lost in her own world.

As she walked them downstairs, Caitlin whispered, "Are you gonna tell Gran?"

"I'm afraid so, kid. We'll see what Alice thinks. She might want to call the police now that we know for sure someone's been messing with her will," Kit replied.

To her credit, Caitlin didn't argue. Instead Kit heard her swallow loudly and whisper, "I wish I could come with you. Mum means well, but she doesn't talk about her feelings. She just drinks about them."

Kit wasn't sure what to say, but luckily Laura stepped in. "Is there someone you want us to call for you? A friend or something?"

"No. There's no one I really talk to. No one I want to talk to either, not about this shameful shit. Go ahead and leave. I'm really tired anyway, so I think I'll go to bed."

Laura put an arm around Caitlin. "Tomorrow morning I want you to call me, okay? I grew up without a mother and was raised by an aunt who I couldn't speak to about things. I'm not sure I can help you, but I know what it's like to need someone to listen."

Kit saw Caitlin glance at Laura and then give her a bland smile. Inwardly, Kit winced. Laura wasn't aware of it, but many Greengagers saw her as some sort of saint and not a real person. It was doubtful if Caitlin would want to talk to the flawless Laura about being fooled by an older bloke and stealing. Still, Kit was going to find someone to help this girl. Someone who listened. Someone who had a parental feel to them. She only had to figure out who that was.

When Caitlin had said goodbye and gone back inside, they ambled towards the car. The heavy silence made it obvious that they were both lost in thought.

"So…" Laura said.

"So," Kit echoed, "um, I'm going off to Liam's house. Did you mean what you said in there? That you're coming with me?"

"Why wouldn't I come along?"

"I'm not sure what's going to happen. He might get…" Kit waved her hand in the air, searching for a word that wouldn't scare her girlfriend. "Angry or something."

"That's exactly why I don't want you to go alone. Besides, you're the one who always says that I know everyone and everything that happens here on Greengage."

Kit chuckled. "Yeah, all part of being lady of the manor, huh?"

"Shush you. It's only because I really care about this island and the people on it. Also, I have a good memory for people and their actions. I might be able to dredge up some facts about Liam to make him talk."

Kit knew when she was beaten. "Okay, come along. Just be sure to follow me if I start running."

"Dearest, if I thought Liam would do anything that we would need to run from, I'd call the police and take them with us. As I said, he's a bad egg, but he's never been violent or involved in anything worse than anonymous letters and petty theft. He doesn't even do drugs except for the occasional marijuana."

Kit halted and shot her a glance.

"Don't look at me like that, Kit. I may be naïve at times, but even I know that the small criminal element on this island bring in drugs from the mainland. I keep an eye on the dangers around here. That's why I'm sure Liam isn't likely to hurt us."

A few steps more, and they were standing by the car. Laura opened the passenger door for Kit and motioned for her to get in. For a second, Kit couldn't move. She had a sudden urge to either kiss, hug, or inappropriately grab the woman she loved.

"You are something else, Laura Rosalind Howard. You know that, right?"

Laura laughed, and as always in her warm voice it sounded like gentle summer rain on moss. Or music. Or something equally sappy. Kit couldn't find the right simile. All she knew was that her heart belonged to that laugh. She hoped desperately that she hadn't damaged what they had beyond repair.

"Is that a compliment?" Laura asked.

"Everything I say to you is a compliment," Kit said. It wasn't sucking up, she meant it with a sincerity she couldn't convey. "Oh, and I want points for remembering your overly posh middle name."

Laura smiled, leaned in for a kiss, and then whispered, "I've missed you."

"I've missed you, too. Now, let's go confront your so-called 'bad egg,' honey."

Kit got into the car, impatience once again overshadowing her other emotions. She was so close to the answers now. Liam would have to bloody talk!

Chapter Twenty-Seven

TWISTY KNICKERS AND TWISTIER CONFESSIONS

The car rattled along towards Nettle Road. Kit found herself wishing that Laura wasn't always so aware of the speed limit. If she weren't, they could have been there by now. Also, Kit realized she *had* put her knickers on the wrong way around. That seam she could feel shouldn't be there. She fidgeted to get comfortable.

Half a century later, they arrived at the row of terraced houses next to Alice's cottage. Kit could see a mop of dark blond hair moving in the window of Liam's end-of-terrace. He was home. They parked right by the house, but as Kit was taking her seatbelt off, Laura's phone rang.

"Ugh. It's Uncle Maximillian."

"Well, you better answer it," Kit said, inwardly adding, *And tell old Max to shove off.*

Laura did so. Answer the call, that is; unfortunately, she didn't tell him to shove off.

"Hello. What? No, I don't know what the difference between a turtle and a tortoise is."

"I think one of them lives in water," Kit muttered, simply to feel like part of the conversation.[1]

"No, Uncle, I don't think it's possible to have a turtle stuffed, nor am I sure it would be ethical."

Kit stared at Laura in amazement. How did she not sound pissed off? How was her voice as normal as if this were a reasonable conversation coming at a convenient point in time? The only sign of impatience was her lips pressing together before she said, "Anyway, I really must get going. When I come home, we can continue this conversation."

Kit peered through the car window, keeping an eye out for that blond head. Yes, he was still walking around in there. Kit's heart picked up speed when she saw that Liam held something to his ear. Must be his phone. Was Jackie warning him? Or Caitlin? Would their soft spot for him be strong enough to overcome his lies and manipulations?

Kit grabbed Laura's arm. "Honey, I have to go. Now. I think someone called to warn him."

Not waiting for a reply, she opened the car door and started jogging towards the house. She heard Laura saying something ending with the word "goodbye" and then the smatter of Laura's kitten heels behind her.

Kit banged on the door, tired of being polite with these people. She was also tired of feeling that seam. How had she not noticed that her knickers were the wrong way around until that stupid tree climb?

Bloody annoying! Is this where the saying "getting your knickers in a twist" comes from?

The door opened with as much vehemence as Kit had put into the knocking.

"What?!" Liam demanded.

Kit took a step forward, about to tell him what. Laura stopped her by replying first. "Hi, Liam. It's been a while since we've spoken, hasn't it? May Kit and I come in?"

"No," he barked.

"Fine. We'll talk out here in the open," Kit said, raising her voice. "About you getting a teenager to steal for you and the criminal activity you were up to with that will."

A muscle fluttered in Liam's sculpted jaw. Kit maintained eye contact. If he thought glaring and shouting would make her back down, he'd never been in a packed London Tube carriage trying to convince a businessman to give up his seat for a pensioner. Kit had. She crossed her arms over her chest and planted her feet. After about thirty seconds of staring, which would've fit in nicely in any gunfight in an old Western movie, Liam stepped aside. Kit and Laura walked into the house, despite its stink of bacon and stale air.

Liam ran his hand through his hair, which had once more fallen into his eyes. "Now that you're in, I suppose you expect something to eat or drink?"

Normally Kit would've said yes. Now, however, she didn't trust her host to not spit in her tea.

"I'm good, thanks. Laura?"

"I'm fine as well, thank you."

"Let's get on with it then," Liam muttered.

He drifted into a room with peeling wallpaper and a sofa that had fallen straight out of 1977. Interestingly, a modern, big, and very expensive-looking TV was mounted on the wall.

Liam threw himself down on the sofa, avoiding eye contact.

Kit stood in front of him, Laura by her side.

After a moment of silence denser than treacle sponge

pudding, Kit shoved her hands in her jeans pockets and said, "We've been talking to Jackie and Caitlin tonight, but then I suppose you're aware of that."

Liam's gaze lingered on the wall. "I dunno what you mean," he said before starting to chew his thumbnail.

"I'm wondering if either Jackie or Caitlin was the one you were just on the phone to."

"Nah."

Kit narrowed her eyes. "No?"

He paused his thumbnail-biting long enough to repeat, "Nah."

Laura cleared her throat. "Liam. This will be much simpler if you're honest. I remember your dad, back when he was my teacher, telling us that we mustn't tell lies and that things are easier if you're upfront from the start."

He stopped chewing as if his thumb had bitten him. "Yeah, well, you must've been like nine when he taught you. He was probably talking about someone nicking a pencil. This is a bit different, Ms High and Mighty."

Kit was about to jump to her girlfriend's defence, but she didn't need to. Laura shook her head wearily and replied, "The point still stands. Being helpful and honest is your best bet here. We know you took the book. Finding out why you did it surely only helps you?"

He scoffed. "How do you know that's true? Because Caitlin told you? Some attention-seeking little kid with a crush on me?"

"Exactly," Laura said. "Her crush made her protect you. Her mother, who also has some lingering affection for you, wasn't sure about 'telling on you' at first either. Still, the truth always comes out." She paused until he deigned to look at her before continuing. "In the end, they both admitted you were behind the theft of the book so you could read the will. When Alice noticed it was gone, you gave it back to Caitlin to hide it—"

"And take the blame for its theft if she was caught," Kit jumped in.

"Precisely. And Jackie knew about it all. This makes them both guilty parties in this situation, so why would they lie?"

He shrugged so hard he almost moved the sofa. "They're protecting their own arses? Or maybe they're wrong?"

"Oh come off it," Kit snapped. "We know it was you, and we're not leaving until you explain."

Liam banged a fist into the sofa cushion next to him. "Bloody hell, fine! I got the pining little bird to nick the book for me. Whatcha going to do about it? Arrest me for borrowing a sodding book?"

"I don't think it's the book that's going to interest the police, Liam," Laura said calmly. "I think it's the will that was in it at the time of the theft."

With a hand running through his hair roughly enough to pull strands out, Liam whispered, "Look, I didn't do it for me. I'm not a moron, I get that I'll be blamed here. And if I don't, it'll be Caitlin. I-I don't want that, but..." His hand dropped into his lap. "I still don't see why I need to tell you to anything."

Kit adjusted her glasses. "Yep, Caitlin might get blamed. Or Jackie for being the mastermind behind it. It's obvious that you care about them. We know about your affair with Jackie." She paused as she thought for a moment. "Actually, someone else you care a lot about was also a suspect. Rachel." She turned to Laura and conversationally said, "Maybe we should call Rach? Ask her to come over here and have Liam explain to her why women he apparently cares for will have to take the blame for him because he won't own up to his actions?"

"Mm. That sounds like a good idea," Laura said.

Liam threw his arms out. "What the bloody hell! Leave Rach out of this! You're supposed to be her friends."

Kit crossed her arms over her chest again. "Then as her *biased* friends, maybe we're not the ones you should be explaining this to. I can call the police right now so you can confess to them."

"Like you'd take it that far," he muttered.

"Hey, I'm only asking questions because Alice wanted me to and because, until I know what happened, I can't decide whether to involve the police. If we were to hear an explanation, though…"

"Piss off," he muttered. He started worrying at that thumbnail again. It looked like it might have started bleeding.

Kit pulled her phone out from her jeans pocket. "Right. I'm calling Rach."

"Excellent, then I think we should ring Liam's father," Laura added. "He's a sweet man, Kit. You'll like him."

"Then the police?" Kit asked.

Laura smiled. "Good thinking."

"Bloody hell!" Liam spluttered. "Fine. Stop. I'll tell you. It'll be nice to get this bollocks over with."

Kit put her phone away.

He scrubbed his face with both hands. When he was done, he said in such quiet tones that Kit had to move closer to hear him, "I did it for Anthony, didn't I?"

"Anthony?" Kit and Laura said in unison.

"Uh-huh. Look, he only needed the will to make a small change. He'd let himself into his mum's cottage one day and heard her on the phone to someone. She was saying that she'd done her will and hid it in a book because she didn't want her sons reading it and, like, fussing about it."

"Hang on," Kit said. "Why would you do anything for Anthony? He's going around telling everyone you're a lowlife thug with about as much brains as a comatose rabbit."

Liam watched his foot which was tapping at great speed on the worn carpet. "Yeah."

"Oh, of course," Laura said, putting her hand to her forehead. "He's making sure no one knows that the two of you are working together by making it seem like he wouldn't touch you with a bargepole. What did he pay you?"

Liam shot to his feet. "Pay me!? He didn't bleedin' pay me for anything. And he'll touch me with a hell of a lot more than just a bargepole!"

Kit locked eyes with Laura. There was no mistaking this. Liam wasn't only

sleeping with Jackie, making Caitlin fall in love with him, and mooning over Rachel.

"You're, um, dating... Anthony?" Laura asked.

"It's more than bloody dating. I don't know what it is he and I..." He trailed off, looking emotional and embarrassed. "All I'll say is that he looks after my interests, and I look after his. It's not like we were really stealing. Anthony only needed the will to check he got a certain, what do you call it, keepsake."

Even Laura couldn't help but give a cynical scoff.

He faced her. "It's true. The idea was to change the will and put it back in the book before anyone noticed."

Kit rolled her eyes. "Change? Mate, you mean *forge* the will."

He slumped back down on the sofa. "I suppose. Anthony only wanted that old necklace, okay! To keep it as a memory of when their family was happy, not sell it like his brother wanted. He said that when he was a kid and they used to go to parties, he'd help his mum put that necklace on." His voice dropped and he mumbled, "It's only a keepsake."

Kit pushed her glasses up. "Is that meant to make it all harmless then?"

Liam squirmed. "Maybe not *harmless*, but it wasn't about the money like it always is with Phillip! Anthony doesn't give a fig if Phillip gets all the dosh or even gets the cottage. He only wants that necklace."

Laura's brows furrowed. "Then why didn't he simply say that when the will was being completed? I'm sure Phillip would've let him have the necklace if he got everything else?"

Liam gave a hollow laugh. "Ha! If Phillip found out how much Anthony wanted that necklace, he'd keep it just to spite him. Maybe even chuck it down the toilet. He hates anything that gives someone else joy. Cold-hearted bastard."

"Anyway," Kit said, "I'm assuming Alice started drawing attention to the missing book and that gave Anthony get cold feet about changing the will?"

"Yeah. He figured she was wary now and would check the will when someone brought it back, so it had to look the same. Rubbish luck, that."

Kit shot him a look. "For you and him, yes. For everyone else, not really."

Liam stood again, fire for once illuminating his blank eyes. "Everyone else? Don't talk to me about everyone else! Do you think Caitlin and Jackie wouldn't love to teach

Phillip a lesson? Like they're not bleedin' tired of him and his shitty behaviour as well?"

"Sure they are," Kit snapped. "However, I'm not convinced that Anthony forging his mother's will to get a necklace does them any good. Nor that Anthony and you did it to help them in any bloody way!"

Laura put a hand on Kit's arm and whispered, "Dearest. Calm down."

Kit nearly shrugged the hand off. How could she calm down when this bloke was trying to make it sound like forgery and theft were a kind service to family members instead of a way to deal with sibling rivalry by stealing jewellery?

While Kit was busy gritting her teeth, Laura asked, "How did you two think you'd get away with this?"

"It didn't pop into our heads that Alice might notice. We were only gonna keep the book long enough to change the will, then we'd put it back and everything would be fine, right? When Alice started making noise about her bookshelf being messed with, Anthony got all edgy, saying that we should've known that she'd keep an eye on the book which had her will in it." His foot started tapping away on the carpet again. "But I don't know. I mean, she quickly forgot that the will was in that book, otherwise she would've told you that the bleedin' *will* was in the book when it went missing. Phillip and the coppers would've taken that seriously."

"True," Kit said. "So, Alice noticed the book was gone and started asking questions. This made Anthony panic and quickly try to return the will."

"I'm not surprised. He always was a bit of a mummy's boy and an anxious personality," Laura interjected.

"Yeah, that bit I get," Kit said. "What I don't understand is why you two didn't stick the will back in the book and put it under the sofa or something, so that it could be found later without any mystery to it."

"Anthony wanted to buy time," Liam mumbled. "He knew Phillip couldn't be bothered helping others, so he said that he found the will laying around and worried that their mum was going a bit bonkers with age. He said he'd take it to the safe deposit box later."

"Thinking that he might be able to forge it before then?" Laura asked.

"Exactly. But Phillip, for once, wanted to pitch in and take the will to the bank with him and bring Alice along, too, to make sure everything was official and stuff. Obviously, money was involved, so now he cared."

"Okay, then what?" Kit said.

"After that, Anthony, like... gave up on the plan. He told me to give the book back to Caitlin, so she'd get the blame if things went tits up, and then dropped the idea of ever getting that necklace." Liam slumped. "I reckon Anthony might be, I don't know, depressed or something. He doesn't do anything but take long bloody walks and freak out about his mum finding out and hating him. That's why he's been stalking you at the library, to see if you've figured it out."

"I knew I'd been seeing him around," Kit exclaimed.

"Yeah, he's acting weird. He doesn't give a shit about his dead career. He certainly doesn't care about me, except for a quick shag once in a while. Which isn't my thing." He fixed them both with his fiery gaze in turn. "I'm not into blokes. I'm straight, okay?"

Kit had a cynical reply waiting, but Laura got there first and in her gentlest voice said, "But you make an exception for Anthony?"

He gave a curt nod. "He's bloody brilliant. Or he was. When I was at school, everyone still ranted about his record sprints and the awards he won. I bet he could've been an Olympian, but he wanted to use his mind to win at life. I mean, shit, did you know he had *perfect* grades?" His tone turned to worship. "The flawless brain in the flawless body. He did everything right, while someone like me only messed everything up. Sometimes I think I fancy him because I want to be him. All that talent, drive, and money. I wonder if that's why it's so nice to be on top of him and make him..." He stopped, red blooming on his pallid cheeks again.

Kit was suddenly so tired. "No need for details, Liam. I don't know why you fancy him. I do know that it's not healthy if it leads to forging wills of lovely old ladies who've helped you. Not to mention blaming and using lonely, vulnerable teenage girls to help you commit your crimes."

"I never meant to hurt Caitlin. Or Alice. Caitlin got a new headband thingy and lots of praise for just doing us a little secret favour. No biggie! Alice, well, she wouldn't have known. She'd have been long gone before her will was read out, right?"

Laura's frown deepened. "So, in your mind, the only one who would suffer was Phillip?"

"Yeah, and that stuck-up, wanking twat had it coming!"

Kit scowled at him. "Oi, there's no need for that."

He ignored her, as she'd assumed he would, and muttered, "Look, this has all blown up to a huge thing. Why are you all up in my arse like this? I only wanted to make Anthony happy and mess with Phillip. That's all."

Kit's weariness grew back into frustration. "Don't give

me that! That's not all and you know it. Don't pretend to be that daft. You know what you've done, the trusts you've broken, and the people whose feelings you've hurt." She pointed at him. "I'm telling Alice everything. Then she gets to decide whether or not we call the police. Not gonna lie, I'm going to recommend she tells them exactly what you and Anthony tried to do and how you used Caitlin!"

Liam rubbed his hands all over his pretty face again, unable to answer.

After a few beats, Laura broke the silence. "What about the note incriminating Caitlin? Did you write it?"

"What bleeding note are you talking about?" he said, sounding utterly puzzled.

He didn't leave that Post-It in the library, then.

That only left one person who could've written it. A certain unemployed architect who'd been hanging around the library the last few weeks.

"In that case," Kit said, "you should know that Anthony wrote a note pinning the blame on Caitlin, and we're pretty sure he tried to make it look like you wrote it. I'd think about that before I tried to protect him again."

Liam's mouth opened, but then he closed it without a sound.

Kit headed for the door. "One last question before we leave you to your conscience. When we pulled up, someone was on the phone with you, and you seemed prepared for our visit after the call. Who was it?"

The last drops of the rebellious, bad-boy charm trickled off Liam. Now he looked like as much of a child as Caitlin, and Kit was reminded that he was only just turned twenty.

"It was Anthony," he admitted. "He'd watched you go

into Phillip and Jackie's house and talk to Caitlin. He said to tell you nothing, or he'd never… shag me again."

Kit was about to answer with something sympathetic, when Liam added, "I wish I'd had the balls and brains to follow that order. Now piss off!"

There wasn't anything else to say. Kit and Laura left. While they walked to the car, Kit was deciding whether to go confront Anthony or stick around to check that Liam would be okay. That was when she noticed that Laura was on her phone and heard the words, "Mr Soames? Hello, it's Laura Howard. I'll be brief. I think you should go to Liam's house and talk to him. He's done something rather silly, and I don't think he should be alone right now."

Kit smiled. That sorted that. Next stop, Anthony Caine, even if his statement was only a formality at the moment. After that would come the hardest part: telling Alice that she was right not to trust her children.

Chapter Twenty-Eight

AT LEAST THERE WAS TEA

K it and Laura were about to drive away from Nettle Road. Laura was explaining where Anthony's flat was when Kit slapped the dashboard and exclaimed, "Never mind. Look over there!"

The light above the front door to Alice's cottage had just flickered on and shown Anthony about to knock. Without a word, Laura switched off the engine. Kit watched the door open to reveal Alice's happy face upon seeing her son.

For a moment, Kit wondered if they should sweep all of this under the rug and tell the sweet old lady that Caitlin borrowed the book and forgot about it. Let her be happy. Maybe they could even get Rach to say she'd borrowed it, so Caitlin didn't get blamed.

But then, Anthony strode in, and as Alice was closing the door behind him, Kit got a moment's view of his mum's smile fading as she peered at his back. That look reminded Kit that Alice knew what her sons were like. First, she hadn't trusted them to see her will, instead hiding it in a book. Then, she'd assumed that they were the two prime suspects for messing with her bookshelf and taking a book. Then she'd known that they were gaslighting her by insisting she was getting senile and making a mountain out of a mole hill. Alice knew something was going on but that no one would tell her the truth. Kit would change that. Even if it meant breaking Alice's heart, she would tell her that she was right not to trust her sons. And that she shouldn't trust Liam either. It was the only way to return Alice's confidence in herself and to keep her safe.

Kit undid her seatbelt and got out. Once more she heard the clicking of Laura's heels behind her as they darted for the cottage.

🐌

Fifteen minutes later, there they were, sitting on the sofa with a cup of tea while waiting for Alice, who was in the kitchen plating up some Garibaldis.

Kit looked around, seeing her own sadness and unease mirrored on Laura's face. Standing by the fireplace was Anthony. He wasn't glaring at them, as Kit would've expected. In fact, he was eyeing a framed embroidery reading: "Family is God's gift. Cherish it always."

Yeah, you stare at that, mate. Then we'll chat, Kit thought as she blew on her tea.

Clearly, Laura couldn't wait that long. "Anthony," she put her cup and saucer on the table, "you must know that we're here to tell Alice everything. Why don't you take this opportunity to be the one to tell Alice why, instead of merely asking for the pearl necklace, you tried to forge her will?"

"Explain why you decided to use Caitlin and Liam to

get what you wanted while you're at it," Kit muttered, drinking some of her tea.

He twisted his whole body towards her, and Kit saw some of that speed he'd apparently been famous for. "Oh, why didn't you go away and shut up when I told you to? You're about to hurt a darling, frail lady. And for what? Nothing happened. She noticed that the will was missing, so I found it and it's now in the bank, in the exact form she wanted it."

"For what? Because she deserves to know the truth," Kit hissed, so she couldn't be heard in the kitchen. "She's already suspicious of who she can or cannot trust, including herself, and I'll be damned if I don't help her like I promised I would."

Laura, like Kit, used hushed tones when she added, "We will leave it up to her if she wants to call the police."

"How generous of you," Anthony snarked. Kit wasn't sure he even noticed how loudly he spoke. His eyes were wild, his nostrils flared, and his flexed body looked ready to pounce.

Alice came in with the biscuits and placed them on the coffee table. She smoothed her skirt underneath her and sat down next to Laura. "There, now we all have refreshments. I suppose now is a good time for you to tell me what's happened here. Most of all," she looked right at Anthony, "I want to know what you meant by 'you're about to hurt a darling, frail lady,' though I'm willing to wager that I know what this is regarding."

Anthony's mouth worked wordlessly for a moment. Then a single word slipped out. "Pearls."

Alice clasped her hands in her lap in a weary manner. "Pearls? You don't mean my triple-strand freshwater pearl necklace? Was *that* what all this was about?"

Anthony's gaze was fixed on the ceiling. He obviously wasn't going to answer. It fell to Kit to explain about Anthony overhearing where the will was, chickening out of stealing it himself and getting Liam to try, and how, when he got caught both times, they came up with the idea to let a teenager with possible kleptomania steal the book.

Then, there was the snag of Alice making a big deal out of the book disappearing. Anthony panicking and pretending to find the will. The book being returned to Caitlin to ensure it was in her possession if everything came out. After all, who'd believe her word against Anthony's? She added that Caitlin had admitted it all to Jackie but that they thought it had been a silly prank and ignored it. Finally, Kit explained how it had all been stirred up again when she met Alice in the post office and decided to investigate who'd disturbed the bookshelf and why. Laura supplemented that this was when Anthony started shadowing Kit and left a note incriminating his niece.

Anthony growled like some prowling jaguar. "It was only a blasted note! Besides, that brat gets away with everything. She would only have gotten a slap on the wrist for taking a book."

Alice gave him a withering look. "What about the rest? The attempted forging of my will? Oh, and have you really been stalking Kit?"

Anthony threw his arms out. "All I've done is keep tabs on who she's been harassing. Did you know she climbed a tree to break into Phillip's house? I was in the bushes and saw all of it with my binoculars."

His demeanour was so sanctimonious that Kit wondered if he realised how sneaking around in bushes with binoculars made him sound.

"Actually, Caitlin let us in," Laura clarified. "That was when she and Jackie admitted everything."

"Yep. Later, Liam filled in the gaps," Kit said. "For what it's worth, Liam, and certainly Caitlin and Jackie, are all apologetic and swimming in guilt. Unlike Anthony here," she nodded towards him, "who happily climbed up from the pool of guilt and dove into a pond of self-right-eousness instead, where he's now flapping about and blaming everyone else for his actions."

Anthony was about to speak but was quickly silenced by the look his mother gave him. Kit presumed anyone would've quieted if someone they loved gave them that look of disappointment, sadness, and anger.

Alice sagged where she sat. "Anthony. I will hear no more excuses or blaming of others. Because the sad truth is that I'm not surprised. I felt certain the culprit was either you or Phillip, and knowing the way you are around your brother, I should've guessed the will would make you do something terrible."

"Mummy, I—"

"What did I just tell you, Anthony? I don't want to hear it. In fact, it's time *you* listen to *me*. I'll have to ponder whether or not I want to report this to the police. I'll certainly have to tell your brother, who will never let you forget this. Neither will I."

All the bluster left Anthony Caine. Wherever it went, his words seemed to follow. He stood silent as the grave, avoiding all eye contact.

Alice turned to Kit and Laura. "I should let you ladies go enjoy the rest of your evening. I'll inform you if I decide to involve the police, in which case they will prob-ably wish to speak to you. If not, I thank you from the bottom of my heart for your help. If you ever need anything from me, you have but to ask."

Kit gave Alice a peck on the cheek. "No need to offer us anything. I was glad to help. Well," She took Laura's hand. "*We* were glad to help."

Laura shook her head with a smile. "That's not completely accurate. I bet you anything, Mrs Caine—I mean Alice—that Kit will take payment in Garibaldis, as well as someone to help her wrangle Mabel Baxter when she decides to interfere with Kit's life."

Despite her distress, Alice laughed at this. "Consider it done. I will be on Mabel duty if ever needed, and there will always be an offer for you both to drop by for a biscuit. I will make sure to always have Garibaldis in my cupboard."

Kit threw a glance at Anthony, who was still as a taxidermy fox. "Right, we'll leave you to it. Call if you need anything, Alice."

Their hostess smiled faintly. "I will. Goodnight, girls."

They let themselves out.

As they headed for the car, Kit gathered up her nerve.

"Baby? Now that's settled… When are we going to talk about our argument?"

Laura rolled her neck, making it pop twice. "Not tonight, please, dearest. It's been a long day and an eventful evening." She sighed. "And I have to get up early tomorrow to smooth things over with Farradays."

"The big client? I thought Maximillian hadn't called them."

Laura adjusted her hair. "He wouldn't have if he, like he said, had been going alphabetically. However, it seems that when he said alphabetically what he actually meant was random as a drunk person with a blindfold on."

Kit chuckled. "Classic Maximillian. Well, um…" She kicked at a leaf on the ground. "I can walk home if you want to hurry to bed?"

"No, certainly not. I want to drive you home. After all," she beamed at Kit, "you do live rather close to me."

Kit felt a smile tugging at her lips. "Yep, seems someone wanted me within spitting distance."

"Charming expression. Now get in the car, beautiful."

Kit did as she was asked. She was still waiting for the sense of relief at having solved the bookshelf mystery to kick in, but all her feelings were focused on the Laura situation now. That, and her desperate longing to wash up, get into her comfy bed, and sleep like the dead.

At least that last one would be easy to achieve.

Chapter Twenty-Nine

NO TEA, BUT AT LEAST THERE'S WINE

The next evening there was a soft knock on Kit's door. She put her book down on the coffee table and answered it.

Standing there in the summer evening with the purples, pinks, and blues of the setting sun illuminating her, making her look like a human representation of the bisexual flag, was Laura. Kit's mouth went dry.

"Can I come in?" her girlfriend asked. "I think we are overdue a chat."

Kit stood aside. "Of course. Have you actually managed to shake your shadow?" She bit her tongue. Why did she say that? Of all the things to mention right now, Maximillian and his constant presence was the worst one.

"I told him I got my period and needed to go to the shop to get some panty liners. He grumbled something about young women today being too blunt and hurried down to the kitchen."

If Kit hadn't been so tense, she'd have laughed at that. Maybe even clapped Laura on the back and congratulated her for the ruse. Now, however, all she could manage was a smile and an offer of tea.

Laura closed the front door. "No, thank you. I'm far too hot after the walk. It's warm tonight."

"I'll get you some water."

Laura gave her a small smile. "I think wine might be more appropriate, don't you?" She held out a bottle she'd been hiding behind her back. Kit accepted it and read the label, some posh white wine with a long French name.

"Thanks. I'll get some glasses, oh, and water as well. I'll be right back."

When Kit returned with a tray holding two tumblers of water and two glasses of wine, Laura was perched on the edge of the sofa. It was hard to imagine someone looking so uncomfortable on such a comfortable piece of furniture.

Kit sat next to her and sipped the cold wine. Laura gulped down half of her water and then hiccupped.

The anxious body language and that adorable hiccup made Kit's heart ache. She couldn't stay quiet. She scoured her mind for things to say that she hadn't already blurted out, like that she didn't want Laura to change or to be uncomfortable with her decisions. Or to hurt Maximillian.

Laura beat her to it. She put her water glass down and announced, "Dearest, I've spoken to Aimee."

Of all the things Kit had anticipated Laura saying, that certainly wasn't on the list. What the hell did Aimee have to do with this?

"You have?"

"Yes, I called her during my lunch break. I wanted tips on how to have this discussion with you. It made sense to start with picking the brains of the person who has known you the longest," Laura concluded before grabbing her wine glass for a long gulp.

Slightly disorientated, Kit wondered if she should:

One: apologise again.

Two: let Laura lead this conversation.

Three: point out that Aimee was a maniac and could give any sort of advice, including tantric sex, as a solution to all relationship issues.

In the end she settled for a feeble "okay."

Laura swallowed her mouthful of wine. "Aimee said that your parents never put you first and that most of your girlfriends only wanted you to save them and help them, meaning they didn't put you first either. She thinks that this makes you excessively sensitive about me not prioritising you."

Kit sat back. "Whoa." She took a couple of deep breaths. "I've never thought about that."

"I see why. Because I think she's wrong."

"What?"

"Well, not wrong. I do, however, think that she's approaching *our* issue from the wrong angle."

"Oh?"

Laura took another gulp of wine. "Yes, because after much soul-searching I've decided that you're not being excessively sensitive here. The fault lies with me. My only real relationship was with Dylan, and while he required my attention, he only wanted it superficially."

"Superficially?"

"Yes. If I spent five minutes on the phone listening to him whinge or bought him a nice present, he was content with that. So, I could continue the way my parents behaved: always sacrificing their own lives and time for the people of this island."

Kit swigged some wine as well. "Makes sense," she mumbled.

"Well, things are different now. I'm in a real partnership with someone who actually wants to be with me. Who actually needs me. And I suppose in seeing your need for me to, not only set aside time for *you*, but to take time for *myself*, I've come to realise…" She looked up to the ceiling and let out a shaky exhale. "That I don't have to sacrifice so much to be a real Howard or to make people like me."

"Oh, baby, I—"

"No, Kit, please let me finish. I'll lose my train of thought otherwise."

"Sorry. Carry on."

"Trying to maintain my parents' legacy by relinquishing my time and mental well-being for others wasn't healthy for me before. However, it's worse now that I'm aware that my deepest desire is to be with you. But I'll never be the sort of person who says 'screw everyone else' and simply does what they want."

"No, of course not. Actually, you're usually not even a person who says the word 'screw' without blushing for forty minutes," Kit said in an attempt to lighten the mood.

Laura gave a limp smile, placing her glass on the table. "I suppose we can all change."

"But I don't want you to change!" Kit objected.

Laura put a calming hand on her arm. "I know, dearest. You keep saying that you want me to stay the way I am and be comfortable with my actions, and I know you mean it. I love you for it. However," she took Kit's face in her hands, "*you* deserve to be put first."

Kit wasn't going to cry. At all. Her eyes were merely a bit foggy from the cold wine on such a warm night.

"Dearest, we need to find a balance where I can prioritise you but also maintain my role as, well, as Laura Howard. And, yes, we've concluded this before, and back then I said I'd try to find that balance. The difference now is," her thumbs caressed circles on Kit's cheeks, "that this time I want to change for both of us. Uncle Maximillian sabotaging Gage Farm, making me feel like a guest in my home, and worst of all making me hide my greatest treasure—my relationship with you—has made me realise that I not only need to prioritise you but also myself."

Kit sniffled as subtly as she could. "Well, thank fu— hrm, fudge, for that."

They both laughed before Kit continued. "You'll carry on dropping what you're doing to look after the Greengagers. And you'll sacrifice a lot of your time, blood, sweat, and tears for Gage Farm and for Howard Hall. That makes sense to anyone who's met you. But, honey, you can only do all that if you look after yourself first."

Laura let go of Kit's face and clasped her hands in her lap. "Which is what you tried to say at my birthday party, I know. I wasn't listening then, but that day in the orchard, I heard you. Obviously, my uncle butchering my business, because I gave him the slack to do that, drove the point home," she said with an eye roll.

Kit laughed while trying to blink away that fogginess in her eyes. "I'm glad you want to make a change for yourself, and not only for me, because I don't think that'd be healthy. Plus, it would keep me feeling like a whinging, demanding brat."

"I know, dearest. Any change I make will be for both of us."

"Good. Only small changes, though. I want you to be the person I fell in love with, just happier and, well, to be honest, around more."

"Consider it done," Laura said in the voice she used when making decisions at Gage Farm. Kit had yet to tell her that the professional-power-woman voice was a major turn-on.

She squirmed in her seat. *Now is not the time, libido.*

"So, what does this mean for the here and now?" she asked.

"I discussed that with Aimee, actually. I asked her if the holiday and lingerie I promised you would be enough to make it up to you. She pointed out that something you'd appreciate even more was right under my nose."

Kit swigged her wine and put the empty glass down. "Okay, what's that?"

"Our main problem. You want me to tell Maximillian about us and I want him out of my house."

"Ding-ding! Right on both accounts."

"Well, one of the reasons I'm here tonight is to ask you if we should tell him together, or if you'd prefer if I did it on my own?" She ignored the soft gasp Kit gave and added, "I would've done it before I came over, but something told me it would be more symbolic if we did it together, as the perfect team we are. That would show him that our type of team isn't only friendship, but…" Suddenly there was a shy look about Laura. "But future marriage material."

Kit was rarely lost for words, but this was an exception.

Laura wants to marry me one day. And wants to tell her uncle. Well, bugger me sideways.

Anything Kit could think to say sounded too prosaic

and feeble. She sat there, hearing nothing but the rush of blood as her heart pounded and her eyes welled up again. Laura blinked repeatedly. Her cheeks were reddening. She looked as vulnerable as Kit felt.

"Y-yes, please," Kit stuttered quietly.

Laura drew her into an embrace and whispered against her neck, "I don't know how to show you how important you are to me other than to try to always put you first and foremost, like you are in my heart."

Kit smothered a sob and tightened her grip around Laura's waist. She ached with regret for all the wasted time she could've spent with Laura, even if Maximillian had been present. She'd wallowed in self-pity these past months. No, if she was honest, she'd been doing that for much longer. Whenever Laura had been busy throughout their relationship, Kit had needed to be put first. Whether she had admitted that to herself or not. Now Laura was very clearly prioritising her, and it opened Kit's tight chest and filled it with warm love and assurance.

She buried her head in Laura's big curls and whispered back, "My turn to be sappy now?"

"Yes."

"You're my home, Laura. The way you show me what I mean to you is by letting me be with you. Even if that is with your uncle hanging around and giving me weird, dead things."

Laura laughed. "We'll get rid of him, and then I'll give you as much of my time and attention as I can possibly free up."

"Without sacrificing what makes you happy," Kit quickly interjected.

Laura broke away so she could lean her forehead against Kit's. "Yes, I've already promised you that. We'll get the balance right. Just remember, what makes me happiest of all is being with you."

"Do you think we have time to be together in a more... naked way?"

Laura quirked an eyebrow. "Dearest, are you actually suggesting a quickie while my poor, heartbroken uncle is waiting for me?"

"You mean the bloke who disapproved when you talked about period stuff? Yeah, I think he can bloody well wait."

Laura ran her hands from Kit's shoulders down her back, until she could slip her hands in between the sofa and Kit's bum to grip it. "This is why I think you might be my soul mate—you have your priorities right. Oh, and a bum that poets should write about," she growled with a squeeze.

Kit attempted her best bedroom eyes. "If you like that, you should come upstairs and let me show you what else I've got."

Laura gave that warm, chiming laugh as she let Kit take her hand and lead her up the stairs. Kit was giddy and hurried them along.

Right now, the world was an extremely good place, but her bedroom would be even better.

Chapter Thirty

GAY SQUAD SAVES THE DAY

K it got off the phone with Matt and returned to her kitchen table. She smiled at Caitlin Caine, who sat on the opposite side slurping a Fanta.

"There we go," Kit said. "I've set it up so that you'll babysit Clark for Matt and Josh once a week so they can have time off for a romantic dinner. In return, they'd like to take you out to the cinema tomorrow. Matt actually talked about making that a weekly thing."

Caitlin shot her a cynical grin. "You're trying to get me some sort of father figure, right?"

"No," Kit said, crossing her arms over her chest. "I'm trying to get you two. In fact, I already have, so there!"

Caitlin laughed while shaking her head.

Kit switched to her serious voice. "I think you need it. Your dad ignores you and your mum isn't great at talking about things. Also, she has problems that she needs to focus on, right?"

"Yeah. She says she's gonna stop hitting on everyone. She's talking about checking herself into a clinic for her drinking problem again, too."

"Probably best. Even if she doesn't and stays around, both your parents are hard on you one second and spoil you the next. Josh and Matt are different. They're a regular, healthy couple with lots of affection and sage advice to give. They love chatting about feelings and listening to people."

"I guess that's cool," Caitlin said with faked nonchalance. She traced a pattern with a few drops of spilled Fanta on the table. "You know, Dad will hate me spending lots of time with other adults and taking their advice. He likes to blame all my shitty habits on spending too much time with Mum, or Gran, or with pretty much anyone else but him."

Kit considered Wing Commander Caine's behaviour and personality and decided that she could live with him being outraged.

"Well, it's up to you if you don't want to spend time with, or take advice from, Josh and Matt." She put her hand over Caitlin's. "I've got to say, though, since your dad doesn't spend time with you, he can't complain when you hang out with people who *do* want to be with you and who want to help you."

"Suppose not. Besides, I think everyone on this island agrees that pissing my dad off is a sign that you're doing something right."

Kit tried to keep from grinning. "You're not wrong."

"Oh, by the way," Caitlin suddenly said, "Gran wanted me to tell you that she's not gonna call the police. She's punishing Uncle Anthony by not talking to him and by changing her will so the necklace goes to me. I told her that it'd piss him off more if she gave it to my dad."

"Probably true."

"Yeah, but she didn't want to reward Dad's, like,

crappy behaviour towards you by giving it to him. So, I get the necklace."

"Good. You can show it to Charlie Baxter to get him back on your good side."

Caitlin had the decency to look embarrassed. "Yeah, I need to apologise to him. I did just want to check the cufflinks out, though."

"There's no need to defend yourself to me."

"No, I guess not. That's pretty awesome, you know," Caitlin said with a tiny smile. "I don't want to get all emotional and shit but thanks. For taking me seriously and for helping set me up with the gays."

"Josh and Matt," Kit said firmly.

Caitlin rolled her eyes. "Yeah, duh, I know their names. I just find it funny that the gay squad is saving me from my messed-up straight family."

"Hey, your grandmother is straight, and she's brilliant."

"True, but I think she's a little freaked out by me."

Kit thought about that. About how Alice had rushed to get Caitlin that drink when they all first met in her cottage. "Maybe, but who isn't scared of teenagers?" She paused, realising that she might be projecting her own feelings on all of Greengage. "Actually, Josh and Matt aren't. Yet another reason why they'll be great company for you. That and the fact that they have a YouTube channel about being a rainbow family and will probably let you guest star in the next vlog."[1]

If Caitlin had looked pleased before, her eyes now sparkled like a Disney princess who had just got the prince, the cute talking animals, *and* the happy ending. The fact that she'd recently dyed her hair candyfloss pink might be leading to that simile.

"Awesome! I mean, I guess that's good. Whatever. Have you got any more Fanta?"

"Sure," Kit said, already on her feet to go get it.

There really was nothing like the buzz of helping people.

Chapter Thirty-One

BADGERS, SUSAN, AND OTHER TREATS

That Sunday, Kit sat on the lawn behind Howard Hall. A picnic blanket was under her and a basket crammed with snacks enough for an army in front of her. She'd just told Laura about setting Caitlin up with two good, caring role models.

Maximillian was there, too, but not listening, of course.

Laura handed Kit a paper cup filled with Gage Farm cherry cordial. "That's great, dearest. Josh and Matt were a good choice."

"I thought so. I hope the three of them will get along, and the guys will get a good babysitter while Caitlin has some decent adults in her life."

"I'm sure they'll be very happy. What's more, it'll irritate the controlling Wing Commander Caine incessantly."

Kit grinned. "Yeah, Phillip getting his knickers in a twist is a brilliant bonus."

"That reminds me," Laura said. "I've cut Tom off from his allowance."

Suddenly Maximillian started paying attention. "Tom? Thomas Howard?"

"Yes. My brother. Your nephew. Howard or not, he now has to pay his own way," Laura declared.

There was a brief pause in which Kit and Laura held their collective breath to see how Maximillian would react.

"Jolly good, dear girl! Is he still in prison?"

"He was never imprisoned," Laura corrected her uncle with relief. "Only detained over a misunderstanding. He's free now, but still in Monaco, yes. As I won't buy his return ticket, he'll have to use his savings or, more likely, trade his charms for some help from his rich lady-friend."

"So, Tom does have a sugar mama," Kit said. "Huh. I wonder if that's made him less of chauvinist pig? Either way, good for you, babe. He needs to take care of himself."

Laura nodded with the air of someone convincing herself that she believed it. "He does. I'm tired of giving him half of my paycheck just because he's my brother. Part of my new scheme to put myself first is making him earn his own money. No more allowance. No more top-up loans."

"I'll drink to that!" Kit said.

They toasted with the cordial, and about thirty years of stress thawed out of Laura's posture.

A bird of prey squawked overhead, and Kit and Laura watched it sail on the wind with endless confidence and grace.

"Wait, it's July," Maximillian muttered out of the blue. "I say, dear girl, when is that nonsensical kitten race?"

Laura didn't bat an eye. In fact, she kept watching the bird. "The kitten race is next week."

"Blimey!" he said, spitting biscuit crumbs. "My silk tie, the one with cat silhouettes on, is still missing. I must buy a new one before the race. After all, it's expected of a Howard to show up and dress up."

"Mm, Greengage has always had a lot of expectations of us. Although, I wonder how many of them we have put on ourselves?" Laura said, throwing Kit a meaning look.

That glance meant it was time. They'd discussed how to tell Maximillian but decided that there was no easy way of doing it. They'd have to slip it into everyday conversation.

Maximillian peered up from his current occupation of throwing biscuit crumbs at an anthill over by the trees. "What's that, dearie?"

Laura clasped her hands in her lap. "I was talking about the expectations on us. For example, I ran into quite a bit of that when I ended my engagement with Dylan and got into my current relationship."

Maximillian dropped his remaining crumbs. "You're in a relationship? I say! Is it serious?"

The final part of the question must have thrown Laura a bit because she blinked at him for a short moment, but she stayed the course. "Yes. I apologise for not mentioning it before. I didn't want to tell you since you were so heart-broken and not in any mood to see happy lovers parading around you."

Seconds ticked away while confusion, annoyance, acceptance, and something which might have been cramps due to wind passed over Maximillian's features.

Kit found herself holding her breath again. His reaction was so vital. Not only because no one wanted him hurt but also because Kit suspected that, in Laura's mind, this would set the precedent for how people would react when she put her own needs ahead of theirs. The problem was that no one else was going to see it that way, much less understand the importance of Maximillian's next words. Least of all Maximillian himself.

He drew himself up. "Laura, I shan't lie, I appreciate that you did not rub your blissful relationship in my face. However, I'm quite recovered now and glad to see you in love with someone."

"It's… not just *someone*," Laura said.

He lowered his eyebrows so they were a cottony shrubbery over his eyes. "I'm not a simpleton. Considering the indiscreet intimacies and love-struck gazes between you two—not to mention that weeks ago Charlie Baxter showed me a tux he's considering for your future wedding—it's obviously Susan here."

Kit allowed herself a moment of shock at that he'd actually noticed something, then got back to the business of her name.

"My name is Kit, not Susan. We've told you many times before. My full name is Katherine Sorel, but everyone calls me Kit. As you're the uncle of the woman I love, I'd like you to do the same." She tried for a smile but felt the muscles in her cheeks straining. Hopefully that didn't make it look disingenuous. There was still so much riding on this conversation.

He made a sound somewhere between a scoff and a grumble. "Certainly. Yes. Kit. Of course. Do you think I would set up my darling niece with a woman whose name I don't know? Don't be absurd."

"Set us up?" Laura said, wide-eyed.

"Why, yes, of course," he said, puffing out his rounded chest. "Why do you think I've been bringing the two of you together so often?"

"You what?" Kit spluttered.[1]

He waggled a finger at her. "Don't interrupt, dear girl.

I felt certain that you were perfect for one another the first time I saw you together. Since then, I have been trying to get you to realise that you have more than friendship between you. I'm glad you finally noticed and decided to make it official."

Laura and Kit stared flabbergasted at each other. Was there a point in questioning the lack of logic in what he was saying? Was there a point in putting him right? Did it matter? No. Not when everything had gone their way.

Kit couldn't help but notice that Laura looked not only incredulous but also quite emotional. She recognised that sensation. This week was turning into one hell of a roller coaster.

Maximillian didn't appear to notice their shocked stares. "Oh, and also, I now feel quite convinced that the progeny of badgers *is* called kits. Feisty little creatures, they are. Although, I suppose your late mother would call them endearing, Laura. She adored badgers."

Laura's eyes glistened, and her voice was croaky when she said, "Yes, they were her favourite. Do you remember when she used to put food out for them on the grounds?"

"Oh, yes," Maximillian said. "I thought it rather ridiculous at the time. Your father, however, lectured us all on the importance of the different animals and forced us to celebrate sharing Howard Hall with so many creatures. Largely because your mother loved them so, I think." He scanned their surroundings. "In fact, she loved the whole estate, even more than those of us born here. I miss her."

"So do I," Laura said quietly. "Every day."

Tears now trickled down her soft cheeks. Kit went to hold her but was beaten to it by Maximillian, who hauled his niece into a brusque hug, almost making them fall over on the blanket.

Kit noticed Laura trying to suppress her crying, probably more for Maximillian's sake than anything else. If the awkward hug wasn't a sign that he wasn't great at displays of emotion, the way he kept gaping and staring around like a fish caught in a net proved without a doubt that he was out of his depth.

After a few seconds, he coughed and boomed out, "Your mother would be proud of you, you know."

"You think so?" Laura said, her words muffled against his chest.

"Oh, yes. Proud of the good person you have become. Proud of the businesswoman you've become, too. And, I dare say, exceedingly proud of the *Howard* you have become. Both your parents would want you to be in love and happy with your ladylove here." He paused as if something had struck him. "In fact, I bet the first thing your mother would have said to Sus... Kit, was that the progeny of her favourite animal, badgers, were called kits."

Laura laughed in between small sobs. "Yes, I bet she would." She sat up. "Oh dear, what am I like? Crying over nothing."

Right as Kit wondered if she should leave them to have this family discussion alone, Laura reached out and took her hand. She brought it to her lips and kissed it. Kit's heart gave a thrilled thump, much stronger than its usual ones.

"You're not crying over nothing, sweetheart," Kit said softly. "You're crying because you miss your parents and because this has all been very emotional. For all of us, I think. Anyway, I'm glad everything is out in the open now."

"Me too," Maximillian said. "I'm even gladder that I just had an idea of where my tie with the cat silhouettes might have gotten to. I wager it is tucked into my socks with the swan print." He stood up and brushed biscuit crumbs off his perfectly pressed trousers.

Kit started. "Wait. Why would you keep a tie with your socks? And what do swans have to do with—"

Laura put a hand on her arm. "Don't. We've gotten this far by not questioning anything. Let's not break the good luck only to figure out the mystery of the cat silhouette tie," she whispered.

Kit peered over at Maximillian, who was meticulously smoothing down his comb-over which the wind had blown out of place.[2] She exhaled, long and slow. Laura had a point. When it came to Maximillian, or possibly to all Greengagers, she needed to simply roll with it.

Laura scooted forward on the blanket. "Uncle, before you go, may I ask one thing?"

"Of course, dear girl," he said, now preoccupied with an ant that was climbing up his shoe.

Laura hesitated but then asked, "Who is Susan?"

Maximillian finished chirping to the ant about the biscuit crumbs he was throwing it before turning to Laura with a blank expression. "Susan? Oh, Susan! That was the nanny in charge of me, Sybil, and your father, when we were old enough to not truly need a nanny but still required supervision." He stared longingly up at the sky. "Susan, short for Susanna, loved books, physical exercise, and always wore a necklace with a unique pendant, a fox kit. As soon as I was a grown man, I would have proposed to that incredible woman, if she weren't as homosexual as the day was long."

With that, Maximillian Howard guided the ant off his shoe and walked away with the air of a man who had said nothing out of the ordinary.

There was a long moment of silence so full of unspoken confusion that it hummed.

Finally, Laura said, "Well, I did warn you that he was something else."

Kit adjusted her glasses. "Uh, yeah. You did."

"And I suppose that ends the need to shelve our relationship."

"Yep."

Laura moved closer. "Also, you sorted out the mystery around Alice's bookshelves."

"True."

"You also managed to help Rachel and Shannon," Laura murmured in a low, affectionate tone. She edged even nearer on the blanket.

"I suppose I did."

Laura sat right in front of her now, invading Kit's personal space to the point that Kit could smell the fruity cordial on her breath as she whispered, "Sounds to me like my beautiful hero has earned treats."

Kit's smile felt so wide it risked getting stuck to her ears. "Really? Treats for me?" She pulled Laura into her lap. "If I'm very good, will you tell me what they are?"

"You're always good," Laura replied suggestively. "So yes, I will. I figured we'd take a two-day trip to London, where we'll eat at your favourite Thai restaurant, visit where you grew up, and go see any West End musical you want, as long as it's within my price range. As an added bonus, we'll visit every bookshop and library we see."

Kit blinked. "Wow. You really do love me, don't you?"

Laura only smiled and kissed her.

"Babe," Kit said cautiously. "You'll be with me for all of it, right? You don't have to stop off to do business or something?"

Laura shimmied forward in Kit's lap so they were even closer. "After these past months apart, it'll be a long time before you can tear me from your side."

Relief hit her like champagne on an empty stomach. "Great! Those are amazing treats. Maybe I should contribute some money, so I don't feel like I'm scrounging off you?" She saw Laura's frown and quickly added, "We can discuss that later. Thank you! So, um, what about the… you know."

One of those expressive auburn eyebrows quirked up. "What's that, my love?"

"You know, um, *the outfit.*"

"Do you mean that skimpy black negligée with white lace trim I bought?"

Images danced through Kit's mind, getting naughtier by the second. "Yes," she croaked.

"I can wear it when I come over to your cottage tonight."

As much as her pulse was working overtime, Kit couldn't stop herself from the obvious gag. "Under something else, right? I know it's a short walk, but you could still be arrested if someone happened to spot you."

Laura tweaked her nose. "Yes, under my dress, you plum."

"Score! Then you will have treated me to everything I could ever ask for. Well, except for one thing, which I think I'll be investing in myself."

Laura ran a warm hand through Kit's hair. "What's that, dearest?"

"A bloody cross-trainer for my cottage. I never want to have to go running again!"

Laura laughed, then took Kit's face in her hands. "We

can go shopping for one later. Right now, there is something *I* need."

"Okay. What?" Kit mumbled, spellbound by the beautiful eyes gazing into hers.

"This." Laura closed the distance between their lips and kissed Kit as if there were no tomorrow. Which there luckily was. And then the day after that, and the many days following that… And hopefully most of those days, they could spend together.

EPILOGUE - THE YEARLY KITTEN RACE

Kit listened as insects buzzed and birds sang their hearts out. Still, they were almost drowned out by the murmuring of the excited crowd. It was a beautiful July afternoon with the air still fresh from last night's heavy rains, though the day warmed under the bright sun.

Perfect weather for Greengage's annual kitten race.

Kit switched her glasses out for her new prescription sunglasses and stuck the regular pair into her rucksack. She slung it onto her back even though its rough appearance stuck out. She'd learned from last year that people dressed up for the kitten race and had conceded to put on a white shirt instead of her usual T-shirt or tank top. The only issue was that Laura had worn an almost identical shirt. Sure, she'd paired hers with expensive-looking suit trousers, high heels, and jewellery while Kit just had a pair of dark blue jeans and her faded Converse. Still, they'd gotten close to the dreaded lesbian-twin-syndrome', but hey, that was a normal progression of any sapphic relationship. It was merely frustrating that Laura looked so much better in the shirt than she did. Kit was trying very hard not to gawk at how the shirt strained a little over those wide hips.

As if sensing that Kit was drooling over her, Laura came sauntering over. "Hello, dearest. Are you all right?"

"Fine. I am starting to wonder if Aimee and George got lost, though. Perhaps I should've met them when they got off the ferry?"

Laura retrieved a hairband from her pocket and assembled her wild curls into a ponytail. "I'm sure they're fine. They've been here before, the island is small, and there is plenty of signage to the main square. I suppose if you're worried you could text her?"

"Nah, you're right, they'll be here soon. I'm just excited to see them! They haven't been here since my birthday."

"Oh, speaking of birthdays, Uncle Maximillian called me from his house to say that he has made the same decision regarding the kitten race as he did on my birthday: the crowds are too much for him."

"Brilliant! I mean, I'm sorry he's been spending so much time in his house after moving back home, especially now that I like him since he's a fan of our relationship, but he's clearly happy."

Laura beamed. "He is. Furthermore, it means you and I don't have to worry about his constant company. I will, however, call to check up on him and my cousins. Later. Much later. Maybe after the weekend."

Their conversation was interrupted by a squealed, "Kitten race!" Shortly followed by, "And Phyllis, Mummy!"

Even if Kit hadn't known her godson's voice, she still could've guessed that it was George based on the shouts about his two favourite things on Greengage. She rushed over to give Aimee a hug and then picked the toddler up and spun him around while kissing his face until his squealing subsided into giggles.

Aimee smiled at Kit and George. "Good. You keep hold of the little squire here and I'll go get myself some booze."

"I thought you might say that." Laura joined them, holding out a paper cup to Aimee. "It's Gage Farm apple cider. Be careful, it's potent this year."

"Music to my ears, mate! It's been ages since I had a drink, or anything else potent, if you know what I mean," Aimee said, winking and taking the cup.

Laura laughed and gave her a hug, careful not to spill the cider. After that, she returned to Kit's side to greet George and to wrap an arm around Kit's waist.

Aimee grinned at them. "Man, it's great to see you two. I've missed you syrupy lovebirds."

"We've missed you, too," Laura replied. "Kit has counted the minutes."

"I'm sure she just wanted other mainlanders here to have her back," Aimee said with a wink and a slurp of cider.

George squirmed in Kit's arms. "Phyllis where?"

"Where's Phyllis? Uh, I don't know." Kit scanned the square, trying to locate Rajesh and that wonky-toothed mutt of his.

Aimee drained her cup and muffled a hiccup. "Don't worry about it, Kit. I have enough cider in me to go looking for that ugly dog now."

"Not ugly. Phyllis pretty," George said with a frown.

The grown-ups glanced at each other.

"*Pretty special* at least, little chum," Kit said, putting

him down. "Go with your mum, and she'll help you find Phyllis and Rajesh."

Hearing an asthmatic bark by the busy sandwich table, George rushed off. Aimee handed Kit her empty cup and followed the running toddler.

Kit watched them go, and that was when she spotted Josh and Matt at the fringes of the sandwich-table crowd. Matt moved his big, beefy self to the right and revealed Caitlin Caine, holding Clark in her arms. She wiped something off his downy head, and Kit had to smile at how confident she looked. Caitlin handed the sleeping baby over to Josh, who said something that made her laugh and that made Matt roll his eyes before kissing his husband's cheek.

Kit had never gotten the expression "warmed my heart," but with the current, toasty feeling in her chest, she thought she understood it. Or maybe that was due to the sun beaming down on her white shirt? She tugged at the offending garment.

Who wears long sleeves when it's 27C? Madness.

Next to the happy couple and their young friend and babysitter was Greengage's leading politician. He had a tiny triangle masquerading as a sandwich in one hand and was using the other to wave Laura over.

"Uh-oh. You're wanted," Kit murmured.

Laura ogled Kit's Converse as if they'd become mesmerising in the last two seconds. "I know. Don't look. I'm trying to ignore him."

"Okay. Shouldn't you go talk to him?"

Laura still directed the conversation to Kit's shoes. "No. He can wait."

Kit put a finger under Laura's chin and gently tipped her face up. "You sure, babe? It's probably events business."

Laura pursed her lips. "That's what I'm afraid of."

"Still, it might be important. Perhaps they've discovered that one of the kittens is taking performance-enhancing drugs, like testosterone-raising catnip or something?"

"Whatever it is, it's not as important as us having some quality time before I get sucked up in all the island madness again."

With that, Laura shielded herself from his view by stepping into Kit's embrace. Surprised but pleased, Kit wrapped her arms around Laura with pride. Greengage had wanted Laura's attention and time, but she had prioritised Kit. She had chosen their relationship before everyone and everything else. Just as she promised.

Kit was going to point out how lost Greengage's events committee was without its leader but thought better of it when Laura hummed contentedly and placed a kiss on her pulse point.

She's right. They can wait.

From the corner of her eye she noticed people taking their seats, meaning that the race would be starting soon.

Kit extracted herself from the hug to wave at a few of the Greengagers. Some waved back, while others nodded towards her and whispered to each other. She could make out words like "detective" and "mystery." She blew out a long breath and let it settle in—the acceptance of her position as the island's amateur investigator and problem fixer. There were worse roles to have in a society. At least she could help people. And yes, have a reason to be nosy.

Kit took Laura's hand and looked around for Aimee, George, Rajesh, and Phyllis. Watching the kitten race next to them had been perfect last year, and she'd like to repeat that if possible. She couldn't see them, but did spot Alice Caine, who was sitting down on a chair currently being softened by the cushion Phillip had placed on it. When she was seated, Anthony came over with a parasol and a glass of cider for her.

"Nice to see they're finally cherishing their mother," Laura said.

Kit, with the cynicism of a Londoner, wondered how long that would last. She worried it had more to do with the fact that the will had recently been changed and could therefore be changed again.

I hope I'm wrong. I hope the Caine brothers have mended their ways.

A smack on the back of her head informed Kit that Aimee had found her. "Oi, sloth. Get a move on! We're sitting over there with Raj."

"You didn't call him that, did you? You know he hates nicknames," Kit said as she and Laura followed Aimee towards some seats to the side.

"Of course not. Now, shift yourselves, lovebirds! I don't want to miss the start. George will start wailing if I'm not there to see the first kitten get bored and fall asleep."

"Really? He looked quite calm today to me," Laura said.

"For now, yes. We had four temper tantrums this morning when I wouldn't let him bring one of those stuffed toys you sent us, Kit."

Kit eyed her. "Stuffed toys? I haven't sent you any of those, Aimes."

"Sure you have, babes. That fox and the hare and—"

Laura interrupted Aimee by gasping.

It took Kit a few seconds more to understand. When

she did, she held out a brief hope that Aimee was joking. "Uh, Aimes…"

Her friend gave her the once-over. "What's wrong? You're paler than bird poo."

"Aimes, you *do* know that the animals I sent you aren't toys, right?"

"What are you on about? What else would they be? I mean I know they're creepily like real animals, but obviously they aren't."

"Oh gosh," Laura whispered.

The disgusted shriek that came from Aimee later, when Kit explained that those were real animals, killed and then stuffed by a skilled taxidermist, made the entire crowd gawk at them.

"Tell me you're having a laugh," Aimee said with such pleading that Kit felt bad about shaking her head.

"Kit was given the animals from my uncle, who is a taxidermy fanatic," Laura murmured, in the way of a debateable explanation.

"Bloody hell! You mean I've let my kid play with dead animals?"

"Well, yeah," Kit said, pushing her glasses up. "But I assumed you knew what they were and would take some funny pictures for Instagram and then bury the poor things. It never occurred to me that you'd be enough of a doughnut to think they were toys!"

Aimee stared into space before whispering, "As soon as I get home, I'm donating them to the biology section of the University of Southampton. Or to anyone else who'll have them." Then she gulped and added, "Oh, god."

"What?" Kit asked.

"George made me kiss them all good night every evening."

Even Laura, quite desensitised to these things mumbled, "Blimey," at that.

They led the shell-shocked Aimee to their seats. Kit was busy watching George staring into Phyllis's mangy ear, and didn't look where she was stepping, so of course her foot landed in a puddle of mud from last night's rains. She cursed under her breath but sat down with the others, accepting her fate.

While waiting for the race to start, she felt the sludge seeping into her Converse and actually smiled. Mud stains brought this adventure full circle, from today to the first day of the bookshelf mystery, when she and Laura had dropped into the mud outside Alice's cottage.

The corners of her mouth went from smile to frown when she realised that she hated mud almost as much as she hated running. Still, it was worth it. For Laura. For Alice. For her friends. For her new family. For all of Greengage, in all its sweet but strange glory.

She sat back, still holding Laura's hand, and waited for the kittens to be released.

NOTES

1. RHINOS AND RELUCTANT DETECTIVES

1. The famous Gage Farm. Read *Greengage Plots* for more info. Or keep reading this book. One mustn't let footnotes dictate reading habits.

2. UPDATING RAJESH

1. Experienced Greengage readers will know that Rajesh hates nicknames, meaning that Kit can't call him Raj, much to her disappointment.

3. SHELVING ROMANCE AND THE TEDDY BEAR TECHNICIAN

1. See the novella *Greengage Holiday Cheer*. Unless you're too busy, of course.
2. This unfolded in part one of the series, *Greengage Plots*. Best not to bore you with repetition. This story is long enough as it is, and we need to move on to more pressing things.

4. A HOTPOT AND RACHEL IN HOT WATER

1. Propriety keeps the writer from explaining this further here. Read *Greengage Holiday Cheer* to find out more.
2. The one-year-old came to them without a name, so they had named him after Clark Kent. Partly because he was also adopted and partly because they said their son was "their little Superman." Sadly, he also seemed to have the hero's Super-hearing power as he always knew when his fathers were trying to have a romantic moment and interrupted it with a Super-wail.

6. MUSTARD HEATHEN AND THE BROOM CLOSET PRISONER

1. To name some: a Vietnamese Vengaboys tribute concert, a dank cave with two guys with terrible body odour. Oh, and Mabel Baxter's bedroom on that fateful afternoon when Mabel got a zip stuck and needed assistance. More about the terrifying Mabel later.

7. TRIMMING THE VEG PATCH

1. Which, weirdly, also smelled of cabbage.
2. Another Greengage luminary and part of the same book club as her best friend, Mabel Baxter. You'll see more of them both later. Unless you give up on the book here. In which case you'll miss not only the sexy times and solving the book mystery, but also more on Maximillian's Susan obsession.

8. CODSWALLOP

1. Short for "Tosser With Head Up Arse". Pardon the bad language; Aimee is like that.

9. ANTS IN YOUR BRA

1. Well, the humans were. Phyllis slept and then she washed her bum. And then slept some more.
2. This refers to *Greengage Holiday Cheer*, in which Ethel talked some sense into Kit. We could all do with someone to talk some sense into us sometimes. Perhaps even to suggest that we're using too many footnotes. Or that we shouldn't eat yellow snow.

10. BARBIE BALLOON

1. Another long story from Greengage Plots, one which you probably wouldn't believe if I told you.
2. A sort of snuffling squeal, a cuteness which belies the fact that a badger could take your face off in five seconds with its vicious claws. So could Laura Howard, but you'd have to push her very far for it to happen. Meanwhile, you'd only have to look at a badger the wrong way for your face to be off.

11. THE BIGGEST TOSSER

1. No really. If you looked up the word "annoyance" in an image search, you'd probably find a picture of Phillip Caine wearing that exact expression.

12. THIS ONE HAS SEX IN IT

1. Some might claim that tea and that scented candle were too autumn-themed for June, but Kit has always been a rebel.

13. SNAIL MURDERERS AND SPILLING TEA

1. A not overly sweet, fruit-filled biscuit that Kit informed Alice she liked at the end of *Greengage Plots*. For you non-Brits, imagine a flat, oblong cookie with a currant filling. Never mind that now, get back to the story.
2. Actually, they were seashells.

14. WHO KILLED THE GLORIOUS BADGER?

1. Although she would still pop down into the orchards to check on them. Laura never stopped working completely. Kit alleges that she even once ran through new recipes of jam out loud in her sleep.

17. A VERY HOWARD BIRTHDAY BASH

1. Scottish expression from the 1700s meaning sexual intercourse, generally adulterous in nature. You learn something new every day, right?
2. See *Greengage Plots* to find out more about the dreadful blonde giants of the Stevenson family, including what Leslie Stevenson did at that year's kitten race.

21. GOSSIP AND A QUIVERING MOUSTACHE

1. Also, her pulse rate was 129. Whether that was due to eating so fast, hurrying out, or the thrill of a classic Greengage scandal, you can decide for yourself.

25. DON'T DIE TO DEATH!

1. The big four-wheel drive cars—like new Range Rovers, which looked to Kit like fancy tractors mated with tanks—that have become popular in some British suburban areas.

27. TWISTY KNICKERS AND TWISTIER CONFESSIONS

1. Tortoises live on land, while turtles hang out in the water some or most of the time. Basically, tortoises don't like to get their shells wet as it ruins the silky finish and lavish shine. (That last part might not be true.)

30. GAY SQUAD SAVES THE DAY

1. There was no reason to tell Caitlin that their channel only had four subscribers. She was trying to make the girl impressed, not make her pity her new role models.

31. BADGERS, SUSAN, AND OTHER TREATS

1. She did so loud enough to frighten a pigeon that had been creeping up on them to steal some biscuit crumbs. It still has a nervous twitch, which manifests to this day whenever it sees humans on blankets.
2. Sadly for everyone involved, he was smoothing it the wrong way, thereby making it look like his hair was trying to run away from his head.

ABOUT THE AUTHOR

Emma Sterner-Radley, a Swedish romance and fantasy writer, got a degree in Library and Information Science because she wanted to work with books, and being an author was an impossible dream, right? Wrong. She's now a writer and a publisher. (But still a librarian at heart.)

She lives with her wife and two cats in England. There's no point in saying which city, as they move about once a year. She spends her time writing, reading, daydreaming, exercising, and watching whichever television show has the most lesbian/sapphic subtext at the time.

Her weaknesses are coffee, sugary snacks and small chubby creatures with tiny legs.

www.emmasternerradley.com

ALSO BY EMMA STERNER-RADLEY

LIFE PUSHES YOU ALONG

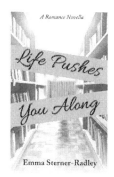

Zoe's on autopilot. Rebecca is stagnating. When change comes knocking, will they open the door?

Twenty-something Zoe Achidi feels safe in her unchallenging life in a London bookshop. Bored, but safe.

Her only excitement comes from pining over frequent customer, Rebecca Clare, unobtainable as this beautiful businesswoman in her forties seems.

One day, Zoe's brother and her best friend bring Zoe and Rebecca together.

While they connect, and it turns out Rebecca is also bored with her life, their meetings remain all business. When things take a turn for the worse, life pushes along.

But will Zoe and Rebecca end up being thrust in the same direction?

If you're looking for an age-gap romance that will inspire you to shake up your life, then look no further.

Take the leap with Life Pushes You Along by Emma Sterner-Radley

LIFE PUSHES YOU ALONG | PREVIEW

by Emma Sterner-Radley

CHAPTER ONE

Zoe watched as one of her favourite customers observed her with what seemed to be desperation. She felt her heart twinge with sympathy.

"So, do you have it?" he asked.

She knew she was going to disappoint him.

"I'm not sure, Mr. Evans. A book with a bird on the cover that was based somewhere with a big forest... that doesn't ring a bell, I'm afraid."

The bookshop's unpleasantly sharp fluorescent lights showed every crease on his wrinkled face as it took on an embarrassed look.

Zoe quickly added, "I know the feeling though. There's lots of books I have been looking for and I can't remember anything but the cover, or a piece of the plot, or half of the author's name. It's a pain."

He nodded. "Yes. Yes, my dear, it certainly is."

"Do you remember anything else about the book? Who was the main character?"

He looked up at the ceiling for a moment. "I suppose she was quite a bit like you, actually."

Zoe felt her brow furrowing. She didn't want to be rude but that didn't narrow it down much. Did he, perhaps, mean that the main character was someone who worked with customers, someone who dressed like her, or someone who was in their late twenties? She hoped he wasn't alluding to the fact that she wasn't white because she wasn't sure if a conversation with this elderly gentleman would stay politically correct if they got onto that subject. She liked Mr. Evans and wanted to continue liking him.

"I see. Um, how was she like me?"

"Young and likable," he answered simply.

Zoe was relieved. It was still just as impossible to find the book he was looking for, though.

"I'm afraid that doesn't give me much to go on. Tell you what, I'll keep an eye out for a book with a forest setting and a bird on the cover. We have your contact details on file, so I can call you if we get it in?"

His face lit up. "That would be splendid! Thank you ever so much for your help."

She smiled at him, happy to be able to help. Mr. Evans put his trilby hat back on, and she couldn't help but smile at his posh, old-fashioned sense of style which perfectly matched his way of speaking.

"Goodbye. I hope to hear from you but if I do not, I shall come in to purchase another book instead."

"You do that, Mr. Evans. Goodbye."

Just as he was leaving the bookshop, he turned around and shouted, "Oh, by the way, it might have been something other than a bird, now that I think about it. I think it was something that flew. So, maybe t'was a bat, a moth, or perhaps a ferret? Anyway, cheerio."

The door closed behind him and Zoe stared into space, puzzled.

Had he meant to say 'ferret'? How the hell was that categorized as something that flew?

Zoe's manager, and the owner of the bookshop, Darren, walked in with a small box under one arm.

He held out the box to her. "We've got a book delivery. Who was that?" He inclined his head towards the door.

"Oh, it was Mr. Evans."

Darren's bushy eyebrows met at the bridge of his nose. "Who?"

"Mr. Evans. You know, the retired bank manager who likes books about nature and sea journeys. Comes in here every week?"

Darren still looked like he was trying to do complicated arithmetic.

Zoe managed not to sigh. "The old guy with the big mole on his right cheek?"

"Oh, that crazy, posh old badger. Right. Anyway, here's the new batch. Put them on the system and then shelve them, will you?"

She gave a curt nod and took the box from him. There was no reason why he couldn't do this himself—well there was one reason and that was simply that he was lazy. He'd stand at the counter and watch her put the books out, and as soon as she was done he'd slink back into the breakroom, leaving her to man the counter as always, while he drank his bodyweight in sweet tea. *No wonder he always needs to use the loo*, she thought as she unpacked the books.

She put them on the system and looked at the packing slip to check the details as she did so.

Her job wasn't the dream that most other book-nerds conjured up when she told them what she did. Yes, she worked in an independent bookshop. However, it was a lacklustre bookshop, where she was overworked, her boss didn't care much about the running of the place, and the clientele was dwindling.

As Zoe began to shelve the books, she looked around at the cheap birch bookcases, faded beige walls, and harsh fluorescent lights and thought about how she had ended up here.

She had been in dire straits when she applied for this job. She had been out on the street since her parents kicked her out. She didn't think she was focused enough for further education, she was down to her last twenty pounds and totally unqualified for any job.

Out of desperation, she had applied for this position and when Darren had asked her, in the interview, why he should hire her and not the other two applicants, who both had degrees and experience, she had broken down in tears. He had grumbled about not being able to stand seeing people cry and after a long chat about her situation, he had agreed to give her the job on a trial basis. She had never known how to thank him for that, and so she merely put up with him as a way of showing her gratitude.

She had just turned eighteen back then and she had stayed in the job for the following eight years out of loyalty, habit, and a feeling that there was no other job out there for her.

She sighed as she placed another book on the shelf. What was she qualified to do? Other bookshops were run a lot more professionally than Darren's Book Nook. Her quick foray into wanted-ads told her that they would demand that she "showed initiative" and "managed her own workload." She was sure she wasn't ready for that. She figured that a trained monkey could do the job she was doing right now and so that was what she would stick with, no matter how much it bored her.

The little bell above the door rang out. Before Zoe had time to turn to see who their new customer was, she heard Darren's sharp intake of breath. She knew immediately who must be at the door. Rebecca Clare.

Their favourite customer was shaking drops of water from her elegant brown coat and looked unfairly beautiful despite her red hair being wet and her glasses covered in little raindrops. Zoe stole as many glances as she dared while Rebecca rid herself of the worst of the rain. She admired the fancy high-heeled shoes, the black stockings, and what she could see of the knee-length black dress under her coat. And that was saying nothing about her face; those stunning eyes and the heart-shaped lips were truly mesmerizing. Especially this close up. Rebecca was near enough for Zoe to be able to reach out and brush her cheek. Not that she was daydreaming about that, of course.

Zoe knew she shouldn't be staring. Not only because it was rude, and borderline objectifying, but because Rebecca was way out of her league. And far too old for her. Zoe didn't know how old Rebecca was but she was certainly older than her own twenty-six years. Oh, and to make Rebecca even more of an impossible choice, she was Darren's huge crush too.

Just as Zoe was dragging her gaze away, she saw Rebecca quickly remove her drenched glasses. The water that had rested on them shot out in Zoe's direction, some hitting the side of her face.

Rebecca looked mortified. "Oh, I'm so sorry. Are you all right, there?"

"Yeah, sure! I'm, uh, waterproof," Zoe replied. She hoped her tone was light and jokey but worried that she sounded as terrified as she always felt when this woman spoke to her.

They had never had any long conversations, she realised. Zoe, and by extension, Darren, only knew Rebecca's name because she had ordered books and they always took contact information to be able to call or e-mail the customer when their book arrived.

Rebecca Clare, RebeccaClare@acacia-recruitment.com, Zoe repeated in her head, stopping herself before she reeled off the memorized phone number too.

The contact information, which showed that she must work in recruitment considering the company's name, and Rebecca's fondness for crime-fiction was all Zoe knew about this woman. Well, that and the fact that she had the sort of presence that you couldn't miss. Despite Rebecca's feminine looks and apparel, there was almost a masculine air to her behaviour. Zoe realised that what she saw as masculine could probably be boiled down to confidence, calm, directness, and a sense of power. Rebecca was polite and friendly but in a way that spoke of a person who you couldn't take for granted.

Either way, Rebecca Clare demanded all the attention of her onlookers without having to fight for it. And that, combined with her obvious beauty, took Zoe's breath away. Just as it was doing right now as she stood with droplets of water running down her cheek and Rebecca smiling politely at her.

Zoe wiped away the water from her face with her sweater sleeve and watched Rebecca dry her glasses on a tissue she had taken out of her pocket. Then she put the glasses back on. Zoe struggled to find something to say. Something normal. Something witty.

She heard Darren clear his throat and come rushing over.

"Mrs. Clare, isn't it? Come to pick up your latest bloodcurdling chiller?" He grinned at Rebecca. Zoe realised that he probably thought it was a charming smirk. It wasn't.

"It's *Ms.* Clare," Rebecca replied casually. "And yes, please. I got an email a few days ago and haven't had time to pop in until today."

"Terrible weather for it, though. You should have waited until tomorrow," Darren said, his strange smile still fixed in place.

Zoe saw Rebecca raise an eyebrow for a brief moment.

"Well, it's meant to rain all week, so planning to only go out when it's dry seems futile. We're Londoners, right? We're experts at dealing with rain."

Darren laughed, far too loudly and for far too long. Zoe wondered if Rebecca was suffering from second-hand embarrassment as much as she was right now. Deciding to rescue the other woman, Zoe put the books down and went behind the counter to pick up the book Rebecca had ordered and put it through the till.

When she was done, she handed Rebecca the thick tome. "Here's your book. I've never heard of this author. Is she any good?"

"Very good. Or, at least, her last three books have been. Here's hoping her latest doesn't disappoint." Rebecca looked down at the book and gave the front cover a quick pat. Then she looked back up at Zoe, with a smile.

Zoe felt herself freeze. She was meant to be telling Rebecca the total for the book, and asking if she wanted a bag but all she could do was stare. The charming smile was bad enough but Zoe had just ignored her own advice – never look this woman in the eye.

Rebecca Clare's eyes were a common blue-green colour, but what made them so dangerous was that they always seemed to glimmer. As if Rebecca was constantly happy. Or constantly flirting. It was insanely distracting and Zoe had to force herself to ignore those gorgeous eyes and just say the total sum. She barely remembered to offer a bag for the book.

When Rebecca had paid and thanked her, she turned on her high heels and click-clacked back out into the rain and out of Zoe's line of vision. Zoe sighed deeply and stopped herself when she realised that Darren could probably hear her.

It turned out that she didn't need to worry about that. Darren was busy staring after Rebecca, looking like an abandoned puppy. Zoe looked around at the shop which suddenly looked ten times duller and knew how he felt.

Published by Heartsome Publishing
Staffordshire
United Kingdom

First Heartsome edition: July 2019